W9-BEL-425

BRACELET OF BONES

BRACELET OF BONES

Kevin Crossley-Holland

Quercus

Quercus

New York • London

© 2011 by Kevin Crossley-Holland
Maps © 2011 by Hemesh Alles
First published in the United States by Quercus in 2014

Any member of educational institutions wishing to photocopy part or
all of the work for classroom use or anthology should send inquiries to
Permissions c/o Quercus Publishing Inc., 31 West 57th Street, 6th Floor,
New York, NY 10019, or to permissions@quercus.com.

ISBN 978-1-62365-112-1

Library of Congress Control Number: 2013913384

Distributed in the United States and Canada by
Random House Publisher Services
c/o Random House, 1745 Broadway
New York, NY 10019

Manufactured in the United States

2 4 6 8 10 9 7 5 3 1

www.quercus.com

for Twiggy

The Characters

In Norway and Sweden

Solveig	*age 14, Halfdan's daughter*
Halfdan	*Solveig's father*
Asta	*Solveig's stepmother*
Kalf	*age 15, Solveig's stepbrother*
Blubba	*age 10, Solveig's stepbrother*
Old Sven	*a farmer in Trondheimfjord*
Peter	*a young priest*
Oleif	*a very old man in Trondheim*
Bera	*Oleif's wife*
Orm	*a Swedish fur trader*
Ylva	*Orm's wife*
Turpin	*Orm's brother*

Aboard

Red Ottar	*trader and skipper*
Torsten	*the helmsman*
Bergdis	*the cook*
Bruni Blacktooth	*the smith*
Slothi	*a trader*
Odindisa	*Slothi's wife, a seeress and healer*
Bard	*age 11, Slothi and Odindisa's son*
Brita	*age 9, Slothi and Odindisa's daughter*
Vigot	*a mercenary*
Edith	*Red Ottar's slave*

On the Way

Oleg	*a master carver*
Mihran	*an Armenian pilot*
Edwin	*an Englishman*
Sineus	*a Slav*
Smik	*a laughter maker*
A shaman	
Truvor	*foreman of the portagers*
Yaroslav	*king of the Rus*
Ellisif	*Yaroslav's daughter*

And also

Bulgar traders
Market stallholders in Ladoga, Kiev, and Miklagard
Monks
Portagers
Pechenegs
Lepers
Varangian guards

Gods and Goddesses, Giants, and Spirits
(Norse unless otherwise indicated)

Ægir	*god of the sea*
Asgard	*world of the gods and goddesses*
Aurvandil	*see* Morning Star *in Word List*
Bifrost	*flaming three-strand rainbow bridge between middle-earth and Asgard*

bogatyrs	*giant heroes of the Rus*
Freyja	*foremost of the fertility goddesses*
Freyr	*foremost of the fertility gods*
Heimdall	*watchman god who was the son of nine waves*
Hel	*realm of the dead. Also the name of its monster ruler, a daughter of Loki*
Loki	*Norse god often called the Trickster*
Mokosh	*(Damp Mother Earth) Slavic and then Russian mother goddess*
Norns	*three goddesses of destiny*
Odin	*foremost of the Norse gods. God of poetry, battle, and death*
Perun	*Russian god of thunder and lightning*
Ran	*wife of Ægir, god of the sea. She dragged down men with her net and drowned them*
Skadi	*goddess of skiing and hunting*
Skoll	*wolf who pursues the sun*
Thialfi	*long-legged son of a farmer who became Thor's servant and accompanied him on a journey to the world of the giants*
Thor	*god of the sky and thunder and of law and order*
Valkyries	*beautiful young women who chose dead men on the battlefield and brought them back to Odin's hall, Valhalla*

BRACELET OF BONES

GREENLAND

ARCTIC OCEAN

ICELAND

SWEDEN

FJORD
STIKLESTAD
TRONDHEIM
NORWAY
LAKE MALAR
SIGTUNA

FAROE ISLANDS

SHETLAND

ORKNEY

PICTLAND

NORTH SEA

ATLANTIC OCEAN

BAL

POLAND

R. HUMBER
YORK
RICCALL
DENMARK

DUBLIN

IRELAND

ENGLAND

NORMANDY

R. DANUBE

SPAIN

ROME

CORDOBA

NORTH AFRICA

GRE

-HEMESH·ALLES-

"Is this it?" Solveig called out.

No trees stood on the battlefield. Nothing but little scrubby, twisted black bushes.

Without breaking his long, limping stride, Halfdan glanced over his shoulder. "You all right, girl?"

It's all dead, thought Solveig. There's nothing left but black fingers, black hands, thousands of them. Stiklestad. What can ever grow in this place again?

She caught up with her father and slipped her hand through his right arm, and he turned and embraced her. He almost crushed her, and Solveig could feel him trembling. She looked up at him, startled.

"I wanted you to see it so you'd understand," Halfdan told her, "and I wanted to see this place again myself. Once more in my life on this middle-earth. Stiklestad to fuel me! Stiklestad to put fire in my belly."

Then the two of them loped across the middle of the battlefield, the fighting-farming Half-Dane and his shining daughter. The gusty night wind had gone quiet, and the sun—at least the bright eyeball glaring through the lumpen gray-brown clouds—had already climbed as high in the skull of the sky as it meant to.

"Today's the battle day," her father reminded her. "The last day of August."

"Five years ago," Solveig replied.

"Harald was fifteen," her father said. "Same as you."

"I'm fourteen."

"Rising fifteen," her father said with a half smile. "Fifteen and rising. But I was ready to follow him, all right. So were many others along the fjord. Harald Sigurdsson, he was born a leader. Mind you, King Olaf thought he wasn't strong enough to fight, but Harald told him, *If I'm not strong enough to swing this sword, I'll bind my hand to the hilt.*"

"King Olaf wasn't surprised," Halfdan continued. "He knew what his half brother was made of. There were three thousand of us, Solva. Three thousand. But even so, there were many more in King Cnut's army.

"I can still smell it. The sharp stink of fear, the thickness of sweat, the sweetness of blood, the scent of grass mangled and trampled, the body of earth gouged and churned. I can still hear it. The clang and the clatter and the moaning and shrieking—"

"Father!" protested Solveig, and she put her warm right hand on his brow. "Now that you've come back here, you can leave it all behind you forever."

"This is the battle that needs to be told and retold," Halfdan went on, "and in this place more than anywhere, to honor all the men who died here. The wolf chased and swallowed the sun. It was still early in the afternoon, and by the time the sun was born again King Olaf lay dead." Halfdan pointed. "Just over there. I was in the shield rampart around him. I lost my footing, I stumbled, and one of Cnut's men slashed the back of my right knee. The bastard cut right through my hamstring."

Solveig grabbed her father's arm, and her eyes flooded with tears.

"That's why your right leg's shorter than your left." Solveig gulped. "But you're still as tall as a pine tree. Always getting in your own way. Odin knows how many times you've cracked your head against the lintel."

"I know," said her father. "I'm like one of those clumsy great frost giants I'm always telling you about. And over there, see, just by that knoll, that's where your uncle—"

"Eskil!" exclaimed Solveig.

"Your mother's best brother. One man cut him down and another hacked off his right leg."

Solveig screwed up her face.

"He was only eighteen. And marrying that September." Halfdan grimaced. "Where was I? Yes, the shield rampart. Harald's wounds were worse than mine. Much worse. Cnut's men beat him to the ground. One arrow was sticking between his ribs, and another had pierced his stomach. Blood was spitting out of that one, and because of the barb it was impossible to pull it out cleanly. But Harald would rather have been the cause of his own death than allow Swedes to kill him. He just grabbed the arrow shaft and ripped it out of his own stomach.

"After that, Harald lost half his blood and some of his guts as well. That's when I called over to old Rognvald—he was one of the king's earls—that I knew a farm hidden in the forest . . ."

"Ours, you mean," said Solveig.

Her father nodded. "A safe house."

Solveig shook her golden hair and stared in admiration at her father.

"You'd have done the same, Solva. I don't know quite how—Rognvald white-haired and me with my severed hamstring—but we half carried Harald, half dragged him." Her father frowned. "I can't remember much about it. Except how much it mattered. More than anything. That and the pain."

"I remember," Solveig said. "Well, I half remember. You and Asta arguing because she didn't want Harald in the house."

"She was afraid for Kalf and Blubba."

"Afraid!" Solveig exclaimed scornfully. "I remember that saying you told me."

"Yes," said Halfdan. *"Fearlessness is better than a faint heart for anyone who puts their nose out of doors. The length of my life and the day of my death were fated long ago."*

"That's right," said Solveig.

"She was afraid for you too, Solva."

Solveig sniffed. "I can still see Kalf and Blubba stretching a sheet of canvas between the rafters and you putting Harald over your shoulder and somehow getting him up the ladder."

"Earl Rognvald only stayed for one night," Halfdan went on. "He said he'd never be safe, not in Norway. He kissed Harald's forehead—it was so pale and cold—and said he'd be waiting over the mountains in Sweden."

"I didn't know that."

"Harald's recovery took weeks, not days. Months, in fact. By then it was winter, so Harald had to lie low. And wait. He wasn't much good at that."

"I'm like that."

"Yes, Solva, always impatient! But that was the time when Harald and I talked. We talked and talked. We told stories. We laughed."

"I remember how he laughed and how he loved your stories."

"He brayed. He shouted with laughter, and our turf walls shook. But then came the day when Harald asked me which way Earl Rognvald had taken into Sweden. He was planning to escape east and south with him and other survivors until they were strong enough to return and fight again and win back the kingdom of Norway. I told Harald it was best to sail down the fjord, because I'd heard of a traders' track leading west over the mountains from Trondheim. But he said, 'No, that's not the best way. Not for Rognvald. Not for me. I don't want to be recognized.'

"So I led him along the string paths through the forest, along the sheep runs east into the Kjolen Mountains. Each of us carried an ax, and Harald was wearing his sword as well, under his cloak. We each had a sack over one shoulder stuffed with food—smoked mutton and good whey cheese."

Solveig nodded and patted her left shoulder.

"Ah!" exclaimed her father. "You made it?"

"I always do. And we've got carrots. And pink plums."

"You're right," Halfdan said. "It's well after midday. I'm hungry."

"Over there?" suggested Solveig. "There's a bit of grass by that bush."

That was when she saw it. It was jammed inside the twisted bush, and at first she thought it was a piece of canvas, then a wedge of pine wood.

"What is it?" her father asked.

Solveig pulled it out and held it between her fingertips—a blade of bone, stripped by sea eagles, bleached by frost, sharpened by time.

Halfdan took the bone and inspected it. "Poor sod!" he said. "His shoulder blade. One of us? One of them?"

Solveig closed her eyes. "Any of them," she murmured, and she gently shook her head. "Eskil. All of them."

"I know," Halfdan said.

Solveig secured the bone inside the waist cord of her felt cloak and stroked it. "I'm going to carve it," she told her father.

"Or Asta could use it. For smoothing."

Solveig screwed up her face.

Her father shook his head and gave a rueful smile. "You and your stepmother."

Solveig opened her bag. She pulled out a tatty old piece of cloth and, inside it, whey cheese and pink plums. As soon as she'd broken off a nugget of cheese and swallowed it, she lay propped up on her left elbow and looked at her father with her left eye—the violet one—and then with her right.

"Well?" Halfdan asked her.

"Was she tall too?"

"Your mother?"

Solveig nodded. You always know what I'm thinking, she thought.

Halfdan looked at his lap. "Yes," he said slowly. "Tall. Very tall. So it's no wonder you are."

"And golden?"

"You know she was."

"I know. But when you talk about her, you make her alive to me."

"Siri . . . Always so alive."

"She's still alive for me." Solveig hesitated. "I like the way you say her name."

Halfdan put a plum in his mouth, drew the juice from it, and spit out the stone.

"I was telling you about how Harald escaped," he said, "and how I led him east over the mountains. Mile after mile, me limping, Harald wearing a broad strap to hold in his guts."

"Before you left," Solveig said, "Harald took both my hands and swung me around and around. Until I was giddy. 'Your father,' he told me, 'your hamstrung father, he's still worth double any other man. Don't you ever forget it.'"

"Is that what he said?" asked Halfdan, grinning.

Solveig tilted her head to one side, and her eyes shone.

"On the third day," Halfdan went on, "Harald told me it was time I turned back. Time I went home.

"'Nothing matters more than loyal friendship,' he said, 'and by Thor, you've come farther than you needed to. But in the end, Halfdan, each of us has to stand on his own.'

"Then Harald delved into his cloak, and he drew out a wad of bog cotton." Halfdan paused, then reached into his own bag. "Like this," he said, and he gave the wad to Solveig.

Solveig's eyes widened.

"Loosen it," her father told her.

As soon as she did so, Solveig could see gold, gleaming. Then she saw the whole brooch. She gasped.

It was almost as long as her little finger and as tall as the distance from the main joint to the tip. Incised on it was a boat with an oblong sail, much the same shape as the brooch itself. Two people were sitting in the boat, both facing in the same direction. The one in the bows was certainly a man, a man or a god, but the smaller one in the stern . . . both arms outstretched . . . Solveig couldn't be sure.

A huge snake ribboned out of the waves, over the boat, and down into the water again, and he was biting his own tail. Solveig examined him. He was much thicker than the whippety smooth snakes she sometimes surprised on the hillside.

"It's so—kingly," said Solveig. "So heavy."

Halfdan turned the brooch over in her hand. "Harald scratched two pairs of runes on the back: ᚺᛋ and ᚺᚠ Harald Sigurdsson and Halfdan son of Asser.

"'I owe my life to you,' Harald told me. 'That's why I'm giving you this.'"

"You've never shown me," said Solveig accusingly. "You haven't even told me."

"I've never told or shown anyone," her father replied. "You're the first and only."

"Where do you keep it?"

Halfdan narrowed his eyes and smiled. "It's as precious as my own blood. It's worth more than our farm and all our animals."

"And Harald gave it to you," said Solveig, wide-eyed.

"And he told me that he'd sail to Kiev, because Yaroslav, king of the Rus, had given shelter to King Olaf and would be sure to welcome him.

"'And then I may sail south of south,' Harald told me. 'South as far as Miklagard itself—the golden city. I may join the Varangian guard—the troop of Vikings serving the emperor. But be sure of one thing, Halfdan: I'll send for you. Yes, when the time's right, I will send for you.'

"'And I will come,' I promised him. 'I will come.'

"Solva, my Solva, I can still hear the words Harald Sigurdsson sang before we embraced and he went east and I went west:

'Creeping, creeping, now I go creeping
from forest to forest. Dishonored. Lame.
But who knows? My name may still become
famed far and wide before the end.'"

"You swore it," Solveig repeated. "You swore you'd go."

Halfdan nodded.

"Would you take me?"

Her father smiled. "But you'll be wanting to marry before long. If I take you, what would I be doing? Stealing your years."

Solveig frowned.

"Marry, yes, and become a mother."

"There's no one here . . ." Solveig began. "Anyhow, not if it means being like Asta."

"Solva," her father rebuked her tenderly.

"No one," Solveig repeated. "None of the boys on the fjord. I'd rather sail with you. Will you swear to take me?"

Halfdan stared gravely at his daughter. "In my heart I will."

Solveig smiled weakly.

"I swear it, Solva."

"Your heart swears you will," Halfdan's daughter told him. "But not your eyes."

2

The earth moved.

The first day of September. Almost autumn. Almost sunset. Solveig always forgot just how much she loved this between time, and then, instinctive as an animal, she remembered.

"Why don't you sleep out?" her father had suggested. "You always do that at the start of autumn. Clean under the stars."

Then Halfdan wrapped his arms as tightly around her as he had at Stiklestad, and for a second time she could feel he was trembling.

"The best time of year for it," Halfdan said in a husky voice. "The stars—you can almost pick them."

"Let me go, then," said Solveig, laughing yet troubled, wrestling free. But what she meant was: "Never let me go."

"Go on, then, Solva," her father told her.

Up on the high ground behind her farm, Solveig leaned against a silver birch as slender as she was, and she stared at the fjord, nothing but silver glitter as it snaked its way north, nothing but orange flame as it wound south and west toward the setting sun.

There were flames up on the hillside too, the flame leaves of the sumac that had already scented autumn. In the springy moss around her, Solveig found plenty of blueberries. Most she dropped into the leather pouch attached to her belt, but some she chewed until her tongue and lips were as blue as a changeling's.

"That's what you are," her stepmother, Asta, sometimes told her, with her mouth full of nails. "A changeling. Your watchful eyes, one gray, one violet. And they're too wide apart. You're not young, you're not old."

Solveig sighed.

When she pressed one ear to the mossy rock, Solveig could hear it grumbling, as far off as her first memories.

She wasn't afraid. But she knew something must be happening, maybe down in the dripping caves, home of the greedy dwarfs and their smithies, and maybe much farther, nine days' ride through freezing mist and darkness, in the world where the dead live.

But when she lay flat as a plank and pressed her other ear to the rock, the earth was slumbering again. Solveig could hear nothing but her own soft breathing and a mosquito whining.

Then she lay back and linked her fingers behind her head. She thought about Stiklestad and how her father was haunted by the battle and always would be and what runes she should carve on the shoulder blade she had found. She watched the bleeding sun slide down into the water. She shivered and wrapped herself in her sheepskin—the skin of one-eyed Tangl.

Night rode across the sky, and the rime that dropped from her stallion's mane stiffened Solveig's sheepskin. The hoarfrost stiffened her limbs too.

Waking in the middle of the night, she lay and wondered at the thousands and thousands of stars.

I know I'm up here on our hillside, she thought, but it's so strange; I feel as if I'm in every other place as well and here in this time but in every other time too.

Closing her eyes again, Solveig dreamed the story her father had once told her about the bride who vanished on her wedding day. Solveig was the bride, and she had wandered a little way away from the wedding feast and danced with the fairies, supposing they were guests. And then she drank their wine . . .

When Solveig returned to the feast, everything looked different. The farm of her bridegroom's family had disappeared, and there was no sound of singing or fiddling or laughter.

Then she met an old woman, sitting outside her cottage, and the old woman took one look at her and screeched, "I know who you are. The bride! The bride of my great-greatgrandfather's brother."

With that, Solveig—the bride who came back—dropped down dead. She dissolved into a heap of dust.

When Solveig woke, it was broad daylight. She stood up and stamped like a colt to be sure she was still flesh and blood and bone. Then she swung her arms, rubbed the stars out of her eyes, and yawned.

Gazing down, she saw her own farm was still there, all right: the hearth smoke was rising right through the turf roof as usual. Both cows lowed as soon as she greeted them. And Kalf, chopping wood in the yard, ignored her as usual.

Solveig found her stepmother in the little dairy. After her dream, Solveig was even quite pleased to see her.

"Good morning and good morning!" she caroled.

Asta looked up. "Good for nothing," she grunted.

Solveig frowned.

"Your father's gone." Asta smacked her wooden scoop against the side of the churn, and its slender stem snapped. "Now look what you've made me do."

"Gone where?" asked Solveig.

"Hel, for all I care."

"Trondheim, you mean?"

"They came for him."

"Came? Who did?"

"Harald's men. Last night."

"But he's . . ." The back of Solveig's neck was freezing. "But he's . . ."

"Gone!" cried Asta, and she spit on the marl floor. "Gone to join Harald."

"Where?"

"How should I know? East to Garthar. South to Kiev and Miklagard. That's what they kept saying."

"But . . ." Solveig gasped. "He said . . ."

"Since when," demanded Asta in an acid voice, "were men and promises close companions?"

He knew, thought Solveig. He knew. That's why he took me to Stiklestad. That's why he wanted me to sleep up on the hill.

"How long?" she asked. "I mean, how long?"

"Don't ask me."

Solveig was wordless. She felt as if she had dissolved into a pile of dust.

"Still," said Asta, "I'll be all right, won't I? I'll be just fine with Kalf and Blubba and you, Solveig, you dreamer."

Solveig walked out of the dairy. She walked away from the farm and down to the fjord. She sat cross-legged at the end of their little wooden jetty.

He'll send for me, she thought. Just as Harald has sent for him. He swore he'd take me with him. Didn't he?

But she began to shiver in the broad sunlight.

To begin with, she choked back her tears. But then she began to sob. She sobbed—she couldn't stop herself—and her tears dripped between the planks of the jetty into the salt water.

All day Solveig kept going over everything her father had told her at Stiklestad. Each word. Each silence and gesture. His trembling.

She understood why her father wanted to follow Harald. But what she couldn't understand was why he hadn't told her. All she felt was her own desolation and helplessness.

That night, Solveig could see Asta sitting on her three-legged stool by the fire. Her sweep of copper hair glinted in the flickering light. Her stepmother moaned, and then she began to pray and redouble her prayers.

Asta prayed to Thor for Halfdan's safety. She prayed to Freyja to give her strength of mind, strength of heart. She prayed to all the guardian gods for Kalf and Blubba. She even prayed for Solveig, and then she tossed her head, and hawked, and spit into the fire.

Solveig lay as still as a stone seems to lie. Through half-closed eyes she saw her stepmother stretch out on her sleeping bench and heard her sigh as loud and long as a seventh wave breaking.

Then Kalf and Blubba barged in.

"Beware!" proclaimed Kalf in his high-pitched voice. Although he was fifteen, his voice was still breaking, one moment quite gruff, the next squeaky.

"Beware of a creaking bow," Blubba said.

"And a yawning wolf," said Kalf.

"Beware of new ice."

"And a pretty girl's pillow talk."

Both boys guffawed.

"Kalf! Blubba!" Their mother's voice cut through the darkness. "Enough!"

"Beware of a stepfather," Kalf went on, "a scuttling stepfather. Come on, Blubba!"

But Blubba didn't join in. He knew what Solveig must be feeling.

"Blubba!"

"Enough!" their mother cautioned them.

Before long, both boys had fallen asleep, and so had their mother. Solveig lay in the thicket of their breathing, their growling and snorting, trapped and unable to escape.

My father, she thought. My father. She moaned like a wolverine, one long, low warbling moan. Then she banged her head against her pillow sack.

In the high skies, stars froze and the moon marbled. Then kind clouds closed the sky lid, and down came the rain.

Solveig was first to wake.

It was still raining. She could feel it without hearing it.

She felt so drained. As if her head were too tired to think and her heart had run out of feeling. Then she remembered all over again. And as soon as she remembered, warm under her sheepskin, she shivered.

Solveig put both arms around her pillow sack, drew it close, and buried her face in it. That was when she felt it. A lump. Hard and edgy, flat almost. She poked her fingers inside the pillow's woolen casing, then reached in almost up to her elbow, splayed her fingers, and burrowed into the down. There! She had it, and she was almost sure she knew what it was. She closed her right hand around it.

The fire in the hearth was nothing but gray ash. And the last light from the little oil lamp suspended from a rafter was no brighter than elf-fire. Solveig stood up and stepped over to the door. Barefoot, she walked out into the rain.

3

When winter closes its fist, when the ice age cracks its bones and the wolf age moans, you cannot follow, you cannot lead, you cannot stray far from your own hearth. All you can do is scratch the half-frozen earth for blighted turnips and carrots, and water your goats and cattle and bleating sheep, and feed them with hay, and drill holes through the ice and let down a baited line for pike or herring or mackerel; all you can do is drink ale, and chew dried meal, and gnaw your chilblains, and wait.

Days became shorter, though sometimes they were so dazzling that they stuck little pins into Solveig's eyes. Nights became longer.

On some mornings, Kalf worked in the little smithy. He stoked the furnace, then he smelted the block of iron he and Halfdan had brought back from Trondheim and began to hammer out a new cooking cauldron. Not only this. Kalf put new edges on all the knives and axes, even Solveig's carving knife, and a new edge, too, on the blade of his tongue. He never missed a chance to cut his stepsister with a keen word.

Bright-eyed Blubba worked alongside his brother. Whistling and singing snatches of song, he worked long strips of iron, winding them around their old milk vat where it was coming apart at the seams, and secured them with iron nails. And once, with Solveig, he walked over the hill to the birch copse, and the two of them axed a tree and together dragged it back to the farm. On sunny mornings, Solveig went down to the jetty with a basketful of filthy clothing and washed it all with soap stinking of mutton fat, gritty with wood ash. Then she laid the clothes out to dry from one end of the jetty to the other, weighted with stones, but by the time she went back to collect them, they were all stiff as boards.

"Our old sail," said Asta. "More holes than fabric. It's like a colander."

"It's all right," Solveig said.

"It's not," retorted Asta.

It wasn't so much Asta's words as the way she said them, and what she did not say, that hurt Solveig.

"Hard work, Solveig, I know it's hard. But you and me and Kalf and Blubba, what are we meant to do? Your father's not half the man Einar was."

Solveig glared at the marl floor.

"No one pushed Einar around. He would have stayed loyal to the family."

Solveig's eyeballs grew hot.

"What are we meant to do?" Asta repeated. "We must work all the harder."

Sometimes Asta narrowed her eyes and saw straight into her stepdaughter's head.

Once, while Solveig was weaving coarse cloth for the new canvas sail: "You wouldn't get as far as Trondheim. Wolves would eat you."

And again: "Words! Words! Words make promises. Words break promises."

And for a third time, while Solveig was cutting wax for new candles: "You're just a girl, Solveig. Fourteen winters old. You're soft as beeswax."

Kalf overheard his mother. "Soft, and stuffed with secrets."

Solveig's fingers tightened around the handle of her knife.

"Me and Blubba never know what she's thinking."

"I know, all right," said Asta in a cold voice. "I know exactly what she's thinking."

Solveig's eyes were hot. She glared at the beeswax and jabbed at it.

"But I do know . . ." Kalf said slowly.

Solveig held her breath.

"I do know she's hiding something . . . and I'll find out what."

On some evenings, Asta drowsed beside the hearth, worn out by her day's work, and Kalf and Blubba fooled around in the dark outside or drank themselves stupid with ale, but Solveig sat upright on her bench and scoured and scraped at a piece of walrus bone. She shaped it into a kind of oval, and then she began to inscribe it with runes.

My father, she thought, his real name is Asser Assersson. His mother was Swedish, but his father was Danish. That's why everyone calls him Halfdan.

I can't remember my mother. She died to give me life. Sirith she was called, but my father calls her Siri. When he says her name, his voice is always gentle.

He's the only one who shortens my name. Solva, he says. Solva. Sun-strength!

He doesn't care about Asta in the same way he still does about my mother, and it's the same with Asta. She still loves Einar, her first man, Kalf's and Blubba's father. He was drowned.

What I believe is my father needed a woman and Asta needed a man. For comfort. To make a household. To bring up their children. They argue half the time and sometimes go to bed bitter.

I think my father must be glad to have escaped Asta's tongue. And Kalf's as well. They're as sharp as each other.

He's never liked Kalf, and Kalf's never liked me.

Actually, I don't think Asta minds my father going all that much. She complains, all right. And it's true, we all have to work harder without him. But . . . but you promised. You must have known it was our last day together. You must.

"You're fourteen, Solva. Rising fifteen . . . Fifteen and rising."

Were you just waiting for me to grow up before you went away?

One day, a young Christian priest from Trondheim, Peter, came to talk with Asta and the other folk living along the fjord about building a church.

"King Olaf and his warriors," he began, "sailed back from Garthar to reclaim his throne and kingdom—and he fought in the name of the White Christ."

"Much good that did him," said Asta.

"At Stiklestad, three thousand men fought alongside the king," Peter went on. "Norwegians, Swedes, shoulder to shoulder."

"Not because they were Christians," Old Sven said. "Because Olaf was our rightful king."

The young priest sighed and clasped his hands. "But it was one man against ten, the huge heathen rabble loyal to King Cnut. The largest army ever seen in Norway. But although King Olaf died, Christ, the Prince of Peace, will live forever."

"Don't you preach to me about that battle," Asta told him.

"There's not a family along this fjord who didn't lose a father, a son, a brother," added Old Sven.

"What I don't understand," Solveig said to the priest, "is how the way of the White Christ can be carpeted with blood. You keep saying he's the Prince of Peace, but King Olaf and his army whirled their battle-axes. How can you forgive and wreak vengeance at the same time?"

The young priest, Peter, gave Solveig a pitying smile. "We forgive those who are willing to be baptized; those who are not, we must strike down."

"Most of the families living along our fjord have been baptized," Asta retorted, "but they still worship Odin and the other gods as well."

The young priest shook his head. "I will pray for you," he said, "and visit you again."

On another day, Blubba asked Solveig why her father had left them and sailed away.

"He's gone because he promised to," Solveig told him. "He's honoring his promise."

Blubba frowned.

"He promised Harald Sigurdsson that he would follow him. Can you remember him?"

"Not really."

"He was even taller than my father."

"I remember that."

"And he had a loud voice and a loud laugh."

"Yes, I remember."

"When he fought with my father at Stiklestad, he was fifteen and you were only four," Solveig told Blubba, and then she sat him down beside her. "He was born to be a leader, Harald was, and you can be sure he and my father will come back and avenge King Olaf's death."

"When?" asked Blubba.

"Do you know," Solveig went on, "when Harald was just three, he told his half brother—King Olaf, that is—that what he wanted most was warships? Not food, not board games, not weapons. Warships!"

"I wish Halfdan would come back," announced Blubba.

Solveig swallowed loudly. "What about you?" she asked Blubba. "What would you choose? What do you want most?"

Blubba gazed at his stepsister seriously.

"Well?" she asked.

"You used to be happy," Blubba said. "And smiling . . . and laughing. I want . . . your days to be all like that again."

"Oh, Blubba!" cried Solveig. Tears sprang to her eyes, and roughly she drew Blubba to her, and then she sniffed and pummeled his back.

Not a day passed without Solveig thinking about what her father had said, and not said. Without wondering where he was and whether she could follow and find him.

She had never been farther away from her home than the market at Trondheim, and even then not on her own. But home isn't home, she thought. Not any longer. There's food and shelter here, I know, but such sadness, such pain.

Even the wolves, she thought, even they would be better than this.

Solveig inscribed the runes, so that the point of her awl bit into the oval of walrus bone: "SOLVEIG THE SUN-STRONG FOLLOWED . . ."

"Solveig!" rasped Asta. "Will you stop that? You're scouring my skull! Stop all this scratching and scraping before you drive me mad."

Solveig stayed her hand.

"Or else work outside. The days are lengthening, aren't they?"

Praise be, thought Solveig. Praise Odin and Freyja and Thor and all my gods. Praise the White Christ, even. Yes, the days are getting longer.

My winter's almost over.

The ice is breaking up.

The morning before she left, Solveig told Asta that spring was on the doorstep.

"There are many false springs," Asta replied.

"Can't you feel it?"

"And it's better not to think about it," Asta warned her. "Otherwise you won't be able to think of anything else."

Then Solveig blithely announced, seeing as spring was in the air, it was high time the little shed beside the jetty was mucked out. "And as my father's not here," she went on, "I'll do it for him."

"As you please," said Asta in a dry voice.

So her stepmother suspected nothing when Solveig walked down to the jetty, five hundred paces away, three times that day. But each time she went, Solveig was carrying more of the things she needed to take with her—food, and fresh water in a little keg, clothing, her carving tools and grindstone and a little sackful of bones—and she stowed them all in the upended back half of her father's old coble where he stored oars and bailers and nets and lines and weights and floats and the like.

The first time she went down to the jetty, Solveig actually did muck out the shed—for a short while, anyhow—to salve her conscience. And on her third trip, she checked the rigging of their boat, perched on the end of the jetty. Then she got down on one knee and poked at the frazil ice with an oar. The crystal needles were as thin as her own fingernails and at once gave way.

Solveig's heart quickened. Her blood began to sing.

Before she went back to the farmhouse for the last time, she picked her way along the shore to the family's sloping graveyard. Bitter little wavelets were dashing themselves against the rocks at the bottom end of it.

Solveig wandered between the graves of her mother's parents and grandparents and great-grandparents she had never known, and then she knelt in the sopping grass beside her mother.

"Sss," hissed the north wind. "Sss-sssss."

Solveig put her right hand over her heart. "I feel afraid," she told her mother. "I've never felt so afraid. But I've never been so sure of what I have to do. Mother, my mother, my journey will either lead me to my father or lay me down like you."

It was too early in the year for even a pale aconite or a nodding snowdrop, but Solveig scouted around and collected a handful of little white pebbles. Carefully she arranged them at the foot of her mother's tilting stone: snowflakes, teardrops, a white petal shower. Then she stood up and hurried back to the farm.

That evening, Solveig grew nervous. Very nervous. She didn't feel hungry, and that night she didn't sleep much. She kept telling herself she must wait until first light, but then she became afraid she might fall into a deep sleep just before dawn.

She sat up in the dark. Quietly she dug out the gold brooch hidden in her pillow sack. She felt for the holes in her reindeer skin and put her hands and arms through them. Then she stood up and picked up her sheepskin. But with her first step she kicked the iron poker lying between her bench and the hearth.

Asta was instantly awake. "Who's that?" And then: "What is it?"

"Me," said Solveig in a hoarse voice. "Only me." Her heart was hammering.

"What is it?"

"My stomach," said Solveig. "Cramps in my stomach. I've got to go. I've got to."

Both boys were snoring.

"I can't wait," groaned Solveig.

"Close the door," Asta told her. Then she sighed and lay back again.

The moment Solveig felt the night chill on her cheeks she was alert—alert to the terrible risk of leaving and to all the pain of staying.

I can go back in, she thought. I still can!

But then, all at once, she was striding away from the farm. Now she was running, and the east wind was springing after her. And when it moaned, Solveig was sure it was Asta, calling.

Solveig didn't look back until she reached the jetty, but as soon as she did, she could see that the sky over the hills was just beginning to turn pale. Not yet green, not primrose.

Quickly, Solveig shoved the boat down the sloping ramp into the water. Then she hurried back to the upended coble and carried out the few things she had to take with her.

Solveig stared at the farm, still masked by night. Then she turned back to the dark and dancing water.

Yes, I can, she thought. I can. They'll be sorry about the boat but not sorry about me. Old Sven will help Kalf and Blubba to cut the planks to build another one.

At the end of the jetty, Solveig got onto her knees. She was out of breath.

"Ægir," she prayed, "don't shout at me with your rough wave tongues. Ran, don't snare me with your drowning net. Lift me and carry me to Trondheim."

Then Solveig stood up. She felt in the pocket of her reindeer skin for the walrus bone she still had not finished carving.

SOLVEIG THE SUN-STRONG FOLLOWED THE STRONG SUN EAST AND SO . . .

Solveig laid down the disk at the end of the jetty.

"You, Kalf and Blubba . . ." she whispered. "Asta, you . . . Will you find it? And you, wind and waves and days and hope, will you help me complete it?"

Then Solveig edged down the ramp on her bottom and scrambled into the boat. At once she realized she hadn't untied the painter.

"Solveig! Solveig! Where are you? Solveig!"

She was sure she could hear Asta calling her.

Solveig picked up her carving knife. She hacked and slashed at the painter. She severed it.

4

As soon as Solveig had rowed the first few strokes, she realized the tide was so strong that it was taking her in the wrong direction, farther up the fjord, away from Trondheim. She shipped her oars and scrambled over to the mast and pulled up the old sail.

Asta's right, she thought. It's a rag of a thing. Less like a sail than a colander.

Then she remembered her stepmother's bitter words: *"You? You wouldn't get as far as Trondheim. Wolves would eat you."*

At least there aren't any wolves out here, thought Solveig. There are other things, though. Things I can't see. Things without names.

For a little while, Solveig could still see their farm in the breaking light. Then she thought she could. Then she knew she could not.

Everything, she said to herself. The farm, this fjord, they've been everything to me.

She could feel tears welling up.

What am I without this water, this earth? This is where I was born. Where my father taught me to fish, and told me stories, where he showed me how to carve the runes, and . . .

Solveig swallowed loudly.

"You know all I am," she whispered. "Will I ever see you again?"

But then she tossed her head.

Where will all this get me? I must look ahead. I'm following my father.

Running across the wind down the widening fjord, Solveig had soon traveled farther from the farm than she had ever been on her own. To begin with, she listened to each creak of the little boat, and stared at each dark wave welling up in front of her, and bit so hard on her lower lip that she tasted her own blood. But after a time, she began to yawn. She trailed her right hand in the freezing water, and when she raised her fingers to her sore lips, she could hear her father telling her the tale about the salt in the sea.

". . . But once he'd got it started, Solva, the skipper couldn't stop it. The quern stone ground more and more salt, just as it had ground a whole waterfall of herrings and broth, and ground so much gold its owner was able to plate his whole house with it. The quern stone ground and ground, and in the end it ground so much salt that it sank the ship. But even then, Solva, the quern didn't stop. It's down there on the seabed, grinding. That's why the sea's salty."

While Solveig was still listening, and at the same time wondering why tears taste salty, she realized that someone on the waterside was waving to her. Waving and shouting. He was too far away, though, and she couldn't make out what he was saying.

He can't be after me, she thought. How can he? Has Asta . . . No, that's nonsense. All the same, she might get Sven or someone to follow me, to bring me back.

Almost at once, there was a terrible grating. The boat jolted and pitched Solveig forward. It was as if some god had ordered the quern stone on the seabed to grind the boat into sawdust.

Solveig didn't know what it was, not at first. Then she saw. Her boat had collided with a thick sheet of ice, and the boat was so light that it was lifting its nose, its whole body, while the ice slid under it.

One of the seams in the bottom of the boat began to ooze where the grim ice had gouged it, but as far as Solveig could see, there were no other wounds.

Otherwise, she thought, my journey would be over already. Before it had really begun. But if the ooze grows into a leak, I'll have to start bailing. That man on the waterside, he was warning me.

First the wind fell away to nothing; then the tide turned and began to push the skiff downstream.

It's a good thing the tide takes much longer to drag back to the sea than to fill up the fjord, thought Solveig. The same amount of water ebbs as comes in, I know that, but it feels as if Ægir is helping me on my way.

Solveig drifted. She yawned again. She felt quite warm inside her reindeer skin.

When the wind and water are as soft as this, she thought, sailing's as easy as deep breathing. If I close my eyes, it feels as if I'm sliding south, all the way to Miklagard. I know! Sailing's never easy, not for long. The sea's a shining trickster and often dangerous. I must be watchful.

Solveig reached for her little water keg and held it up to her mouth and turned the tap. Much as she would have liked to drink deep and then splash fresh water over her salt-sticky face and hair, she took no more than a few sips.

If you're crossing a mountain or sailing down a fjord, she thought, *always be sure to take enough food and water.* That's what Odin says.

Then Solveig untied the neck cord of her leather bag, pulled out a lump of dried mutton, and cautiously sucked it.

Early April. The day's small store of light was soon drained. The Lodestar and the dragon, the hunting dogs, the great bear and the little bear began to glitter, and the moon wore a silvery-white halo.

Was it really only now that Solveig realized she wouldn't reach Trondheim before dark and not even by midnight?

She gazed at the water around her, and in the almost-dark it was shining.

Things, she thought. Things I can't see. Sea serpents, sea snorters. Wild men. Things without names.

All at once, the night sky thronged with black wings and wailing and shrieking. Skuas, terns, and cormorants circled Solveig as if her skiff were a bright beacon, and she buried her head in her arms. They peck your eyes out, she thought. They do if you're dead, and they drill into the soft spot in your skull even when you're alive.

But when Solveig opened her eyes again, the night birds had all gone. As if they had never been.

They were flying from world to world, she thought. Wild and wailing.

The darker the night sky, the more the water shone. The little skipping wavelets were luminous.

Then Solveig saw the ghosts of Stiklestad swimming through the water, white faces up. And all around her she began to hear voices, insistent, soft as a snowfall:

Cut me
Carve me

Tell me
Sing me

I laughed
I was young

I sang
I loved

Say my death
Say I'm life

Sing now, Solveig
Now and forever.

"I will!" cried Solveig in the darkness. And then she thought, I'll carve runes for you on your shoulder blade. I must sing life, otherwise I'm half dead myself.

Brighter and brighter, the Morning Star gazed at Solveig.

I know about you, she thought. You're Aurvandil's big toe—the one that froze because it was sticking out of the basket strapped to Thor's back when he rescued Aurvandil from the giant world. So Thor snapped you off and threw you into the sky.

But I'm all right, she thought sleepily. I'm warm enough inside Tangl's skin and my shawl.

All at once, Solveig's sail began to flap as wildly as an imprisoned seagull.

Solveig stretched, she yawned, she shook her head. I fell asleep, she thought. Where am I?

And at once she sat bolt upright.

Around Solveig were waves, nothing but waves, the sides of waves, gray-green and glassy, sinuous, the tops of waves, bristling, baring their teeth, the troughs of waves, death-dark and bottomless.

Solveig's skiff was light as thistledown. One moment, she was deep in a shadowless grave, the next whisked and lifted onto a sunlit peak. Up, down, down again, up.

Solveig's stomach lurched. She felt weightless.

But then she launched herself at the little mast and grabbed it. Standing with both arms wrapped around it, Solveig stared around her, and as her boat lifted again, she could see in the distance behind her the blue-green stone malt houses and granaries of Trondheim.

While she had slept, tight as a clam, she had been swept right past them.

Solveig was aghast. Aghast and terrified.

If my boat weren't so light, she thought, the waves would have broken right over us. From in front. From behind.

She clenched her fists until her knuckles were white.

Then Solveig knelt down and cautiously grasped the steering paddle, eased the skiff around toward land again, and gripped the oars.

But as she did so, a wave swept under its bows and lifted and carried it.

I don't know whether I'm making any headway at all, she thought. But what else can I do?

A few drops kicked up and splashed Solveig and streamed down her face. She licked her salty lips.

"Heimdall!" she cried. "Son of nine waves. Son of nine mothers. Guide me. Save me from Ran and her drowning net."

Solveig's mouth was dry and her tongue felt too big, but she didn't dare stop for a moment to gulp down some water. It was a long time before she was sure she was coming closer to land and at least an hour before she was able to make her way back into calm water. She was completely soaked and shivering. She knew she had kissed fingers with death and escaped with her life.

Solveig sat to her oars. She braced her shoulders and pulled the skiff away from the mainstream, looking over to the bank until she saw a little staithe where she could come in.

A very old man was standing there beside a wreck—its ribs were slimy green, slimy black—and he watched as Solveig beached the boat on the gravel waterfront.

Solveig stepped out of her skiff, and at once she reeled sideways and fell forward onto her hands and knees.

The old man kept his distance. His white eyebrows were bushy and had lives of their own.

Slowly Solveig uncurled herself and looked up at him.

"You fool!" he said angrily.

"I didn't mean to." Solveig shuddered.

"Madness! In an oozy old skiff."

Solveig's skin was blue, and her teeth began to chatter. "I fell asleep."

The old man spit into the gravel. "Who are you, anyhow?"

Solveig didn't reply.

"Your name."

"I . . . I . . . It got left behind."

"Where from?"

"A day back. All day yesterday and last night."

"That long!" exclaimed the old man. "You've been in the boat that long?" He glared at Solveig. "Human, are you?"

"Of course I am," Solveig replied.

The old man hoicked his thumb over his right shoulder. "Come with me."

"I'm all right."

"I'm telling you. You're bone cold."

Solveig's shaking legs nearly gave way when she dragged herself after the fierce old man as he led her to his shack—it was really little more than that, nothing like as roomy as Solveig's farm. An old woman was sitting by the fire.

"Bera!" barked the man. "Look at this!"

Bera didn't need asking twice. She put an arm around Solveig, sat her down in her own place, and draped a loosely knitted scarf around her shoulders.

Solveig shook. She couldn't stop shaking. And for the first time, her eyes filled with tears.

"Carried right out, she was," the man told his wife. "In an oozy old skiff. I saw her just after sunrise."

Bera, the old man's wife, put a bowlful of warm turnip soup between Solveig's trembling hands.

"Levanger?" croaked the old man. "Is that where you're from?"

Solveig jerked her head sideways.

"Thought I'd seen the last of you. That's what I thought."

"More soup?" asked Bera, and she gave Solveig a knowing smile.

Solveig was still shaking so much that she had difficulty holding the bowl without spilling it.

"Well, she's not come down from Asgard," the old man said. "The gods always complain about food on middle-earth. They're always greedy for something better."

"Says you, Oleif!" his wife scoffed.

"He's right," said Solveig. "Red Thor killed and cooked his own goats. Oh!" She pulled back her shoulders and looked up at the old couple. "I'm sorry. I haven't said so much as a word. I was so cold."

"I know," said Bera kindly.

"Not from Asgard," her husband repeated, "and not a ghost. I don't think she is."

The old woman pinched Solveig's cheek. "Of course she's not," she said. "Pink and pretty."

"But not welcome under this roof," Oleif said. "Won't say who she is. Won't say where she's from. On the run, maybe."

"Come on, Oleif," said Bera. "Come and sit in your chair."

"On the run, are you?" the old man asked Solveig.

Solveig took a deep breath. She closed her eyes.

"I'm following my father."

Oleif's eyebrows quivered.

"To the market?" asked Bera.

Solveig shook her head.

"Go on, then," Oleif told her.

"Miklagard."

"Where?"

"Miklagard. The great city. The shining city."

Oleif spit into the fire, and it hissed at him.

"It's a thousand miles away," Solveig explained.

"Moonshine!" said the old man.

"It is! It's after Garthar. South."

"Right," said the old man scathingly. "A thousand miles, but you couldn't keep awake as far as Trondheim."

"It sounds like the beginning of an old story," Bera said.

"A story with a bad ending," added her husband. "You're not going anywhere, my girl. You're sailing back home."

"I'm not!" Solveig replied fiercely, and at once she stood up and stepped across to the open door.

The old man's eyebrows jumped.

Bera patted the air between her husband and Solveig. "Not so fast, Oleif," she said. "We don't know her story. We don't even know her name."

Oleif sniffed. "I'm getting Peter, then."

"Who?" Solveig asked.

"Peter. The young priest. He'll know what's best."

"No," Solveig protested.

Bera shuffled over to the door and took Solveig's arm. She looked her full in the face with her misty, knowing eyes. "We've seen worse than you," she said. "Much worse. Last week that little girl . . . all bloated, she was. Yes, we've lived so long, we've seen almost everything. Sit down again, now. You're so cold still. And soaked. What did you say your name is?"

Behind Solveig and the old woman, there was a snort.

Old Oleif had fallen asleep.

At once Bera took Solveig by the arm and shepherded her out of the shack.

"First you," the old woman said quietly, "and now him. He's always doing that."

Solveig gazed at Bera. I can trust you, she thought. I think I can.

"Come on," said Bera, smiling. "While we can. He's not as heartless as he makes out." And she led Solveig away from their shack.

"I'm strong as the sun," Solveig told the old woman.

Bera shook her head. "Don't talk in riddles, girl," she said.

"I'm Halfdan's daughter."

"Halfdan," said the old woman encouragingly. "Halfdan . . ."

Then Solveig told Bera about her father and Harald Sigurdsson and Stiklestad and Asta and Kalf and Blubba, and everything, almost everything.

"Maybe the gods are with you," the old woman said. "Maybe they've put a mouthful of wind in your sails."

"I haven't got sails," Solveig replied. "Only a rag of a thing."

Bera waved a leathery hand. "Enough to bring you here. Maybe I can help you."

"Where are we going?"

"Down to the market."

Solveig shook her head.

"Step by step," the old woman told her. "Sometimes forward, sometimes sideways, even backward. That's the way you make a journey." Bera took Solveig's hand. "I've lived here all my life, and I know who's coming, who's leaving, where they're going. I'm taking you to our friends."

"Who?"

"Turpin and Orm and his wife, Ylva. Swedish fur traders."

"Swedes?" exclaimed Solveig.

"They can't help that," replied the old woman. "None of us can choose our parents."

"I thought the trappers lived away north," said Solveig.

"They do. They bring their furs down to Trondheim, and the traders take them on."

"Where to?"

"They can speak for themselves," the old woman said.

"Miklagard," Solveig told the traders.

Sitting on their mound of skins and fur, Turpin and Orm and Ylva pursed their lips.

"Miklagard," Solveig said again, hoping she sounded more confident than she felt.

"Some man, is it?" Orm inquired.

"Her father," Bera explained.

"That's what they all say," retorted Orm.

Ylva gave Solveig a look, half fond, half pitying. "You've no idea," she said.

"Is that where you're going?" Solveig asked her. "Miklagard?"

The three fur traders gurgled.

"Miklagard," Solveig repeated. "It's after Garthar."

"We know where it is, all right," Orm said. "No, we're going to Sigtuna."

"Sigtuna," said Ylva. "Over the mountains."

That's the way Harald went, thought Solveig. The way my father's gone. It must be.

"And across Sweden," said Orm.

"It's where Baltic traders sail from," Ylva explained. "A port on the lake of Malar. Fourteen days from here."

"Will you take me with you?" Solveig asked eagerly.

Turpin swung his bear head from side to side and growled to himself.

Orm and Ylva said nothing.

"An extra mouth," said Turpin. "You wouldn't last, anyhow."

Solveig clicked her tongue. "I'm tougher than I look," she told him. "I can carry my share."

Orm slowly stroked the squirrel furs he was sitting on and considered Solveig—half girl, half woman, her wide-apart eyes, one violet, one gray, how tall she was, the way she planted her feet so firmly on the ground, her determination.

"And I'm rising fifteen," Solveig added, pulling back her shoulders.

"Have you got some skill?" Orm asked her.

"Carving," Solveig said at once.

"Carving what?"

"Fishhooks. Pins. Runes."

Orm looked at his brother and Turpin looked at him. They were men of few words and often understood each other without using any words at all.

"On this condition—" said Turpin. "Whenever we stop, you're to carve until sundown and give us whatever you've carved when we reach Sigtuna."

"Oh, yes!" said Solveig eagerly. "Yes, I will."

"Our packhorses carry our furs," Ylva explained. "We walk."

"What's this one?" asked Solveig, pointing to a shiny brown fur.

"Sable. Sable marten," said Orm, and then he pointed straight at Solveig and grinned. "And what about you? What's your name?"

Solveig shook her head. "Halfdan's daughter," she said.

Orm frowned. "When we reach Sigtuna," he said, "you'll have to find a boat sailing to Ladoga."

"No," said Solveig. "Miklagard."

"Baltic traders sail only as far as Ladoga," Orm told her. "And if you ever get that far, you'll have to pick up traders heading south for Kiev."

"Step by step," said Ylva.

Turpin growled softly and stood up on his throne of furs—sable and squirrel and pine marten, reindeer and black bear. "All right," he announced. "Tomorrow morning. At first light."

Solveig's face brightened. "I'll be as strong as the sun," she assured him.

Solveig meant it. She meant it with her head and heart. She just hoped she could be as strong as her word.

5

Solveig led the way along the narrow path between shoulders of blue-gray rock. Then, at the top of the pass, she turned to face Turpin. In the wind, her felt cloak flapped. The sun at her back made a halo of her golden hair.

Turpin sheltered his eyes with his hairy right hand and appraised her.

"What?" she asked, and she tilted her head a little to the right.

Turpin growled softly. "You remind me," he said. Then he walked past her.

Sun and wind and scudding gray-brown clouds, stinging April showers, and one snowfall: days passed.

Did you see this? Solveig wondered. Father, did you see all these huge boulders, hundreds and thousands of them, strewn all over the slopes, looking like an enormous flock of sheep? Did you wash your face in this freezing, frothing milky river?

The way hill paths were windswept but forest paths springy with pine needles; the way mountain air was so clear that single sounds—a clinking bell at the neck of a goat standing on a far ridge, a mountain man splitting logs with an ax and maul—sailed right across a valley; and how the earth was beginning once more to open her eyes: masses of tiny white flowers with yellow pupils, these and the dew tracks of wolves and weasels and snowshoe hares, the spraints of roe deer and that underwater hush when snow is falling, the feel of new moss, spongy and shocking green, the taste of the morning so clean it could have been the day on which the world was created; yes, Solveig saw and heard and felt it all.

At dusk, when the traders had stopped for the night, twice in ramshackle old barns and once in a shallow cave but otherwise in the open, by bright moonlight and firelight Solveig carved a strip of maple.

"What are you carving?" Ylva asked her.

Solveig didn't reply.

"It looks like a handle for a hammer."

"Or a long spoon," suggested Orm.

Solveig edged closer to the fire, and the aspen logs snapped and popped.

"In this half-light," said Solveig, "one thing turns into another. I can see all sorts of things."

Orm looked at Ylva. He slowly shook his head and put his right forefinger to his temple.

"Even when I do know what I'm carving," Solveig added, "it's better not to tell."

"What are you talking about?" Ylva asked.

"Making," said Solveig. "It's better not to talk about it until I've finished it."

Ylva frowned. "Why?"

"I can't explain it," Solveig replied. "But what I'm making needs all my strength, all my head and heart, my body too, every ounce. Talking instead of doing leeches me. Words weaken me."

After the four of them had eaten and drunk a few mouthfuls of ale, Solveig stretched out, and before long Turpin began to tell her about . . .

". . . summer. This journey when it's high summer. There's still snow up on the glaciers, but all these meadows, they're eye-bright with the spires of lupins, creamy, pink, purple . . . and we roast yellow mushrooms and pick red berries . . ."

Turpin's voice sounded to Solveig like the buzzing of summer bees.

"And trout . . . we tickle them and take them and grill them . . ."

"Listen to you!" said Ylva.

"Ah!" growled Turpin. "I was forgetting. Yes, the mosquitoes . . ."

But Solveig had already fallen asleep.

Turpin got up and shook out a fur—in the darkness it was difficult to see quite what, but it smelled of black bear— and laid it gently over Solveig.

"She reminds me," he said.

For a while the three of them sat in silence around the fire.

Turpin rubbed his arms and then stretched and groaned. "My Tola!" he said. "Tola! What father can bear the loss of his daughter? Part of him is lost with her; as long as he lives he goes on searching for her."

The fire sighed. It whistled.

"Not that Solveig will reach Miklagard," Turpin observed. "That's not a likely story. Still, she's following her father, and I mean to help her. When we reach Sigtuna, we can take her to the skipper—Red Ottar."

Ylva drew in her breath between her teeth.

"He'll like her," said Turpin.

"And enslave her," Ylva replied. "He'll demand favors."

"Over my dead body," Turpin said. "Solveig will carve for him. He's got a slave girl already. No, I know Red Ottar. He'll take her aboard and give her passage to Ladoga."

"My friend," said Turpin. "I've brought you a treasure."

"Pff!"

Threads of Red Ottar's saliva glistened in his red-gold beard; some sprayed his companions.

"Hear that, Slothi? Turpin's brought us a treasure."

Slothi uncoiled himself and smiled a twisted smile.

"A treasure," the skipper repeated, treasuring the very word. "Since when, Turpin, have you done anything but fleece me with your stinking fleeces?"

Two of the men laughed, and a gat-toothed woman clapped her hands.

Solveig looked at them. Red Ottar and the pretty young woman with glistening dark brown hair, sitting at his feet; two middle-aged women; a girl and a boy, both much the same age as Blubba; and four other men, one with a black tooth, but one much younger, tall and dark-haired, who gazed intently at her with smiling eyes.

"Nothing for nothing," Red Ottar said. "Go on, then, Turpin. What treasure?"

Turpin simply turned his head toward Solveig and opened the palm of his right hand.

And the Baltic traders, they all looked at her. Ten pairs of eyes, unblinking.

"Nothing for nothing," Red Ottar said thoughtfully. "What do you want of me?"

"She can carve," Turpin told him. He shrugged off his shoulder bag, loosened the leather tie, and opened it. "Just look at these. These pins, this platter with runes around it."

Red Ottar sniffed. Then he put his right forefinger to one nostril and shot snot out of the other.

"She's come with us from Trondheim."

Red Ottar took a step toward Solveig and stood right in front of her.

"On the run, are you?"

Solveig shook her head.

"Too many beatings?"

Solveig flinched, but she gazed straight into Red Ottar's eyes and didn't blink.

"Or worse," said Red Ottar. "Put your carving knife into someone, did you?"

"No," said Solveig, much louder than she meant to.

"She's looking for passage," Turpin said. "Safe passage. She'll pay with her carvings."

"Hear that, Bruni?" Red Ottar said. "An assistant for you."

Red Ottar looked up at Solveig. She was almost a head taller than he was.

"Why?" he barked. "Why, then?"

"I'm following my father," Solveig replied. She opened her eyes wide.

The skipper grimaced and shook his head. "Alone?"

Solveig nodded.

"And where in the world is he?"

"Miklagard." Solveig paused. "I think he is."

"Miklagard," Red Ottar repeated. "I see . . . Hear that, everyone? Miklagard."

"A shining city for a shining girl," said the handsome young man.

"Never at a loss for words, are you, Vigot?" said Red Ottar.

Vigot gave Solveig a crafty smile. "Not on your own, surely?"

Red Ottar slapped his thighs, and then he threw back his head and laughed in Solveig's face. All the traders scoffed and jeered.

Red Ottar jabbed his forefinger into Solveig's neck. "This . . . this girl . . . what did you say your name is?"

"I didn't," Solveig replied.

"Go on, then," said Red Ottar.

Solveig never took her eyes off Red Ottar, not for one moment. "Nothing for nothing," she replied, doing her best to keep her voice clear and steady.

Hearing this, several of the traders began to laugh.

And the skipper, Red Ottar, he laughed at himself.

"Your father . . ." he said.

"Halfdan," Solveig replied.

"Never trust a Dane," Red Ottar said. "Not even half a Dane."

"Halfdan?" repeated an older man with very bright blue eyes. He frowned.

"Well, Torsten?" Red Ottar asked him.

"Yes," said the man. "Yes. On my last passage to Ladoga . . . Halfdan."

Solveig could feel cold waves rippling up her spine, spreading across the broad of her back, stiffening her neck.

"Last September," the man added. "Big man. Clumsy. He had a limp."

Solveig realized her breath had grown jerky. She felt her eyeballs burning.

Then the gat-toothed woman took a step forward and waved a scaly red hand in Solveig's face. "I say no," she announced.

"Nobody asked you," Red Ottar replied. "That's the trouble with you, Bergdis. You talk too much."

"I say no," Bergdis repeated with a gleam in her eye.

"To business," said Red Ottar. "The girl's following her father, and there's nothing wrong with that. But loyalty and high hopes, they only get you so far."

"Without them," said Solveig, "you get nowhere."

"Well?" he inquired.

"Solveig," she said, her voice strong and bright.

Red Ottar smiled through his mustache and red-gold beard. "And trust," he said. "That's another stepping-stone. Loyalty and high hopes and trust, they'll get you a long way, but not half as far as Miklagard." Then the skipper gave

Turpin a crafty look. "So," he said, "how come she matters so much to you?"

Turpin lowered his eyes.

"What's she to you?" Red Ottar persisted.

"She reminds me," Turpin said, and he gave a very deep sigh. "And she's to me what she must be to every man aboard." Turpin gave the handsome young man a long, meaningful look. "I want your word and hand on it."

"We're going to Kiev," Red Ottar said briskly.

"Kiev!" exclaimed Turpin.

"There's always a first time. More risk, but more money."

"Kiev," Turpin explained to Solveig. "That's south, far south. Beyond Ladoga. Beyond Novgorod."

"I know," Solveig said. "Yaroslav's the king there."

Red Ottar raised his eyebrows in surprise.

"My father told me. It's more than halfway to Miklagard."

"I'll throw in extra skins, my friend," offered Turpin.

"You will, my friend," replied Red Ottar in a dry voice. "You will! And we'll throw her overboard if she doesn't pull her weight." He looked around his crew of traders. "Yes . . ." he said slowly. "No . . . I see some of you want her aboard and some do not. Some for the right reasons, some for the wrong ones." The skipper turned back to Turpin. "All right!" he said. "We'll decide tonight. Come back first thing."

6

Solveig sat up half the night, carving by the light of the fire. First she cut the teeth in the maple comb to honor her part of the bargain with the three traders, and then she turned to the walrus-tusk flute.

Carving and looking forward . . .

I don't know what Red Ottar will decide, she thought. That big woman with the fish hands, she's against me. Vigot is really handsome, but he knows that he is, and I don't quite trust him. But what if they decide not to take me? What will I do then?

Looking forward and looking back . . . I don't feel bad about leaving Asta. She won't mind that I've gone. But I feel sad when I think of her sitting at home without a man. Some people do things, but others, like Asta, have things done to them. That's when despair darkens the doorstep.

At dawn, Solveig gave the walrus-tusk flute to Turpin.

"To play a dawn song to lighten your day," she told him.

Turpin frowned. "Who says I'm sad?"

"I do."

Then Turpin gave Solveig a grave look and, after that, a bear hug. "May the gods guide you to your father," he said.

While it was still very early, Solveig and the fur traders walked back along the lakeshore past the granary and malt house to Red Ottar's storehouse, and Solveig was carrying her small bundle of clothes, her reindeer skin, and her sack of bones.

"All right," announced Red Ottar. "We've decided to take you."

Solveig's heart lurched.

"Not," he added, "that we all wanted to. Not by any means."

That big woman, thought Solveig. Who else?

"But a crew's a crew," the skipper went on. "We all pull together."

"I'll pull with you," Solveig said.

"You will," Red Ottar replied. And then he turned to the big woman. "Bergdis," he said with an upthrust of his head. "And you, Odindisa."

Slothi's wife and Bergdis stepped forward and stood on either side of Solveig.

"Behold!" exclaimed Red Ottar. "Your two shoulder companions. Not to mention your fellow bailers and oarswomen. They're old hands—they've sailed with me a dozen times—and they will counsel you and caution you. They're accountable to me."

Solveig was aware of Bergdis's warm shoulder leaning into hers and of the cool space between her and Odindisa.

"And if you come to harm," Red Ottar said very deliberately, "so will they." He paused. "Hear that, Turpin?"

"I do."

"I swear it, my friend," said the skipper, wagging his right forefinger. "Now! Five men, four women, two children. We're a team of eleven, and we all have our own duties and bring our own skills. Your skill, Solveig, is to carve and to give me all your carvings to pay for your passage."

Solveig nodded. He's strong, she thought. I like that.

"Your duties," Red Ottar continued, "are to help Bergdis cook and to assist Bruni Blacktooth with smithing and carving. Do you understand?"

"I do," said Solveig.

"You may think we'll have plenty of time once we're under sail," Red Ottar told her, "but it's never like that. There's always something to be done."

Red Ottar turned to Torsten.

"So," he asked, "when can we set sail? What do you say, Torsten?"

Torsten said the weather was set fair. "Not only that. The wind's behind us."

"The wind's behind us, and my rival Ulrik's already ahead of us," said Red Ottar. "He left last night."

"Tomorrow at dawn, then," Torsten declared.

"Once we've sailed out of this lake and through the waterway to the sea," the skipper told Solveig, "our first landfall will be Åland. One big island. Hundreds of little ones. Like the moon surrounded by the stars. It's two days and two nights from here."

"We'll head straight for it," Torsten said, "unless the wind worsens."

"Åland," said Odindisa in a singsong voice. "It's alive with magicians."

"Pff!" spit Red Ottar. He gave Slothi's wife a sharp look.

"You know I sometimes see what others cannot," Odindisa went on.

The skipper clapped his hands. "Nonsense!"

Odindisa turned to Solveig and gave her a look, half wild, half lost, as if she were caught between worlds.

"Åland, then," Torsten repeated. "And after that, east, east all the way to Ladoga. At least five days and five nights from Åland."

"I saw two dancers turned into stone," Odindisa said dreamily.

"Odindisa," snapped Red Ottar, "I'll flatten you into a pancake."

"Shall I show the girl around?" Torsten asked.

Solveig's heart leaped. She couldn't wait to ask the helmsman about her father.

But Red Ottar said, "I'll come too. I've got to check the cargo."

"We've already checked it," Bruni Blacktooth told him. "Slothi and Vigot are both aboard, watching over it."

"Even so."

Solveig could see how proud of his boat Red Ottar was. He led the way across the landing stage and slapped her planks.

"Oak," he said. "Green oak planks. I saw them being split in the forest. She's only a yearling, you know."

"She's beautiful!" exclaimed Solveig.

"Look at that curve and sweep."

"Like waves," said Torsten. "Like my wife."

"She's my sea wife!" said Red Ottar. "The keel's all one timber, forty feet long. Know about ships, do you?"

Solveig shook her head. "Not really. Little ones. Cobles, skiffs. But I've never been aboard a boat half as fine as this."

"Come on, then," said the skipper. His eyes were fox-red and shining.

Oh! As Red Ottar marched Solveig up to the bows and back to the stern and from side to side, she felt so light-hearted that her feet scarcely touched the deck. In her ears she heard words her father used to say:

"My high prancer! My salt stallion!
One curlew calls and my heart
leaps within me, my thoughts roam
over the gold and glitter . . ."

"Pace her out," Red Ottar told Solveig. "Get to know her."

And with that, the three of them marched side by side from bows to stern again while Solveig counted out loud.

"Fourteen," said Solveig. "Four from side to side."

Red Ottar grunted and then nodded, and Torsten slipped Solveig a wink. "Still growing, is she, skipper?" he asked.

"A ship for the gods," said Red Ottar. "Wasted on you lot."

"You can never be sure," Torsten replied. "Some boats do better to sit on the beach than swim in the water."

"The sail's twenty feet high, twenty wide," Red Ottar told her. "Look at that pennant . . . look at these seal-hide ropes . . ."

He's so rough, Solveig thought, and yet he sounds as eager as a child.

"Right!" Red Ottar told Solveig. "We sail when we can and row when we can't. Here are the oarsmen's benches. I row opposite Vigot and . . ."

"You row?" exclaimed Solveig.

"Of course," the skipper replied. "Do you think I sit on my hands? Torsten's our helmsman, and I row opposite Vigot, Bruni rows opposite Slothi. And then you women, the four of you, will each row a half shift and do some bailing with the children."

"Who will I row with?"

The skipper pursed his lips. "We'll see about that," he said.

Solveig pointed to the open hold around the mast. "What's your cargo?" she asked.

"The usual mix," said Red Ottar. He stamped on the deck. "Stowed under here as well."

"Skins and furs?"

"Hundreds of them," Red Ottar said. "I will say this: old Baldy and his brother—what's his name? Orm?—they bring us better furs than anyone else."

"Turpin, you mean?"

"Baldy, yes."

"Why do you call him that?"

"Because he's so hairy! Mind you, they stink the place out. This time we're carrying wax as well—I've never seen so much. Enough to brighten every building in Ladoga . . . and Kiev."

"Furs and wax," said Solveig.

"And weapons," said Red Ottar, "some with decorated blades and pommels and sheaths. The Icelander, Bruni, he made them this last winter."

Torsten interrupted Red Ottar by spitting on the deck, then spreading the saliva under the sole of his left foot.

"What's wrong with you, Torsten?" barked Red Ottar.

But Torsten didn't reply. He just growled.

"Can I see them?" asked Solveig. "The weapons."

"You'll have to wait. They're all wrapped in oilcloth and stowed away under here." Red Ottar stamped the deck again and he laughed. "Look at you. Bright eyes!"

"It's all so new," Solveig said.

"And then," said Red Ottar, "we're carrying honey, barrels of honey. And board games. And, er . . ." he lowered his voice, "precious metals."

"Gold, you mean?"

Dawn.

Gulls mewed. Terns trilled. But as Torsten untied the boat and she began to glide, then gently to rock, all the companions were silent, caught between earth and water—and between what they were leaving and what lay ahead.

It took them all morning and early afternoon to sail from the harbor on the lake of Malar through the waterway to the open sea, and only then did the west wind really pick up.

The waves clapped their hands, and Red Ottar's boat skipped and whistled.

Solveig sat in the stern, aft of the huge square sail. This is just as fresh as when I was swept past Trondheim, she thought.

"Swinging around," Torsten called out to her.

Solveig squinted up at him.

"The wind!" he bellowed.

"My father," began Solveig, "did he . . . ?"

Torsten motioned her to come closer. "Can't hear you," he said. "Not with all this wind slap."

"My father . . ." Solveig began again.

The helmsman clamped his jaw and nodded firmly. "Good man," he said. "Man of words. Man of stories."

"You talked to him?" Solveig asked.

"We were pinned down in Ladoga for two days," Torsten told her. "North wind. Yes, he told me about Harald Sigurdsson and sailing to join him."

"Oh!" said Solveig, feeling disappointed.

"But he was thinking more about what he'd left behind than what lay ahead. I could see that. The farm . . . Asta . . . One evening he told me about Siri . . . Sirith."

"My mother!" said Solveig eagerly.

"But," said Torsten, first considering Solveig, then laying a warm hand on her left shoulder, "it was you. You, Solveig."

Solveig held her breath.

"Yes," said the helmsman. "He told me how much . . . how most of all, he was missing you."

Solveig felt so hungry. For all that Torsten had told her, she ached for more. As if however much he told her, it could never be enough.

On the other side of Torsten, Vigot hauled in his fishing line and grasped a glittering, jerking sea trout; he took the hook out of its mouth and smacked its head against the gunwales.

Vigot gave Solveig a calculating look. "They can't resist me," he said, and he smiled.

I can, though, Solveig thought. The one who really can't resist you is you!

Red Ottar and Edith were sitting in the shadow of the groaning sail. He was winding a piece of Edith's long dark hair around her left ear . . .

Bergdis was preparing the fish Vigot had already caught, tossing their entrails overboard, where they were snapped up by screaming gulls before they even touched the water . . . Bard and Brita were crouching over some board game, and their father, Slothi, was half watching them. Bruni Blacktooth was searching for something where the cargo was stacked, quietly swearing to himself. And away on her own in the bows, Slothi's wife, Odindisa, was reaching out with both arms, far out over the water, singing and saying.

She's silver-eyed, thought Solveig. Sharp as a scythe. Was she for me or against me?

All around Solveig, the traders were at their business or leisure, and slowly the chariot of the sun journeyed downward, chased by the wolf Skoll, always yapping and snapping just behind her.

"The ravens!" screeched a voice right behind Solveig.

"Oh!" gasped Solveig.

"The ravens!" screeched Bergdis. "Thought and Memory—I can see them sitting on your shoulders."

Solveig scrambled to her feet. "I didn't see you," she said.

Bergdis waved her filleting knife, and it flashed in the sunlight. "I need your help, and I need it now. Come sundown, there'll be eleven hungry mouths and empty stomachs aboard this boat."

"What shall I do?" she asked.

"The same as me. Heads off! Tails off! And then gut them." Bergdis gave Solveig a shrewd look. "To be a Viking woman," she said, "you have to be a man as well."

"What do you mean?"

"You'll find out." She tapped her chin with the point of her filleting knife. "Follow me," she said, and she waddled down the deck.

Bergdis's little hearth, just an iron plate surrounded by four iron fenders, was down in the hold, well protected from the sea breezes. There she and Solveig grilled their first meal aboard—the sea trout and mackerel caught by Vigot—and added cold mash of turnip and carrot. And after they'd eaten this, washed down with cloudy ale, Solveig felt too tired to begin carving. Anyhow, the light was failing fast.

"Nothing goes to waste." That's what my father says, thought Solveig. He'd tell me that even if my carving hasn't become part of my journey yet, my journey will become part of my carving.

I like the way he plays with words, and it's true, master carvers and poets do bring their days and years—their life journey—to their work.

That's why Odin says we should listen to gray-haired singers. *Though they hang with the hides and flap with the pelts,* he says, *and though they rock with the guts in the wind, shriveled skins often give good advice.*

But believing, self-believing . . . that's what matters most, isn't it? Some people scoff at me and tell me I'll never reach Miklagard. Even Turpin did to begin with. But I will! I will for as long as I believe I will.

Solveig unrolled her reindeer skin. She curled up beneath it, and before she had fallen asleep, her two shoulder companions lay down on either side of her. She could feel the way in which heavy-breathing, full-bodied Bergdis lay close to her, and she sensed the distance between her and silent, stick-thin Odindisa. She put both hands to her heart.

Father! My father! I never thought you wouldn't be there when I came down from the hill. Not for one moment. How could you have left without telling me? How could you?

Solveig sighed and stretched. She gazed at the helmsman, sitting in the stern and holding the steering oar, his face lit by his night lantern.

Just when night is darker than dark, in the hour of the wolf, Solveig and Red Ottar and all the traders were woken and shaken by the sail's huge wing flapping, the pine mast groaning and the whole boat jolting and shuddering. Sheets of salt spray stung them, and Torsten was standing and yelling, bawling into the night.

Everyone staggered down the deck and pressed around him. Then Solveig was thrown right off balance, tripped over a wooden chest, and went sprawling. Vigot helped her up and clicked his tongue. "Throwing yourself at my feet!" he said.

But Solveig quickly shrugged him off—she was as scared as everyone else.

"What?" cried everyone. "What is it? What's happened?"

"Out of the way!" shouted Red Ottar. "Torsten! What was it, man?"

Torsten just went on staring over the stern, staring and pointing.

"Whatever it was," he said. "Whatever. Out of the dark, back into the dark."

"Away with you!" Red Ottar called. "Away! Back to your bedding!"

Hollow-eyed, Torsten turned to the traders.

It wasn't until early next morning that Torsten told everyone what had happened.

"It loomed up," he said. "It swam out of the dark. One moment it wasn't there, the next it was."

"What did?" everyone demanded. "What was it?"

"A ship. Pitch black. Darker than night."

"Even its sail?" asked Solveig.

"That as well. The only pale thing was the lookout man, standing in the prow. Big man," he told Solveig, "rather like your father, but I could see right through him."

Solveig stiffened, and Odindisa sucked in her breath through her teeth.

"I yelled at him, but he didn't reply. So then I angled this steering paddle and prayed for strength. Almost wrenched off my arms, it did."

"But for you, Torsten," said Red Ottar, "we'd all be at the bottom of the Baltic."

Torsten squared his jaw and raised his eyes to Asgard. "Don't thank me," he said. "Thank your sea wife!"

"Wave knock," said Edith, as if she were remembering something. "Wave thump. Scream."

"That's the point," Torsten said. "Ships sound. Bows slice. Hulls creak and pennants rap. But this one didn't. It was completely silent."

"I warned you," Odindisa said. "Magicians. I sensed them when I reached over the water. They were on their way out from Åland."

"Says who?" asked Red Ottar in a scornful voice.

"I say so," Odindisa replied, and she spread her cloak a little.

"Sendings," said Bruni.

"What?" asked Red Ottar.

"Back home in Iceland," Bruni said, "there are magicians who know how to cast death spells and how to raise people from the dead. They know how to make Sendings."

"What's that?" Solveig asked.

"Vapors. Sendings can grow themselves as big as giants or small as flies. They board boats and cross oceans and put people into such deep sleep they never wake again."

"Tell us later, Bruni," Red Ottar told him. "There'll be plenty of time for your stories."

"Sendings are not imaginings," said Bruni. "In Iceland we all know about them."

Torsten glared at Bruni. "You can send yourself one for all I care."

"Magicians from Åland," Odindisa repeated. "Magicians or ghosts. We'd do better to avoid the islands."

"Why?" asked Red Ottar. "They weren't after us."

"He's right," Torsten said. "Otherwise we'd never have escaped."

"I'm not changing course," the skipper told Torsten. "Not because of a silent ship."

"We must make a sacrifice for our escape," Odindisa said. "Otherwise Ægir . . ."

"What?" asked Bruni. "What can we sacrifice?"

"Something living."

The traders looked at each other. They looked at Bergdis.

"Ægir and Ran won't think much of mice or rats," Bergdis said, "even if we can catch them. So . . . apart from ourselves . . . the only living things are the three chickens."

"That settles it," Red Ottar said. "One of them."

So Bergdis told Solveig to fetch one of the chickens from the cage beside the mast. "The plump one. The black one."

Solveig shook her head. "It's such a waste."

"A waste?" said Torsten. "A waste to sacrifice to the gods?"

"Oh, no," said Bergdis, smiling. "She won't go to waste. All the gods want is the chicken's spirit."

When Solveig returned with the squawking black chicken, she saw Bergdis had slipped on a strange bracelet. She and Edith examined it.

"It looks as if it's made of little finger bones," Solveig said, and she counted them. "Seven of them. Braided and lying side by side."

"Is that what they are?" Edith asked.

Bergdis didn't reply. She just looked at Edith, and her eyes glittered.

Then she pulled out of her deep cloak pocket her filleting knife, the same one she'd brandished over Solveig's head. She grabbed the chicken from Solveig, held her up, and with a scream slit her breast so that her blood and gizzards spewed over the deck.

The traders got to their knees. Edith retched; all the others gave thanks to Ægir and Ran.

"When we sailed from Sigtuna," Bergdis warbled, "our sea horse was kicking and prancing. But the black ship swam out of the dark. You guided Torsten's hand, you gave us safe passage . . ."

After Bergdis had finished, Torsten said, "Don't forget the ale. Ægir's always thirsty."

"He can have mine," gurgled Edith, and she retched again.

"Half the mug behind us and half before us," Red Ottar told her.

So Edith threw her ale onto the thirsty waves.

"Ægir and Ran be praised," said Slothi. "And Christ be praised."

"What?" snapped Red Ottar. His bull neck turned red and the veins stuck out. "How dare you? I'm not having anyone call on the White Christ on my boat."

"You're no husband of mine," Odindisa told Slothi in a low, cold voice. "Christ . . . Christ."

"You can worship the gods and Christ at the same time," Slothi said. "That's what I do."

"He brought war to Sweden," the skipper went on. "Blood and death." He rounded on Solveig. "And to your country too. When King Olaf came back from Kiev and fought in Christ's name at Stiklestad."

Solveig slowly nodded and closed her eyes. "I know," she said under her breath, and she remembered the ghosts of men who died at Stiklestad swimming in the water as she sailed to Trondheim.

Red Ottar looked at her thoughtfully. "You've been there?"

"And never left," Solveig replied. "Whoever goes to Stiklestad never leaves Stiklestad. That's what people say." She looked gravely at Red Ottar.

"They had their time," Red Ottar said, "and it was their time to die. Right! Let's hear no more of Christ. His men killed my brother and my brother's son."

Then Bergdis turned to Solveig and gave her the mangled remains of the black chicken. "Pluck her," she said. "Save what you can for the pot."

So Solveig sat with her back to the mast and plucked the luckless chicken. The sea wind swept away the feathers, even the sticky ones. Scenting the blood of their own sister, the remaining two chickens squawked anxiously inside their cage.

Torsten. He knows something about Bruni, thought Solveig. There's bad blood between them.

Solveig had a lump in her throat. And, quite suddenly, her troubled tears were dropping onto the chicken's carcass.

Blood, she thought between sobs. Lifeblood washed away by tears.

The mood of the crew was sober all morning. And during the afternoon, a light sea mist dipped and rose and shape-changed around them, and everyone felt imprisoned inside their own heads and hearts. Everyone except for Vigot. He whistled like a finch and announced that stillness and mist were bad for fish but good for fishermen.

"Mist made by Ålanders," Odindisa told Solveig, who was standing with Torsten in the stern. "They make mist when they want to keep people away."

"What nonsense you do talk," Torsten said. "Hot and cold make mist when they mix too quickly."

"How many islands are there?" Odindisa asked.

"I don't know."

"Exactly," said Odindisa. "The magicians raise them and sink them. The number's always changing."

"Odindisa," said Torsten, reaching out and tapping her forehead, "that's where the mist is. Nothing but mist."

"You'll see," Odindisa warned him.

As it was, Torsten could see well enough to guide the ship in to Åland. While Bergdis and Odindisa hauled down the great sail, the four men—Red Ottar with Vigot and Bruni with Slothi—readied themselves at the oarsmen's benches and quietly rowed the boat into the harbor.

It was already almost dark, and not until next morning could Solveig see where they were. It was a mangy, ragged, drafty kind of place, its waterfront peopled by no more than a dozen or so traders and suppliers. A home for shrieking gulls and prowling cats, punctuated by fish guts and piles of sodden, stinking seaweed.

It's not what I expected, Solveig thought. Not at all. Or are the gulls and the cats all magicians?

During the morning, Solveig and the traders busied themselves securing more provisions. Then Red Ottar told the crew they were free to come and go until nightfall.

"And wherever you go and whatever you do," he said, "find yourselves better spirits. No ship makes good headway against argument and ill feeling. They're just as dangerous as floating ice or submerged rocks." The skipper looked around at his crew so intently that each was convinced he was singling them out. "And you can be quite sure," he warned them, "if there's further argument, one of you will be leaving this boat. Even if we're at sea."

Solveig decided to go off on her own.

Eleven of us, she thought. It's so cramped, and sometimes I feel as if I can't breathe. No wonder we keep squabbling.

I know I should be carving, but I'll wear my waist pouch. I'll walk along the foreshore and collect bones.

Almost as soon as she heard her leather soles slapping against the gangplank and then stretched her long limbs— her legs and her arms as well—Solveig began to feel better. She inhaled great gulps of air, stinking of seaweed and fish guts; then she expelled all the air again until her lungs were flat and empty and she was coughing.

Solveig left the little harbor behind her and picked her way along the strand. She saw a yellow-breasted bird she'd never seen before. It was hopping, hopping in front of her, looking at her sideways, whistling.

You're leading me on, Solveig thought. And I'll follow you. But then she thought: What if you're a magician? Are you going to catch me and cut off my hair?

Solveig was so busy watching the bird and telling herself stories that she didn't hear the footsteps behind her.

"Ah!" said the voice. "We're heading the same way, then."

Solveig whirled around and at once slipped on a slimy rock.

"Careful!" said the voice, and a pair of hands clamped around her slender ribs and helped her up.

Solveig looked into her helper's eyes.

"Vigot!" she exclaimed. "Were you following me?"

"No."

"Liar!"

"Well," said Vigot, "you're worth following."

The young man leaned toward her with his mouth half open, as if he were ready to swallow Solveig's least response. But she turned her head to one side, raised her right hand, and pushed it gently but firmly against Vigot's chin.

"You've got strange eyes," Vigot told her.

Solveig shrugged. "I can't see them," she said.

"One gray, one violet. Like a changeling."

Solveig grinned. "That's what my stepmother says."

"Not young and not old."

"That's what she says too," said Solveig, frowning. "Anyhow, your eyes are strange too."

"How?"

They're like fishhooks, she thought. And I can't help looking at them.

"How?" Vigot asked again.

But Solveig just shook her head and kept her mouth shut.

"Where are you going?" Vigot asked.

"I'm following that bird."

"And I'm following you," Vigot said, and he laughed.

"Go away," said Solveig.

But she didn't wholly mean it, and Vigot knew she didn't.

"All right," Solveig said. "If that bird cuts off my hair . . ."

"What do you mean?"

". . . and makes a net to catch a tide mouse, you'll have to save me."

Vigot shook his head and smiled.

When the two of them had crossed a beach of gritty sand and then climbed a green rise, they were surprised to see almost below them a large group of huts and several long-houses with turf roofs.

"So that's how it is," Vigot said. "The harbor's just a harbor."

"And look," added Solveig. "See that track? That leads straight from the village to the harbor."

"A less interesting way," said Vigot with a shady smile.

In the middle of the village, quite a crowd had gathered, and Solveig saw they were watching a wrestling match.

Almost at once, everyone around her yelled. One of the young men had thrown the other and pinioned him, and that was it: the contest was over.

Then Solveig realized that Vigot was no longer standing beside her.

"Wait!" he shouted. "Wait!" And he pushed his way through the crowd. Then he looked back over his shoulder at Solveig. "You'll see," he called out.

No, she thought. What if we're not back in time? What if . . . I don't know.

Vigot walked straight up to the young islander who had just won the contest. He pointed at him and then at himself. Then he fished in a pocket and pulled out a little piece of hack-silver the size of a fingernail.

The young islander nodded and smiled and for his part held up what looked like a silver thimble, then laid it on the ground beside the hack-silver.

Vigot stripped to the waist, and the crowd whistled and booed and cheered.

The moment Vigot and the islander grabbed hold of each other, Solveig could see how lithe and deceptive her companion was. He wasn't as muscular or sturdy as his opponent, but he made up for that with his speed and his feints.

All the same, the islander was the first to strike. He reached out and tried to grab the back of Vigot's neck. Vigot leaned back, but his opponent clawed his right cheek from his ear down to his chin, drawing blood.

Then Solveig saw how rough Vigot could be. He caught the islander's arm and twisted it behind his back. The young man bucked and writhed, but Vigot wouldn't let him go. He forced him down onto one knee, groaning.

Solveig was dry-mouthed. She wanted Vigot to win, and she wanted him not to win.

As it was, Vigot did win. He forced the islander onto both knees and then flat on his face. But after the young man had submitted, Solveig saw Vigot give his arm a terrible extra twist. Then Vigot kicked him hard in the ribs so that he lay in the grit, groaning.

Vigot swept up his own piece of silver and the thimble as well, but the villagers were angry.

They yelled, and one young man made a dive for Vigot's shirt. Vigot tried to grab it back, but two more men restrained him.

"Give it back!" Vigot shouted, but by now he and Solveig were in the middle of a scrum, and Solveig was slapped around the face and elbowed in the ribs.

"Out!" yelled Vigot. "Come on! We've got to get out!"

Then he seized Solveig's right hand. He dragged her behind him, and the two of them broke away from the crowd and began to run along the track leading straight back to the harbor.

"Oot!" howled the villagers. "Oot!"

They spit at Solveig and Vigot, and several boys threw stones after them.

By the time the two of them were sure the islanders were no longer following them, they were both gasping for breath.

"You fool!" cried Solveig.

"He asked for it," panted Vigot.

"He gave in. You were cruel."

"He played foul."

Solveig didn't believe him. "It was you who played foul."

"There's only one way to defeat foul play," Vigot said, "and that's with foul play."

Solveig was still gasping. "There was no need. You put us both at risk."

"Pff!"

"You did," she said angrily. "We could have been stoned."

"Are you hurt?" asked Vigot, putting his left arm around Solveig's shoulder.

Solveig brusquely shook him off. "Who taught you to wrestle like that anyway?"

Vigot shrugged.

"Your brothers?"

"I have no brothers."

"Your father, then?"

Vigot shook his head. "Dead to me," he said.

"Your mother—where's she?"

Vigot shrugged, and Solveig could see he didn't want to talk about her or any of his family.

As soon as Solveig and Vigot walked up the gangplank, Red Ottar and Torsten advanced on them. The skipper narrowed his eyes and slowly drew his fingernails over his own right cheek.

"Well?" he asked. "Love tracks, are they? A woman's claws?"

"Wrestling," said Solveig. "He was wrestling."

"Not with you!" Torsten exclaimed.

"Of course not," said Solveig, and the blood rushed to her own cheeks. "Over there, in the village. There was a contest."

"You won?" Red Ottar asked.

Vigot nodded.

"And the prize?"

Vigot showed Red Ottar and Torsten the silver thimble.

"Vigot cheated. The whole village turned against us," Solveig said. "They yelled at us and chased us."

Vigot glared angrily at Solveig, but she said nothing more.

"Where's your shirt?" Red Ottar asked him.

Vigot clamped his jaw and thrust his chin in the air.

"They grabbed it," said Solveig. "They wouldn't give it back."

"Disgraceful!" barked Red Ottar. "Both of you. We're traders, not raiders. They'll be waiting for you on our way back."

Solveig knew that if she tried to say more, it would only make matters worse.

"Right!" said Red Ottar, clapping his hands. "The stew's ready. Chicken stew. We'll be off at dawn, won't we, Torsten?"

"Ægir willing!" Torsten said.

"He'd better be," the skipper retorted. "This is where our journey really begins."

"Not mine," said Solveig.

"What do you mean?" Red Ottar asked. "Staying here, are you?"

"No," said Solveig. "I mean, I've been on my journey since the day my father left home."

"Then it's high time you started to pay for it," Red Ottar snapped. "That's what we agreed, isn't it? Instead of making us enemies, you should be carving."

8

Solveig watched as Slothi drew the game board on the pine planking with a piece of chalk and then asked Bard and Brita to set out the walrus-bone chessmen. "Now remember," he told them, "you don't have to kill all your enemies. The best players win without spilling too much blood."

"How?" Brita asked.

Slothi reached out and tapped the top of his daughter's head. "By using what's in here," he said. "Wits. Cunning. If you can win without too much slaughter, that's more satisfying."

I wish my father had taught me chess, thought Solveig. It's more interesting than checkers. More sly. It makes my brains ache.

But what was really aching was Solveig's heart. Seeing Slothi play with his children made her miss her own father.

"What's in your bag, Solveig?" Bard asked her.

"It's a sack," Brita corrected him.

"Bones!" said Solveig.

"Bones!" exclaimed Bard. "Human ones?"

"No. Well . . . yes. One is."

"Let's see," said Brita excitedly.

"Bard!" warned Slothi. "Brita! You're like a whole swarm of buzzing flies."

"She doesn't mind."

"Do you, Solveig?"

"I'll show you later," Solveig told them. "You're going to play chess, and I'm going to carve. That's how I'm paying for my passage."

On her own, Solveig quickly opened her little sackful of bones, rummaged in it, and pulled out the wad of bog cotton. She checked that no one was watching . . .

However often Solveig looked at the precious gold brooch, her heart beat faster each time. That man in the bows, she thought, I still don't know who he is, but I quite like not knowing. I can make my own mind up. And the smaller one in the stern, arms outstretched, I don't know who she is either, but the longer I look at her, the better I know her.

Solveig turned over the brooch.

ᚺᛗ and ᚺᚠ. HS and HA.

I know. I'll cut two more runes next to these. ᛋᚺ— Solveig Halfdan's daughter.

Then she quickly wrapped the brooch up again.

It's all right to keep it here, thought Solveig. No one's going to delve down to the bottom of this sack. And no one aboard would steal anything. I don't think they would.

So Solveig got to work on the antler of a red deer, and she scraped it and began to shape it for a good part of the quiet afternoon before setting it aside. Then she stretched and closed her hands to ease the ache in her fingers.

I'll finish off the walrus pin, she thought. I'll decorate it with long wavy lines. Like wavy hair. Like the salt waves all around me.

But no sooner had Solveig put the point of her awl to the pin than the boat shuddered and the awl slipped.

Solveig pressed her lips together and frowned. She held the pin tight between her right thumb and forefinger, and, clamping her arms tightly to her sides so as to keep it steady, she pointed the awl at the pin again.

"Ah!" said a voice. "My apprentice."

"Ow-wow!" exclaimed Solveig, frustrated at being unable to incise the bone and at being interrupted.

"What's wrong?" asked Bruni Blacktooth.

"I'm not."

"Not what?"

"Your apprentice."

"The wise craftsman always know there's more to learn. It's like climbing a mast. The higher you climb, the more you see. Now then, you're decorating that walrus pin."

"I can't," Solveig told him. "The boat keeps trembling and shuddering."

Bruni grunted. "Put the pin in your left hand," he told her. "Yes, and the awl in your right hand."

"But I'm left-handed."

"Now, Solveig, slowly bring the pin to the awl, not the awl to the pin. You see? This way you have better control."

Solveig nodded. "Yes," she said. "I never knew that."

"Mind you," Bruni went on, "young women can't carve. Too soft. Neither can old ones." Bruni leered at Solveig, and she could smell his foul breath. "Still, they've got their uses."

"Is that what you think?" Solveig asked fiercely.

"I've never met a single woman who's a good carver. I've never met a good woman, for that matter."

Solveig tossed her head. "So were you against me coming?" she asked in a sharp voice. "The same as Bergdis?"

Bruni ignored Solveig's question. "But as it is, my dear," he continued, "we're yoked. Yoked!" He put an arm around Solveig's shoulders.

"No," said Solveig angrily. She pulled away, and as she did so, she drove the soft heel of her left hand, just below her thumb, into the point of the awl.

Solveig screamed as lightning flashed in her thumb, and the muscles separated. Then hot red blood spurted over her gown, and when she sucked her hand, she smeared her face with blood as well.

Solveig cried furious tears. "Look! Look what you've made me do."

"I'll bind it," said Bruni.

"Get away!" sobbed Solveig. "I'll do it myself."

Solveig's thumb ached. Her fingers were stiff, and her whole hand was red and hot. Her left wrist and forearm throbbed.

For two days she sat in the prow or by the mast, her hand swaddled with greasy strips of cloth.

Bergdis scolded her because she couldn't help with the cooking. And Red Ottar was annoyed because she couldn't carve.

Strange birds with dark wings and pointed tails were following the boat, and Solveig trundled to the stern to ask Torsten about them.

"Skuas," said Torsten. "Of a kind. You don't often see them this far out to sea."

"So why are they, then?"

Torsten gazed at Solveig, and she found herself thinking she had never met anyone with so clear a gaze, an unblinking gaze that could see over all the rolls and scrolls of the ocean to the edge of the world.

"Why?" Solveig asked again.

Torsten flexed his broad shoulders. "I can tell you truths about tides and stars and winds, the breeding grounds of walrus, the feeding grounds of whales. I can tell you about birds too. But . . ." The helmsman spread his arms wide and slowly shook his head.

"They're not the same as the ones in our fjord," Solveig told him. "They've got sharper bills and tails."

"Sharp as awls," said Torsten.

Solveig sucked in her breath and screwed up her face.

"I saw the way Blacktooth was talking to you." Torsten looked her square in the eyes. "And pawing you. You be careful."

Not long after Solveig had gone back to amidships, Edith came and sat down beside her.

"Aching?" she asked.

"All over. And shivering."

Edith screwed up her eyes and nodded.

"Not just my hand."

"Your heart," Edith said.

Solveig shook her head in frustration so that her golden hair swung from side to side. "Ohh!" she cried. "What if I never get to Miklagard?"

"I know," said Edith, and she very gently squeezed Solveig's right arm. "I do know."

Solveig sucked in her cheeks and swallowed loudly.

"Expect the worst," Edith told her. "Anything better will be a mercy then. Even small pleasures will become great wonders."

Solveig stared at Edith. Her dark hair keeps flapping over her eyes, she thought, like the fringe of a glossy long-haired pony. And she always looks as if she's smiling even when she's not. She soft-foots around like a sweet shadow.

"Expect the worst? Is that what you have to do?" Solveig faltered. "Well, I do know you're Red Ottar's slave girl. His slave woman. But . . ."

Edith crossed her legs and drew her shawl around her. A black beetle fell out of it and hurried across the deck.

"See that?" said Edith. "Free. Free to go where it wants."

"Without knowing it is," Solveig replied, "or where it's going."

"Which is better?" asked Edith. "To be free and not know where you're going or to be enslaved and know?"

"That sounds like a riddle," Solveig said.

"You do know I'm English?"

"Yes."

"Do you know where England is?"

"South."

"South and west," said Edith. "Opposite Denmark. Beyond two groups of islands."

"Shetland . . ." said Solveig.

"And Orkney."

"Oh! That's where Slothi's chess pieces come from."

"Yes," Edith said. "He told me that."

"I like the way you speak our language," Solveig told her. "The way you try it out, as if each word is like stepping on new ice."

"It is," said Edith with a smile, and she edged closer to Solveig. "Do you want to know . . ." she asked, "what happened?"

"Oh!" breathed Solveig. "Everything."

"A gang of Swedes attacked our village."

"Why?"

"Something about a curse. A curse that old Hilda . . . she was our wise woman . . . a curse she put on them."

"What did they do?"

"They killed Hilda, and then they speared my father . . ." Edith put both hands to her throat.

"No!" cried Solveig.

"He was the headman. They dragged me away from my own children."

"Children?" gasped Solveig. "You've got children."

Edith lowered her head and raised two fingers.

"Oh, Edith!"

"Emma," she whispered. "Wulf."

"No," wailed Solveig.

Edith grabbed Solveig's arm, the wrong one, and Solveig flinched but she bore the pain.

"Then . . ." Edith went on, swallowing furiously, "they carried me to their boat. I was screaming. They threw me down and bound me. They sailed me to Sigtuna."

Solveig stared at Edith, speechless.

Edith nodded. "Yes," she said in a voice cold as stone, "and they sold me."

"To Red Ottar?"

Edith nodded again.

At that moment, Brita and Bard rushed past, yelling, and Edith at once burst into tears. Solveig put her right arm around her.

"It's Emma," she said in a choked voice. "And Wulf. It's all right otherwise."

"All right?" said Solveig angrily. "Being Red Ottar's slave? To do with you as he pleases?"

Edith looked at Solveig through her veil of hair and tears. "Solveig," she sobbed, "Ottar's not a bad man. He's good, as men go. But this is how it is for most women. Drudgery from daybreak to dark, and then after dark succumbing to your man's desires. It's dangerous, carrying babies and giving birth. It's painful when men slap you or thrash you or even worse. That's why we must expect the worst. That's why we must take what small pleasures there are."

Solveig shook her head. She felt so sad for Edith, so angry at what she'd heard.

Edith smiled, though. She put two fingers to her lips and lightly touched the top of Solveig's head.

Talking like this, thought Solveig, it's like having a sister. I hope we'll be able to talk again soon. I think I could tell her about my father and everything.

"Yes," Edith told her, "I believe Ottar will be good to me." She crossed herself. "And I believe I'll have a better home in heaven."

"You're Christian!" exclaimed Solveig.

Edith and Solveig were able to sit down together the next afternoon while Red Ottar was sleeping off a tide of ale. But Solveig had only just begun to tell her about her father when the helmsman came right up to them.

"Torsten!" exclaimed Solveig. "I was telling Edith about my father."

Torsten nodded. "Land," he said. "Land. We'll be in the estuary of the River Neva before dusk."

Solveig and Edith stood up. With Torsten, they watched the fuzzy blur on the skyline begin to turn blue and green.

"I must wake Ottar," said Edith.

But as if he were possessed of some sixth sense—some inner alertness—the skipper woke himself. He stretched and got to his feet.

"All hands to the oars!" he roared. "All hands! Bergdis with Odindisa! And you, Edith, you with cack-handed Solveig."

Edith smiled at Solveig. "Whether you can or not," she said.

9

"Solveig," Bruni called out between one stroke and the next, "some of us think you should be a man." Then he looked across at his fellow oarsman. "You should too, Slothi!"

Red Ottar and Vigot guffawed. So did Bergdis, who was sitting in the hold, plucking a chicken.

"If a horse could laugh . . ." Red Ottar called out, pulling at his oar, "if a horse could laugh, Bergdis, it would laugh like you."

For a while the crew kept their own counsel as they strained at their oars.

"All right!" said Solveig. "Cover my hair, then."

"You'll need more adjustments than that!" Vigot sang out.

Everyone guffawed again. Except Edith. She just sighed loudly. And then, less loudly, "The same old gibes, time and again."

With the steering paddle lashed, Torsten was able to leave the helm for a few minutes. He stepped up to the oarsmen, flexing his forearms.

"Want a turn?" Bergdis asked him.

"Like you want to be plucked," Torsten replied. "How's the hand, Solveig?"

Solveig pulled her oar. "Women," she said, "seldom complain."

The five men jeered.

"Solveig's right," said Edith.

Bergdis looked up. "You men think women should be more like you. We know life would be better if you were more like us."

Red Ottar twisted right around on his bench. "You gat-toothed, loudmouthed harridan!" he exclaimed. "Just how should we be more like you? I'll remind you, I'm your skipper."

"We'd all be lost without you," Bergdis said in a mocking voice. And then she added, under her breath, "I'll stuff you, Ottar, like a festival chicken!"

"You're jealous, Bergdis, aren't you?" Vigot chimed in. "Jealous of men. Jealous of youth."

"I'm who I am," Bergdis muttered.

Then, once more, the three pairs of oars pulled together—in unison if not in harmony.

Standing just in front of Solveig, Torsten loomed over Bruni.

"Got a wife, have you?" he asked.

Bruni didn't reply.

"Got a wife? I said."

"In every port," Bruni replied.

"Back home in Iceland?"

"I have," said Bruni in a measured voice.

"Norwegian, is she?"

Bruni threw down his oar and stood up. "Who told you that?" he asked, and he planted himself right in front of Torsten and glared at him.

The helmsman stared back at Bruni, unblinking. "I thought as much," he said in a dark voice. Then he spun around, strode back to the stern, and unlashed the paddle.

Solveig felt confused. What is it between them? she wondered.

Before dusk, Red Ottar joined Torsten in the stern. "How about that strand over there?" he asked.

Torsten gazed at it. "Easy enough," he replied. "Shallow. Sandy."

Red Ottar slid his hand along the gunwale. "Run her up gently, then," he said.

The skipper called over to Bard and Brita. "The hold's awash!" he told them. "I want you to start bailing as soon as we beach her. Understand?"

"Yes," said the children.

"Yes," Red Ottar repeated. "You can sing for your supper."

It was cold that night, the stars glittered, and the crew slept under their sail as well as their furs and skins.

At dawn, after breaking their fast with cold herring and a lump of bread, they were on their way again, but even so it took them all day to row and sail up the River Neva into a lake so wide they couldn't see across it. That evening, they had to beach their boat for a second time.

Before she lay down, Solveig heard wolves howling.

"Garthar," said Vigot.

Solveig looked puzzled.

"The wolves of Garthar."

Solveig hugged herself.

Vigot eyed her. "If you want," he said, "you can come and sleep under my skin."

Solveig thrust out her chin. "I'd be safer with the wolves," she said.

The next day Red Ottar and his companions hugged the shoreline of the great lake until they came to a wide waterway.

"Nearly there!" Torsten sang out. "Two hours up here."

"Two hours!" exclaimed Vigot. He turned to Solveig. "Two hours and we'll be tying up in Ladoga. I'll show you everything. The Earth Town. The fortress. The best market on the whole eastern way."

"Except for Kiev," Torsten said.

"Kiev," repeated Red Ottar, savoring the word.

"But we'll need a river guide," the helmsman told him. "I don't know all the twists and turns and sandbanks and . . ."

The skipper held up his right hand and silenced him. "We wouldn't have gotten this far," he said, "without a good helmsman. You've done us proud, Torsten."

"Thank Ægir and Ran," Torsten replied. "Thank the spirits of all the drowned men."

"I'm thanking you, man," insisted Red Ottar. "Each of us has his own skills, but some matter a great deal more than others."

In the blue hour, when everything's chancy and uncertain—earth and water, thought and feeling—Red

Ottar and his crew paddled quietly up the wide waterway leading from the lake into the harbor of Ladoga. They ate and drank aboard, and while they did so, Red Ottar told them about the town's Swedish ruler and the people who lived there.

The skipper was in such a good mood that he ruffled Solveig's golden hair. "Ladoga," he said. "Ladoga, where Garthar begins. So what's the best part of a journey? The beginning or the middle or the end?"

Sobs of wind. Now and then a skuther. And a whistling as it tore at the rigging.

Solveig lay between sleeping Bergdis and Odindisa and looked up at the sail that the crew had stretched from gunwale to gunwale as a makeshift tent.

Then she reached up and trailed her finger pads across it. It's well woven, she thought. It needs to be. Like a wife who endures blusters and bruises. But here and there the warp and weft are not so tight. And look, the salt wind has scoured this patch here and almost worn it away.

Solveig lifted her head and peered through one of the sail's wind eyes. Fluffy ribbons of pink cloud. A flock of little scooting shorebirds, flying low.

This is the time of day I like best, she thought. A sort of no time when there's all the time in the world.

Ladoga's got a Swedish ruler . . . that's what Red Ottar said. But he didn't tell us why. All the names of people and places, they muddled me. Them and that ale . . . Solveig screwed up her eyes and felt her temples throbbing. I think he said Swedish earls have ruled here for

Edith looked at Solveig, and Solveig looked at Edith, and they both laughed.

Solveig could see at once how well the fortress of Earth Town was sited, overlooking the bend where the wide waterway leading north from the lake met the great river.

"Volkhov," said Torsten. "That's the river's name. And we'll ride her halfway to Kiev."

"Ride?" said Solveig.

Torsten smiled. "On the back of our sea beast," he told her.

The quay lay right beneath the walls and guardhouses of the fortress, and several boats were already tied up alongside it. Two of them looked very much like Red Ottar's, but at the far end Solveig saw a strangely shaped vessel. It wasn't clinker-built, and it was very broad in the beam. Like a barrel, almost. It had quite a short mast, and its pennant glittered in the early-morning sunlight. Then Solveig noticed that there were at least a dozen smaller craft tucked into the harbor walls—cobles and knarrs and skutes and little boats without masts, good only for rowing, as well as a couple of hulks lying up on the quay itself, thick with barnacles and weed.

"First things first," Red Ottar announced. "You, Bruni, and Vigot, sort out the gangplank."

Before long, the whole crew was carrying boxes and rolling barrels down the gangway onto the quay, no more than fifty paces from another Viking trading boat.

"Ulrik," observed Bruni. "Your rival, Ottar. Your twin."

"A twin I can do without," Red Ottar replied.

"He always gets here first."

"But always sells the least," the skipper added. "And buys the least as well. If you don't sell much, you can't buy much."

Once the crew had carried everything down onto the quay, Odindisa and Bergdis set up trestle tables and began to lay out their wares: hides and furs—sable and red squirrel, black bear, reindeer—hunks of wax, board games of checkers and chess, boxes of salt, two wooden platters glistening with honey scooped out of one of the barrels.

"What about the weapons?" Bruni asked.

"Tomorrow," said Red Ottar. "Or the day after. We need something new each day."

"And the carvings?"

"Three combs and a few oak beads," said Red Ottar scathingly. He looked straight at Solveig, unblinking, and the roots of her hair tingled. "You'll have to do better than this," he warned her. "Much better, or you'll end up as fish food."

Bergdis stared at Solveig, silver-eyed. "I warned you, Red Ottar," she said loudly.

Then Bergdis took Bruni's arm, and the two of them walked several steps away along the quay.

They're talking about me, thought Solveig. They're both against me.

"Right!" Red Ottar told Solveig. "I want you and Slothi to watch over our goods. If you need to ease yourself, call Edith, and she'll stand in for you. There's a place at the end of the quay. Understand?"

"Yes," Solveig said. "And I'll carve as I keep watch."

"No, I want two pairs of sharp eyes keeping watch at all times. If anyone looks like buying, give me a shout and I'll come down with my weights and measures."

So while the remainder of the crew busied themselves aboard and went on errands into Earth Town, Slothi and Solveig kept watch over the merchandise, and Bard and Brita, chasing up and down the quay, used them as a base for their games.

The very first men to approach them came not from Earth Town but from the strange-looking boat moored at the far end of the quay.

"Bulgars," said Slothi knowledgeably. "That's a Bulgar boat. They come up the Volga and around to Ladoga. They'll be after our furs."

"Do you know them, then?" asked Solveig.

Slothi shook his head. "Look at their beards. Each as long as the other. And their baggy trousers. Red as rowan leaves in October. Bulgars! I'd recognize them anywhere."

"Have you often sailed here?" Solveig asked.

"Seven years," Slothi said. "Several times each year."

Each of the Bulgar men gave Slothi a handclasp and then bowed politely to Solveig.

Solveig wasn't quite sure what to do. She put out both her hands, one uncovered, one bandaged, but the Bulgars ignored them. Then one of them said in rather thick Swedish, "Allah go with you!"

"Christ go with you," Slothi replied at once. "And the gods go with you."

"What's Allah?" Solveig asked.

"Their god," Slothi told her. "You'll be meeting plenty of new gods!"

The Bulgars were indeed interested in all the furs, especially the more valuable ones. They pinched them and rubbed them between their fingers, talking quickly to each other as they did so.

"Their condition," Slothi told Solveig. "Their color. Their thickness. Look! Now the age of the animal."

"How do you know?" asked Solveig.

"By watching them," Slothi said. "Look how that man keeps turning over the sable. There! Smelling it. Checking how well it's been cured."

When Brita and Bard ran up, pink and breathless, and flopped down on the hide of a black bear, the two Bulgars smiled broadly at Slothi and nodded.

They grunted and growled like bears themselves. Then one of them bent down and squeezed Bard's left shoulder. He put his thumbs on the boy's cheeks and forefingers on his brow; then he pulled his eyes open and stared into them.

"Leave me alone," complained Bard.

The other man, meanwhile, pinched Brita's bottom as if he were testing whether she was ready to be plucked and roasted. Then he put both hands on her cheeks, dragged down her jaw, and peered inside her mouth.

"Stop it!" cried Brita. "Why are you doing that?"

"That's enough!" said Slothi, and he drew his daughter to him.

But the Bulgars only nodded and smiled, and then they examined another hide, all the while talking thickly to each other. They sauntered away, and then they strolled back again.

The older man stroked his beard. "How much?" he asked.

"Which ones?" said Slothi, spreading his palms. "The red squirrel . . . the sable marten . . . How many?"

"Both."

"Both what?" asked Slothi.

"Children."

"No!" cried Solveig.

"No! No!" said Slothi, half frowning, half smiling. "These children," he said, pointing to himself, "they're mine. My children."

"Ah!" said the Bulgars, much surprised.

"No slaves?" one man said.

"No," said Slothi. "Certainly not."

The other Bulgar pointed right at Solveig. "Slave?" he inquired.

"No!" said Solveig loudly. "Of course I'm not." Her heart hammered in her chest.

The man stuck out his lower lip and rubbed his thumb and forefinger extravagantly.

"Tell them!" demanded Solveig.

Then Slothi linked arms with Solveig. "My companion," he told the Bulgars. "Good boatwoman. Good sea woman."

"Ah!" said the men. "Ahh! No slave." And they nodded at Solveig, but they still went on eyeing her and Solveig's heart went on thumping.

"Next time," Slothi said. "Slaves next time, maybe."

So the Bulgars each gave Slothi a handclasp, and with that they sauntered off again.

"They'll buy our hides and furs," Slothi told Solveig. "You'll see. But if they think they'll get a better price by keeping Red Ottar waiting, they're mistaken."

"What did you mean?" Solveig demanded. "Next time, maybe. Red Ottar doesn't sell slaves, does he?"

"Not unless they come his way," Slothi replied. "Believe me, they're not the best cargo."

"He wouldn't sell Edith?"

Slothi laughed. "No, no! Not Edith."

But what about me? thought Solveig. What if I can't pay my way?

"Actually," said Slothi, "I'll tell you a secret. Red Ottar's very pleased with Edith, and he wants to buy her a gift."

"She's like my older sister," Solveig told Slothi, "except I don't have one."

Slothi smiled. "We all need one of those," he said. "They tell us to ourselves. Yes, Red Ottar has asked Odindisa to choose a brooch for her from the fine craftsman here and say charms over it."

"Oh!" exclaimed Solveig. "I do wish I could see his workshop."

10

Bruni and Odindisa set off for the workshop, taking Solveig and Vigot with them.

"I'd rather be fishing," Vigot grumbled, "but I'm short of hooks. Bronze ones. You're sure this man . . ."

"Oleg," Bruni told him.

"You're sure he'll have a good supply?"

"He did last time. And a fine fish knife with a bone handle."

"Bergdis guts them," Vigot said. "I catch them."

On their way, the four of them walked through the cemetery—it stood on a grassy knoll, looking out to sea.

"Rus and Swedes and Finns and Slavs and Balts—they're all buried here," Bruni told them.

"All together?" asked Solveig.

"Why not?"

"But they don't all worship the same gods. I mean, Christians can't be buried alongside us. Not in Norway. Not unless they worship the old gods as well."

"True enough," said Bruni. "But the men who settled here were all far from their first homes. They may have been divided by their faiths, but they were united by their trading. Bulgars and Arabs—a few of them settled here too. They all lived together, and now they lie together."

Solveig examined a roughly dressed stone rather taller than she was.

"I think I can read these runes," she said.

> *"Alrik raised this stone for his son.*
> *He plowed his keel on the Eastern Way*
> *and breathed his last in Ladoga.*
> *Bergvid he was a brave lad."*

"Old or young," Vigot said, "Odin doesn't care. A brave lad, cut down in battle."

"You can't tell that," Odindisa replied. "He may have caught fever."

"Or drowned," added Bruni.

Solveig looked at the memorial stones all around them. She stared out to sea.

"What survives of us?" she asked. "Here on middle-earth."

But Bruni and Odindisa and Vigot were all so caught up in their own thoughts that none of them replied.

Then Solveig heard her father's words: *"One thing never dies nor changes: the name you earn during your lifetime."*

What survives, she told herself, is just runes, some so salt-eaten it's no longer possible to read them. No! That's wrong. Each stroke of each rune in this place was carved with love, with tears. That's what survives of us. The longing that binds daughter to father, mother to son.

Solveig remembered going to her mother's grave on the evening before she left the farm, and kneeling in the lank, wet grass, and talking to her. She realized her eyes were blurred with tears, and she sniffed and wiped them away with the bandage on her hand.

"Ghosts," observed Bruni. "No one can escape them."

"No one should want to," Odindisa said. "We should give them peace. We should lay ghosts, especially our own." But then she grabbed a rune stone to steady herself, gasped, and fell to her knees.

"What is it?" asked Vigot, and he quickly looked around him. He knew, as Bruni did, that Odindisa could see what they could not. They'd followed her when she traveled into what has been and foretold what will be.

"Did you see him?" Odindisa whispered.

"See who?" asked Bruni.

"Standing here. Waving."

"Who?"

"Bergvid." Odindisa was trembling. "Bergvid was. Brave lad! Warning us to turn back, back home to Sigtuna."

Bruni and Vigot and Solveig all stared at one another.

Odindisa closed her eyes. "Come and gone. And now I'm a sodden rag."

"All white," said Bruni.

"And moon-blue," said Solveig.

"Go back to the boat," Bruni told her.

"Shall I come with you?" offered Solveig.

"No," said Odindisa. "You go. You'll be glad." Then she opened her eyes and gazed listlessly at Solveig. "Slothi . . . did he tell you?"

"About Edith?" Solveig said. "He did, yes."

"You must choose it, then. You'll know which. You'll recognize it."

With that, Odindisa got unsteadily to her feet and turned back toward the boat.

"She's walking between worlds," observed Solveig.

"Lurching," said Vigot.

"There's an old woman in our fjord like that," Solveig told them, wrinkling up her face, "and we never know how much to believe."

"In any case," said Bruni, "Red Ottar's not going to be put off by a ghost. Not likely!"

For a while the three of them watched Odindisa, and then they continued into Earth Town.

"You see that building over there," Bruni told them, "the big one with the conical roof . . ."

"It looks like a squatting troll," Solveig said. "Some trolls wear hats like that."

"Earl Rognvald's house," Bruni said. "He rules this town. Red Ottar told you."

Solveig smiled and tapped her head. "He did? I fear the ale was speaking more loudly than he was."

"Do you know why the Rus are Christian?" Bruni asked her.

"I didn't know they were."

"You don't know much," said Bruni. "There was a king in Kiev who decided it was time for the Rus to choose one faith."

"Why?" asked Solveig.

"Stop interrupting me," Bruni said testily. "I wasn't there, but the Swedes, and the Finns, and the Balts, and the Slavs, and the Bulgars, and the Khazars, and the Arabs all had different gods, I suppose, and . . . I don't know." Bruni waved his hands in exasperation. "So this king, Vladimir, sent his ministers to many, many countries to find out about their religions. They rode into Asia, they sailed the length of the Great Sea, and when they reported their findings, the king thought that Islam—the faith of the Arabs—was the best religion."

"Why?" asked Solveig.

"But then his ministers told him that the followers of Islam never drink liquid that's fermented or distilled."

"What?" said Vigot. "They don't drink ale?"

"No! Not ale or cider or wine or any ardent spirit."

"What do they drink, then?"

Bruni shrugged. "Moldy water. Milk."

Both Vigot and Solveig slowly shook their heads.

"When Vladimir heard that," Bruni told them, "he shook his head like you two. He said that a religion forbidding ale would fall flat on its face."

"In Norway too," said Solveig.

"So then the ministers who had traveled to Miklagard . . ."

Solveig's ears pricked up.

". . . they told the king how glorious the Christian church was, the great church of Hagia Sophia, and all the ceremonies inside it. 'On earth,' they said, 'there's no splendor to compare with it, no beauty to better it.'"

Solveig's eyes were shining.

"So King Vladimir decided the Rus should be Christian," Bruni said. "But you can be sure most of them worship their old gods as well. In fact, I've heard there's even a word for it. Garthar, they say, is *dvoeverie*—a country of two faiths."

From the moment she lowered her head under the lintel and stepped into the little log room, Solveig felt she had crossed into a magical world.

It was hot and stuffy and sooty, and everywhere, on each surface, in each corner, lay treasures such as she had never seen.

Here, a pile of glass beads, forget-me-not blue and mossy, pearly, crocus yellow . . . there, a piece of amber almost as large as a kneecap . . . there, a stack of rivets . . . two silvery birch baskets . . .

Solveig could scarcely look closely at one object before her eyes were drawn to another. She felt quite breathless and would willingly have stayed right there for the remainder of her life.

There was a stirring in the inner room. Then the tatty piece of curtain dividing it from the workshop was swept aside, and out jumped—out bubbled, almost—a slight little man with a head too big for his body. He had such a warm and open smile, and the whites of his eyes were almost as pink as pink roses.

"Oleg!" exclaimed Bruni.

"Bruni!" exclaimed Oleg.

The two men embraced, and, with their hands still on each other's shoulders, they appraised each other and laughed.

Bruni gestured to his companions. "Vigot," he said. "Solveig."

"Welcome!" said Oleg. "Man . . . woman . . ." He smiled sweetly at them and slowly locked his fingers.

"No!" exclaimed Solveig. "No, we're not!"

"Not what?" asked Vigot.

"Man and wife," said Solveig. She felt her blood rush to her face. "He thinks we're married."

Vigot just laughed. "She keeps begging me!" he told Oleg.

"My young friends have heard about you," Bruni said. "The smith of smiths!"

"Stuff!" said Oleg.

"Whoever wants to learn should work with you. Not that women ever make good carvers."

"I have two apprentices," Oleg replied, "and that's enough for me."

Solveig saw how restless Oleg was—picking things up, putting them down again, blowing soot from surfaces, pulling at his clothing, as if he couldn't keep still for a moment.

"Solveig wants to learn," Bruni told him.

Oleg smiled at her, and she could see that although the whites of his eyes were rosy with so much smoke and rubbing, the irises were brown as chestnuts and glistening.

"For one . . ." Oleg said warmly, "for one, success at swordplay . . . Do you know this song?"

". . . For one a devious mind for chess,
For one strength in wrestling . . ."

"That's you, Vigot," said Solveig accusingly.

"For one the hawk on the fist . . ." Oleg continued. "And for one the skill of the craftsman. What I think is . . . the craftsman's workshop is a crossing place."

"How?" said Solveig.

"Let me ask you this: Is anything beautiful unless it's useful? And is anything truly useful unless it's also beautiful?"

"No," said Solveig. "They go together. Please show me."

That was what Oleg did. He showed her the drinking cups he had just thrown on his wheel in the inner room. He showed her the decorated bone handles and arrowheads and rivets and nails and pieces of polished and cut amber and dress pins . . .

Then Oleg dug into a pocket, pulled out a bronze key, and unlocked a solid hinged wooden box. It contained several pieces of metal jewelry, and the moment Solveig saw the bronze brooch, she knew it was the one. The one for Edith.

Like a little double hammer, handle end to handle end. No . . . like a double cross. Two silver eyes in each of the hammerheads . . . Solveig couldn't take her eyes off it.

Oleg laid the brooch on Solveig's right palm. She felt how heavy it was, and when she turned it over, she saw how finely Oleg had fashioned the pin catch.

The craftsman took it back and peered closely at it. Then he pressed the brooch to the top of his workbench and picked up a little hammer.

At once Solveig noticed how still he had become. When he's talking, he's all movement and busyness, she thought, but when he's working, he's so quiet. So still.

Oleg gave the fastening the lightest tap, and then a second, smarter one, and eyed it again. "That'll do," he said. "Yes, poems, sagas, tapestries, ships, harps and pipes, swords, brooches—each has its own material, but they all have to be well wrought."

"This is the one," Solveig told Oleg.

"One what?" asked Bruni. "What are you talking about?"

"Ask Odindisa!" Solveig replied. And then she told Oleg, "Odindisa, she'll come here tomorrow and buy it. I'll come back too, if I can."

Oleg smiled. "I'll be waiting for you both," he said.

How old is he? Solveig wondered. His skin's unlined, almost. He's got no hair, though, except those pale patches over his ears. He's supple and quick, but his eyes are age-old.

Oleg's sandy eyelashes flickered, and he gave Solveig a knowing look. "All ages," he said with a merry laugh.

After this, Vigot bought seven bronze fishhooks, and once the craftsman had wrapped them up in a scrap of oily sealskin, Bruni said it was time they were getting back to their boat.

"Our skipper's a slave driver," he told Oleg with a wink at Solveig and Vigot. "Anyhow, Solveig wouldn't want to be out with men like us after dark."

"She wouldn't want to be out without you," Oleg said. "That's for sure."

"I can look after myself," Solveig protested. "I'm rising fifteen."

"Exactly," said Oleg with a rueful smile.

Then Oleg pressed something into the palm of Solveig's injured hand and closed her fingers around it.

"You have a maker's eyes," he told her. He stretched his thumb and forefinger. "Two colors. Wide and dreaming."

Solveig opened her left hand. A violet-gray glass bead nestled in it, shining with a quiet inner light.

"Oh!" she exclaimed, holding it up to what little light there was. "It's beautiful!"

"Your third eye," murmured Oleg.

"Subtle as a fish scale," Vigot observed.

Swiftly Solveig stepped toward the craftsman and embraced him.

"Not much of a man," said Vigot disparagingly as the three of them strode side by side out of Earth Town. "An overgrown dwarf or something."

"The best smith and carver I've ever met," said Bruni.

"More skilled than you will ever be," Solveig told Vigot.

"All he wanted to do was talk about his . . . stuff."

"What did you expect? We didn't go to see him to talk about the weather."

"He made it all sound . . . well, as if it matters more than anything else in the world."

"It does," said Solveig. "To him it does."

"Makers like nothing more than to talk about their work," observed Bruni. "It's what's most alive for them."

"Mmm!" agreed Solveig, smiling. "I can't explain it exactly. But for me, well, meeting him was like taking a step onto the rainbow bridge."

"Heh?" inquired Vigot.

"That little workshop. It's like the bridge between middle-earth and Asgard. Between humans and gods. For me it is."

"You mean," said Bruni, "that when men make something fine . . ."

"Yes," said Solveig. "Somehow, the gods strike a spark in them."

"With strike-a-lights!" said Vigot.

"No, you don't understand."

"There's a story," Bruni told them, "about how Odin won the goblet brimming with the mead of poetry. He shared it out between all the gods, but now and then he offers a drop or two to some human."

"That's what I mean," said Solveig eagerly. "It's like that."

"He didn't ask us anything about our journey," Vigot said. "The crew . . . the cargo . . . where we're going."

"He asked you what kind of fish you want to catch," Solveig reminded him.

"All kinds," Vigot replied, and he flashed her a handsome smile. "Big ones, small ones, they can't escape me."

Bruni grunted. "Thinking about girls again, are you, Vigot?"

"And fish," said Vigot.

"You've got a mind like a cesspit."

"And you're my teacher," Vigot retorted.

Bruni gave Vigot a scornful look, and his thick lips parted. "So says the pot," he sneered. Then he glanced at Solveig. "Ignore him," he told her. "Vigot and his fish, they've reminded me of something."

"What?" asked Solveig.

"Hooked, are you?" said Bruni, and his mouth fell open again. "Listen to this! Thor went out fishing, and do you know what he used for bait?"

"A turd," said Vigot.

"No," said Bruni. "He baited his hook—his very big hook, Vigot—with the head of an ox.

"In the depths of the sea the monster was waiting, the Midgard Serpent coiled around our middle-earth. He let go of his tail and snapped at the bait, and the sea frothed like ale. It fizzed. But Thor hauled up the monster. Then he reached for his hammer and whacked the serpent's head. The Midgard Serpent tugged, and the huge barb tore at the roof of his mouth. He jerked his head from side to side, he wrenched . . ."

Bruni grunted, he spluttered and spit like the Midgard Serpent—and he woke all the sleeping dogs of Ladoga.

No more than a couple of hundred paces from their boat, Solveig and Vigot could hear yowling and yapping, and it was coming closer.

"You and your monster!" snapped Vigot. "You've woken them all up."

Then two huge hounds came bounding along the quay toward them, snarling.

Bruni stood his ground and roared at them. But that only maddened the dogs all the more. They mobbed the three companions. Solveig could hear them panting and smell their foul hot breath.

"Clear off!" yelled Vigot, picking up a paddle lying beside the Bulgars' boat.

But even as he did so, one of the hounds snarled and jumped at Solveig, knocking her off balance.

"Run for it!" yelled Bruni.

But Solveig couldn't do anything of the kind. She stumbled backward, she clawed the air, and then both hounds leaped at her. She could see their gleaming eyes. Their pointed teeth.

Solveig shrieked. She tried to fight them off.

But one hound bit deep into her left calf, and the other sank his teeth right into her slender neck.

Solveig screamed. She screamed as never in her life before. And then she heard a massive clout—a thwack!— and felt the heavy body of one hound collapsing on her.

"Got you!" shouted Vigot. "You hellhound! Now you!"

The other dog didn't give him a chance. Seeing the dreadful fate that had befallen his companion, he ran off with his tail between his legs, howling.

Vigot turned back to the first hound. He gave him a poke with the paddle and then whacked his head again. The hound slathered strings of spittle and blood all over Solveig's back and shoulders.

"Get him off!" spluttered Bruni. "Come on!"

So both men dragged the heavy hound off Solveig's body, and then Bruni knelt beside her.

"Girl!" he said. "Solveig! You're safe."

Solveig was curled up as if she were unborn. Her bandaged left hand was clamped to her neck. With her other, she clutched her bleeding calf. Her whole body was shaking. And when she heard Bruni reassuring her, she began to sob.

Bruni put his hands under Solveig's shoulders and tried to help her to her feet, but she had no strength in her calves and thighs. No kick in her limbs, no force in her body except for her palpitating heart. So when Bruni relaxed his grip, she just slumped down on the quay again.

"Come on, girl," Bruni encouraged her.

But Solveig lay in a heap, shaking and sobbing.

Bruni sniffed and scratched his right ear. "Nasty!" he said.

"Hellhounds," said Vigot. "Killers."

Bruni stared at him. "Like you," he said thoughtfully.

"A good thing too," Vigot replied. And then, more fiercely, "Isn't it?"

Bruni got down on his knees beside Solveig. "I'll carry you back, girl," he said.

"I'll carry her," said Vigot.

But Bruni slipped his arms under Solveig's back and hips and looked up at Vigot with a challenging smile.

Still Solveig couldn't stop sobbing. Bruni was rocking her in his arms, like a baby almost, and she felt utterly unable. She wished only that she'd never left home. With all her head and heart and torn body, she wished she had never come.

11

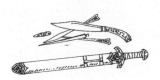

Solveig's blood raged around her body. At one moment she sat up, not knowing where she was, and reached out, gabbling gibberish no one could understand. At another she lay back, soaked in her own sweat, gasping for breath. She screamed; then she lay so silent that her companions thought words had left her forever; she trembled and moaned.

Odindisa nursed Solveig all night. She laid her head across her lap, she said and sang spells over her and rubbed honey into her wounds; she pounded thyme and mint and other herbs and mixed them with a yolk and fed them to Solveig, fingertip by fingertip.

"As long as the bites don't blacken," she told everyone. "As long as her wounds still hurt her . . ."

At times, Solveig half heard voices around her.

"Wrong. We were wrong. We should never have brought her."

"The Norns are against her."

"Scarcely a day's carving."

"Sell her!"

"A fool's errand! . . . No more chance than a frog flying to the moon."

But although Solveig could hear snatches and knew they were talking about her, she was unable to reply.

In the middle of the night, Solveig had a waking dream. She was a tiny girl again, no more than two or three, and so terrified that her limbs locked and she was unable to move.

She could see her grandmother Amma standing over her and hear her frosty voice.

"I've told you before, Halfdan. Her eyes aren't right, and she's a weakling. You should have done it right away."

Solveig's father sat hunched over a bench, still as a stone.

"You should have left her out on the ice," Amma went on. "Food for the wolves. We did that in the old days. It's cruel, I know that, but the weakest in the litter can bring down the whole pack."

"Enough!" Halfdan growled.

"Especially when there's scarcely enough food to go around. A slip of a daughter. The last thing you need now that you're on your own."

Solveig's father stood up, and in doing so he knocked over the bench. "I made my choice," he said, "and I'd choose the same again."

"She's a death bringer," Amma said bitterly. "She's already killed her mother. Sun-strength! She's a weakling and she . . ."

"No," interrupted Halfdan. "Solveig is my blood and I'm hers. I did as I promised Siri, and she would curse you for what you've said."

"I warned you, Halfdan," Amma said, and she clenched her bony fist. "I warned you Sirith would die in childbirth. You mark my words, the day will come when Solveig's weakness will harm others—maybe her own father."

"Enough!" said Halfdan again. Then he scooped up his little daughter, and in her waking dream, Solveig could feel him holding her tight, very tight.

When Solveig opened her eyes, soon after dawn, this dream was still with her, bleak and painful. But she was still being held.

Then she saw Odindisa gazing down at her and realized she was lying in Odindisa's lap.

"You've come back," said Odindisa, smiling gently.

But Solveig couldn't escape the night voices she had heard all around her. "What will he do with me?" she whispered.

"Who?"

"Red Ottar. He won't sell me . . ."

"Never!" said Odindisa dismissively. "Over my dead body. I tell you, if you weren't so strong, your bites would have done for you! You'd have died in the night."

Strong? That was the last thing Solveig felt. She felt weak and frail.

"You've . . . mothered me," she whispered.

"Now then. Did you talk to Oleg?"

Solveig sighed. She felt too tired to reply. She closed her eyes.

"I thought you would," said Odindisa. "And you found the brooch."

"It's so beautiful," Solveig whispered. "I told Oleg you'd come for it."

Odindisa clicked her tongue. "Red Ottar's changed his mind."

Solveig opened her eyes again. They felt so heavy-lidded.

"I'll buy it all the same, with Slothi's hack-silver. I'll buy it and tell Red Ottar later."

"But . . ."

"He's always changing his mind. Like a weather vane. To begin with he'll be angry, but then he'll be pleased . . ."

"How well you know him," Solveig murmured.

Odindisa didn't reply. She just narrowed her eyes and gave Solveig a sly look.

Then Solveig remembered the glass bead Oleg had given to her. Did I drop it on the quay? she wondered. Did Bruni or Vigot pick it up?

While Solveig was still wondering, Vigot appeared—as if by thinking of him she had somehow summoned him. He looked down at her, sharp-eyed.

"You again!" said Odindisa. "Vigot has been our regular night visitor."

Solveig gazed up at him and gave him a smile as pale as the first aconite. "You saved me," she said. "You saved my life."

"What did you think I'd do? Stand and watch?"

"Shhh!" said Solveig gently, and her eyes filled with tears. "I'm thanking you."

Vigot twisted his long fingers. Then he rubbed his right cheek where his wrestling opponent had gouged it.

"Still sore?" Solveig asked him.

"Not as sore as you."

Solveig wondered whether to ask Vigot about the violet-gray bead, but she didn't want him to think she was accusing him, so she decided to ask Bruni first.

Solveig's next visitor was Red Ottar.

"If she weren't so strong," Odindisa told him, "the neck bite would have finished her."

"Strong, is she?" said Red Ottar, staring at Solveig. "First your hand . . . Now this."

Red Ottar could see Solveig was trembling, but that didn't stop him.

"A treasure! That's what Turpin called you. A bagful of bad luck—that's what I say."

Somewhere within her, Solveig rebelled. She refused to allow Red Ottar to wound her further.

"The gods are against you."

"No!" she said huskily, and she screwed up her eyes. "If they were, I wouldn't be here now."

"I'm giving you one more chance," the skipper told her. He shook his red head and then jammed his right thumb against the tip of her nose. "Anyhow, you're needed on the quay. As soon as you can."

"She's not well enough today," said Odindisa.

"Today's the day to display our weapons," Red Ottar told them. "Those fine scramasaxes! And that sword with the runes, the one Bruni made last winter."

"I haven't seen that yet," Solveig said in a weak voice.

"You won't forget it. It cuts itself into your skull."

Solveig blinked. "I've got enough wounds already," she said.

"And then tomorrow," the skipper went on, "we'll put out the carvings." He glared at Solveig. "Such as they are. The weapons, the carvings, yes, and we've got to find a river pilot. Three men are coming aboard this afternoon."

"Three?" said Odindisa.

"So we can choose the best. Everyone can have their say—for or against."

Solveig hoisted herself onto her elbows. She was bright-eyed, flushed.

"Lie down, girl," Red Ottar told her. "You're feverish."

Red Ottar soon dismissed the first pilot to come aboard. He sported a long, wispy fair mustache and had an annoying way of nodding the whole time while Red Ottar put questions to him—questions he slowly repeated before getting under way with his long-winded answers.

"Now you're asking me how many days from Novgorod to Smolensk," repeated the man. "Aren't you asking me that?"

"I am!" barked the skipper. "I'm asking you, not the other way around. Have I got to wait until the Volkhov freezes over?"

"Until the Volkhov freezes over? Is that what you're asking?"

"Get out!" Red Ottar said. "Torsten, ask him to ask you if he knows his way to the gangplank!"

The second pilot looked as mushy as a bag of slops. In fact, he even had some difficulty sitting down, and he sounded out of breath the whole time.

"Like your food, do you?" Red Ottar inquired.

"I do," said the man with a squashy smile.

"So I see. You've piloted boats all the way to Kiev?"

"Mustn't tell a lie," the man replied. "That's what my mother always said."

"Well, have you or haven't you?" demanded Red Ottar.

"Yes," said the man, and he gave a high-pitched giggle. "Yes, I have! If I'd said no, I'd have been telling a lie."

Bard brayed with laughter, and that made Brita laugh as well, but all the companions eyed each other and knitted their brows.

"Got you!" the fat man gurgled.

"Giggle, gaggle . . . gurgle!" Red Ottar exclaimed, waving his right hand. "Take him away."

While the crew was waiting for the third pilot to come aboard, Solveig stood up and leaned against a gunwale. She still felt as unsteady as an old woman, and her neck was so swollen she couldn't turn her head to left or right. But it was the last day of April, the air was soft, and she could hear the shorebirds calling.

Then she became aware that someone was standing beside her.

"Your neck," said Brita. "It looks like boiled reindeer sausage."

Solveig blinked.

Brita took Solveig's arm and studied her neck very carefully. "Can I touch it?" she asked her.

But Solveig was saved from Brita's scrutiny by Bard, who came hopping across the deck. "Hey!" he exclaimed, grabbing his sister's hand. "Come and watch Torsten."

The helmsman had a length of rope between his hands, and before long Solveig heard him saying, "What about a Turk's head, then?"

"A Turk's head?" Bard repeated. "A Turk's head, is that what you said?"

"You're as bad as that first pilot," Torsten told him.

Brita bared her teeth. "What is it?" she asked, as if she wasn't sure she really wanted to know. "A Turk's head."

"A stopper knot at the end of a rope. I'll show you."

"What's it for?" asked Bard. "Oh! I know. When you've threaded the rope through an eye."

"A ring, you mean," said Brita.

"A ring is an eye," Bard told her.

"Why's it called a Turk's head?" asked Brita.

Twice the helmsman twisted the end of the rope back around itself. Then he tucked in the end and held it up, but Brita was still none the wiser.

"It looks like a Turk's headdress," Torsten told her. "You'll see."

"What is a Turk, anyhow?" Brita asked.

But then, from behind her, Solveig heard Slothi saying very loudly, "No! Certainly not. It's too risky."

"He'll change his mind. He always does."

"No, Odindisa."

"You . . . mean-minded Christian!"

They're talking about buying Oleg's brooch, thought Solveig. They must be.

"Slothi!" Vigot called out. "Slothi! Come and have a look at this!"

"Gladly!" said Slothi. He stood up and walked over to the far gunwale, where Vigot had hauled in one of his lines.

"Yuck! What's that?"

Such was the force of Slothi's exclamation that almost everyone turned to see what was going on.

Dangling from one of Vigot's new bronze hooks was the most enormous shellfish. Not a cockle or mussel, crab or giant clam, but a creature covered in mud with a hairy shell and malevolent eyes.

"Let me see!" demanded Bard.

"Me," said Brita, pushing him aside.

"It's disgusting!" Bard exclaimed in delight.

"It's old as old, that's for sure," said Vigot, swinging the creature in front of the children. "Stuck in the mud for years and years, just waiting for you."

"Throw it back," Brita told him.

"What? So it can rise again when the world ends?"

Vigot lowered the sea creature onto the deck, and then he and Slothi and the children poked it and prodded it.

Solveig, meanwhile, was distracted by Bergdis and Edith.

"Three," Bergdis announced, slapping her stomach. "Three I've lost. And I'm very healthy and wide-hipped. Two of them were boys."

"If I have a son . . ." Edith began, but Bergdis interrupted her. "Then I lost my man Jorund. I lost him to Ran."

"Another woman?"

Bergdis snorted. "Of a kind. Ran with her drowning net."

"Oh! You mean the goddess," Edith said.

"Now, Jorund—he was a real man," Bergdis told her. And then more loudly: "Is there anyone aboard this boat red-blooded?"

"Enough, Bergdis!" Red Ottar snapped.

"Red-blooded!" said Bergdis very deliberately. "You, Bruni?"

"I'm warning you," Red Ottar told her.

"Well, there is one," Bergdis confided to Edith in a sly voice, and Solveig found herself leaning forward.

"He knows who he is," Bergdis said. "But men . . . they're seldom satisfied for long."

Solveig heard someone running up the gangplank.

A little man hopped off the end of it, took a big step, and with a jump landed right beside Solveig.

"Mihran!" he announced.

Solveig couldn't help smiling at the very sight of him. He was as little and lightly built as Oleg but much darker-skinned, and his eyes were twinkling, as if to say the best thing to do about life was to laugh at it.

"Everyones know Mihran," the man told Solveig. "Every-ones in Ladoga and Kiev."

Red Ottar stood up to greet the third pilot. "Everyone may know you," he said. "But what about you? Do you know the rivers, the rapids, the lakes?"

Torsten walked up to the skipper's side, still holding the knotted rope, and Mihran immediately pointed at it. "Turk's head!" he said, clasping his hands around his neck and laughing. "Me Armenian. We hate Turkeys!"

Red Ottar snorted, but then he narrowed his eyes. "So you're not from Kiev, then?"

"Me?" exclaimed the pilot. "South. Far south. Sea Black."

"The Black Sea," Torsten corrected him.

"People in Kiev," Mihran told them, "they are Rus. Very tall. Very pale. The king is Rus."

"Indeed he is," said Red Ottar. "King Yaroslav."

Then Mihran sat down with all the crew around him, and by the time he had described the Eastern Way—the long days in gloomy forests, the splendor of Novgorod, the little quiet trading posts, the great lake of Ilmen and the rivers feeding it—and then estimated that the journey would take no fewer than thirty-one days, all this with gestures and laughs and amusing little slips of language, Red Ottar and Torsten and their companions were in no doubt about the pilot's knowledge or his confidence.

When the skipper asked Mihran about the dangers, he immediately held up three fingers. "The portages," he said. He braced his forearms and shouldered the empty air as if it were immovable, and then he splayed his fingers over his eyes. "And the wild beasts," he growled. "'The forests have many, many bears. Wild pigs—tusks."

"And the third danger?"

"Ruffians," replied Mihran. "Human wild beasts."

"We're prepared," Red Ottar told him.

Mihran twisted his black mustache with his right thumb and forefinger and then looked around him. "With these women?"

"I can fight," Bergdis said at once. "May the gods help the man who tangles with me."

Mihran inspected Odindisa and Edith and gently shook his head. Then he considered Solveig.

"Maybe," he said. "Tall. Strong."

"One-handed and one-legged," Red Ottar told him. "And stiff-necked."

"What about me?" Bard demanded.

But Mihran dismissed him and Brita with the back of his hand. "Too smalls," he said. "Too young." Then he held his right hand to his heart. "The real danger is always here, no? Inside, not outside. The one who's afraid. The one who falls ill . . . The one who's a thief."

"You're right," said Red Ottar. "As with the gods and the trickster Loki, so with us. One of our own number."

"Which?" asked Mihran with a wary smile.

"Be on guard against your dark selves," Red Ottar said very slowly, looking from one person to another. "If one of us fails, most likely we all fail."

At first, Solveig thought Red Ottar was talking about her. But then she heard Bruni sucking his cheeks and caught him staring at Torsten; she saw Odindisa drawing Bard and Brita to her side and wrapping an arm around each of them; Edith laid her hands over her stomach; and while Red Ottar was still warning them, Slothi mouthed some silent prayer, stretching out his arms as if he were being crucified. Solveig realized that each of the crew thought that Red Ottar might very well be talking about them.

"Well," Red Ottar asked his crew, "who has any questions? You, Torsten?"

"When the time comes," the helmsman said, and he gave Mihran a friendly nod. "When the need arises."

Then Bergdis asked the pilot about the frequency of the trading posts and what livestock and vegetables she would be able to buy; Vigot and Slothi both wanted to know what river fish they would catch; and Bruni inquired about the best place to buy silver.

"What about you?" Red Ottar asked Odindisa. "Don't you want to know about the river ghosts?"

Odindisa shrugged.

"And . . . what are they called? Sendings?"

"They won't stop you," Odindisa said. "Nothing will."

"How far is it," asked Solveig, "from Kiev to Miklagard?"

Mihran threw back his head. "Miklagard! Ha!" He turned to Red Ottar, smiling. "But you—you go to Kiev."

"That's quite far enough," the skipper replied. "For me—and my sea wife."

"But I'm going to Miklagard," Solveig explained. "To find my father."

Mihran raised his eyebrows and gave Solveig a searching look. Then he pushed out his lower lip and slowly nodded.

"All right!" said Red Ottar, looking around the crew. "All agreed?" Then he, Torsten, and Mihran made their way to the stern, where they began to bargain over the payment for the pilot and discuss when to leave Ladoga.

Before the three of them had clasped hands, Solveig shuffled down the gangplank and padded along to the place where the hellhounds had attacked her.

The ground was scuffed, and when she stooped, Solveig could see globs of her own congealed blood with dog hairs stuck in them. Then she picked up the old paddle with which Vigot had brained the hound and dropped it into the water.

Some of the Bulgars were watching Solveig from their boat, and one of them called out to her and beckoned.

Solveig pretended she hadn't noticed. My third eye, she thought. My maker's eye. One-eyed Odin, in your wisdom, allow me to find it.

12

"Nonsense," said Torsten. "The gods aren't against you."

"Red Ottar thinks they are."

"No, he's just worried about keeping his crew together and selling his cargo," the helmsman assured Solveig.

"Sometimes I doubt myself."

"We all do," Torsten told her. "Look! The sun herself can't burn through all the clouds this morning."

"I didn't know what it would all be like," Solveig said, "this journey."

"Have faith in yourself," Torsten declared. "Your father, he'll be proud of you."

Solveig smiled mistily at the helmsman and ran her right hand through her golden hair.

All that day, Solveig still felt shaky, but by the next morning—their last in Ladoga—she was altogether stronger, and Red Ottar gave her permission to walk to the market with Edith. Bergdis accompanied them, saying she had "certain purchases" to make but without saying what.

On their way through the cemetery, the three of them read some of the rune stones. Bergdis found one raised to Thora.

"My daughter!" she cried. "The same name. Oh!"

Yes, thought Solveig. Memory and caring, they're both in a name.

"First happiness and then war—that's what my name means," Edith told them.

"A very strange name," Bergdis observed. "Edith."

"Not in England. Anyhow, it tells my story. I was happy enough. A good man, two strong children. But then the fighting . . ." Edith sighed. "Yes, the fighting put an end to all that."

"When I came up here with Bruni," Solveig said, "he told us no one can escape ghosts. And Odindisa said we shouldn't want to."

"He would say that," Bergdis observed. "Bruni's pursued by ghosts. Vengeful ghosts. In time he'll meet them."

Yes, thought Solveig, that's true. Time buries, and sometimes, in its own good time, time reveals.

They could hear the tom-tom-tom of the big drum long before they pushed their way through the crowd and saw the drummer and the ring of dancers surrounding him. First they swayed to the left, then to the right, then they joined hands and advanced on the drummer, then they stepped back again.

"A very grim kind of dance," Edith said.

"Grim," Bergdis agreed. "That's what the Finns are. Their idea of singing is a terrible warbling. As bad as a dog howling at the full moon. But I've never seen them dance before."

"How do you know they're Finns?" Solveig asked her.

"Look at their square stone jaws. Some Finns have never smiled once in their lives. And those puffy sleeves—nothing like the ones we wear."

"That's to hide their fins!" Solveig told Edith. "They're half fish, you know."

Edith took Solveig's arm. "Brita might believe you," she said. "Come on now. Red Ottar has given me a silver coin."

"Each to her own," Bergdis replied. "I've got work to do." And with that she disappeared into the milling crowd.

"What's she doing?" Solveig asked.

Edith shrugged. "She doesn't want us to know."

"A silver coin! Why?"

"To spend, of course."

"But, well . . ."

"What?"

"Couldn't you just run away?"

"Run away?" Edith looked astonished.

"Yes."

"Where to? Anyhow, one silver coin wouldn't last long. And then what?" Edith quietly folded her hands over her stomach.

"You're not." Solveig gasped.

Edith gave her a knowing look.

"You are!"

Edith's eyes were shining now.

"Oh, Edith!"

"Bergdis guessed, but you're the first person I've told."

"You haven't told Red Ottar?"

"Apart from him, I mean."

Then Solveig hugged her tight, like a sister, until they were both quite breathless.

"Oh!" exclaimed Solveig, laughing. "I've never held anyone like that."

"This is not what I chose, you know," Edith told her in a serious voice. "I didn't ask Swedes to come. I didn't want to be taken away."

"But you are glad, aren't you?"

"I feel happy and sad at the same time. Ottar's pleased, very pleased—he can be tender, you know. I'm only his slave woman, but I think he'll ease my workload when the time comes."

"I'll help you," Solveig told her.

Edith gave Solveig a loving smile, but even as she did so her features froze. And then, hare-eyed, she looked all around.

"Hear that?"

"What?"

"That voice? Listen!"

"Foreign."

"English!" said Edith excitedly. "Those two men."

At once Edith hurried up to them, but one man immediately turned on his heel and strode away.

"You're English," Edith told the other. "I heard you talking."

The man was quite bulky. He had buckteeth and a ready smile. "So are you, by the sound of it!"

"Oh!" cried Edith. "The first one."

"The first one?"

"Since the Vikings . . ."

Edith could see the man was eyeing the scars around her wrists and her scrappy clothing.

"And now . . ." the man said, "you're a slave."

Edith lowered her eyes.

"The devils! Where did you live, then?"

"Around Ravenspur," Edith said, "and into the Ouse. A town called Riccall."

"Is that so!" the man exclaimed, and he smiled broadly. "God's own country. I know it well. I live in York."

"No!" gasped Edith. Her whole body was sunlight and ripples and shivers.

"I heard about that raid on Riccall, three boatloads of Swedes attacking the Danes settled there."

"My man," Edith told him, "Alfred, he was killed."

"I'm sorry," said the Englishman, and he shook his head.

"What's your name?" Edith asked him.

"Edwin."

"Edwin," Edith repeated slowly, savoring the sounds. "You and your friend, are you trading?"

The Englishman gave Solveig a suspicious look.

"Oh!" said Edith. "Solveig—she's Norwegian and we're boat companions. She can't speak English."

Edwin nodded. "Trading," he said. "Yes, we're traders . . . of a kind."

"What are you selling?"

"Words," said Edwin. "Information. Arrangements, you could say."

"Secrets!" exclaimed Edith. "Are you on a mission?"

"Better not ask," Edwin told her. "Sometimes it's better not to know what you don't need to. What about you?"

"We've come from Sigtuna. I'm Edith."

Hearing the word Sigtuna, Solveig interrupted her. "Tell him we're going to Kiev. Tell him I'm going to Miklagard."

Much to Solveig's and Edith's surprise, Edwin was able to reply, though rather haltingly, in Solveig's own language.

"Miklagard! The golden city." The corners of his mouth twitched. "Quite well known to you Norwegians!"

"Harald Sigurdsson sent for my father," Solveig told him. "To join the emperor's guard."

"Your father?" said Edwin, looking around.

Solveig shook her head. "Last autumn," she said. "I'm following him."

"With your companions."

"Yes, well, no . . . They're going as far as Kiev. Have you been to Miklagard?"

Edwin tapped his head and smiled. "Many times," he replied. "Like you, I suppose. But what I'm asking is why. Why are you following your father? And what will you do when you get there—if you do?"

Solveig shook her head impatiently. "I look after today," she said. "The gods and fates look after tomorrow."

"The gods are dead," Edwin said dismissively. "Christ has slain them." He gave Solveig a friendly smile. "I'm not asking you to answer my questions, just wondering whether you've asked yourself. I wish you both a safe journey. A home from home."

Tears had sprung into Edith's eyes, but by the time she had brushed them away the Englishman had gone.

"I wish he hadn't said that," she sniffed. "About home. First I felt so glad to talk to him. Now it hurts."

"If I'd tried to think everything out, like he said," Solveig observed, "I'd still be sitting at home. Will we see him again, do you think?"

"His teeth stick out like a jackrabbit's," Edith said. "I hope so, though."

"I liked talking to him," said Solveig.

Edith smiled. "I rather think he liked talking to you."

Over their heads there was a great rush of wings as thousands and thousands of little shorebirds flooded over the market, turning back on themselves, rising and waving, for all the world like a dark scarf, a trailing sky scarf.

"Look!" cried Solveig. "Odindisa would know what they mean."

"They mean high tide," Edith said. "I've seen that at Ravenspur. The spring tides drive the shorebirds out of their roosts."

At this moment, a little slip of a man came up to Solveig and cupped her right elbow.

"Oleg!" she exclaimed.

"The gods go with you," Oleg replied.

"This is Edith. She's English."

Oleg smiled. "Let us forgive her," he said.

Edith laughed.

"The best kind of laughter," Oleg observed. "Laughing at yourself." Then he pointed to Solveig's neck.

"Two dogs," she told him. "My calf as well."

Oleg winced, and then he gave her a thoughtful look. "Your eye," he told her. "I saw it."

"Where?" gasped Solveig.

Oleg gestured toward one of the stalls. "On that table over there."

"I dropped it when the dogs attacked me, and I've been searching for it everywhere. On the quay, beside our wares, on the deck, in the hold . . ."

Solveig and Oleg stared at each other.

"Yes, I'm quite sure," Oleg told her. "Makers always recognize their own work."

Solveig narrowed her eyes. "Where from? Who sold it to them?"

"That's what I asked them."

"What did they say?"

"A tall young man. Very watchful. 'Like the blade of a knife.' That's what the stallholder told me. He sold her several things."

Solveig lowered her eyes. "I hoped it wasn't," she said under her breath. She turned toward the stall, but Oleg caught her by the elbow again.

The craftsman reached into a pocket, pulled out the violet-gray eye, and pressed it into the palm of Solveig's right hand.

"Oh!" Solveig exclaimed. "I can't. I haven't got any money."

"I've got this coin," offered Edith.

Oleg waved his hand. "Certainly not! Provided Solveig promises not to lose it again."

"I didn't lose it!" protested Solveig. "It was stolen. I'll cut a strip of leather and wear it around my neck."

"When your wound has healed," said Oleg with a smile. Then he gave Solveig and Edith a small bow. "Those who meet twice meet three times," he said.

"Yes," said Solveig eagerly, "we will. On our way home."

Oleg smiled. "I live in hope," he said, and on his light feet he walked quickly away.

Edith covered her mouth with her hand. "He made me laugh," she said through her fingers. "He looks like an elf."

"Vigot said . . ." began Solveig, but then she shook her head angrily. "He said Oleg looked like an overgrown dwarf."

"Vigot," began Edith very deliberately, "he looks like the blade of a knife."

Solveig bit her lower lip.

"Come on!" exclaimed Edith. "Let's look at everything! Everything old and everything new. Everything we know about and everything we don't!"

"Edie!" cried Solveig. "That's what I'm going to call you. Edie! Everything!"

Late that afternoon, Solveig and Edith slowly walked down from the market in Earth Town to the quay. Edith made her way at once to the latrine, and Solveig limped along to the boat. Red Ottar was standing with Bruni and Slothi at the foot of the gangplank.

"Those furs," Slothi told her, "the ones the Bulgars fingered and smelled and stretched."

"I remember," said Solveig.

"They came back and bought them."

"You said they would."

"Twenty-three of them."

"Twenty-three!" exclaimed Solveig. "Were they good ones?"

"All our furs are good ones," Red Ottar said.

Slothi raised his eyebrows. "But some are better," he added.

"And a very few," said Red Ottar, "are best."

"What price?" asked Solveig.

"Not the worst," Red Ottar replied. "They made us wait long enough. You like buying and selling, do you?"

"And you," Slothi said to Bruni, "you sold three carvings. An ivory brooch and a pin and . . . a fine scramasax."

"This has been the best day," Solveig said.

"It's always like that," the skipper told her. "The pace quickens just before we leave. Mihran's spreading the word that as we're sailing in the morning, we're selling off our sacks of salt and wax."

"Are you?"

Red Ottar gave Solveig a knowing smile. "No," he said. "But it brings in customers. Now, then. Go and give Bergdis a hand."

It was all but dark when Bruni and Slothi brought their merchandise back to the hold, and as soon as Bruni unfastened the chest containing his precious sword and a number of smaller pieces of metalwork, he saw one scramasax was missing.

"When I closed the lid this morning," he told Slothi, "there were three. Now there are two."

"You sold one."

"Yes, I took that one down and left three here."

"You're sure?"

"Of course I'm sure," bellowed Bruni. "And I'm sure I know who's stolen it."

Bruni climbed out of the hold and stood foursquare on deck. "Torsten!" he yelled. "Where are you?"

"Behind you," said the helmsman in a level voice.

Bruni rounded on him. "You! You stole it."

"Stole? Stole what?"

"My scramasax." Bruni Blacktooth glared at Torsten and bucked his head like an infuriated bull.

By now, the entire crew was gathering around the blacksmith and the helmsman.

"Stole it!" rapped Torsten. "Are you mad?"

"You were alone on board."

"I don't steal from my companions," Torsten said. "I don't steal from anyone."

"You thief!"

"Why would I steal one of your ragged knives, you . . . ghastly Icelander? Anyhow, I'll remind you—you brought aboard those Bulgars. Five of them."

Slothi stepped between them. "We did, Bruni. While Vigot looked after the stall."

"It was one of them," the helmsman said. "You mind the blade of your tongue, Bruni. I'm warning you."

"Enough!" barked Red Ottar, and he glared at his crew. "If it was the Bulgars, we can't do a thing about it. But if one of you here is the thief, I'll cut off your right hand."

13

Very early, before the cockerel, before sunrise, two men stood on the chill quay beside Red Ottar's boat. Now and then they spoke quietly; now and then they paced up and down, flexing their arms and stamping.

They watched the boat gently bumping against the quay's fenders—sealskin sacks packed with wool noosed over wooden bollards. They rubbed their eyes and pointed at something waterlogged drifting down the river. A bloated gray corpse, was it? Or part of a tree trunk. Then a mongrel came trotting along the quay, and sniffed, and turned up his nose at them.

At length there were signs of life aboard the boat. Odindisa sat up and, with the crown of her head pressing against their sail tent, murmured her morning invocations and charms; then Bergdis hoicked back her side of the sail, but the moment she got to her feet she started coughing and couldn't stop; missing the warmth of the women who had been lying on either side of her, Solveig curled up, still pretending it was the last night watch.

Down on the quay, one of the men began to sing a dawn song:

"Many a hand must grasp,
Many a fist must hold
The banded blades of oars
Chill with the cold of morning."

Solveig listened. The man was singing of a journey, a journey made not to a destination but simply for the love of journeying. Then she started to think about the little bone flute she had made for Turpin, and she wondered whether, somewhere on this middle-earth, he was playing it at that very moment.

Before long, everyone was on their feet, and that was when one of the men on the quay cupped his hands and shouted.

Solveig recognized him, and her heart gave a little skip. "Edith!" she called.

But Edith was already standing right behind her, wide-eyed and smiling.

So the gangplank was pushed out, and Red Ottar allowed the two men to come aboard. "My name's Edwin," the first man told him in halting Norwegian, "and I'm an Englishman."

Red Ottar screwed up his face as if he'd tasted something bad.

"My friend here is Sineus. Sineus the Slav."

"So?" asked Red Ottar.

But before Edwin could answer, Odindisa asked, "Which of you is the songbird?"`

Edwin pointed to his companion, and Sineus gave Odindisa the most engaging smile, revealing a whole grave-yard of broken teeth. His hair was a mass of rather matted dark curls.

"So?" repeated Red Ottar.

Edwin apologized for bothering the skipper so early. "These fine young women," he said, pointing at Edith and Solveig, "told me that you're bound for Kiev."

Edith took Red Ottar's arm. "We met him in the market," she explained.

"Fine young women," said Red Ottar. "That's the first time I've heard them called that. A half-baked girl on a half-baked journey and a slave woman."

"An Englishwoman," Edwin replied firmly.

"Get on with it," Red Ottar told him.

"Can you give us passage?"

"Give you passage," Red Ottar repeated slowly.

"Can you find room for us?"

"Everyone aboard my boat is here with good reason," the skipper told him. "To man the oars, to guide us, feed us . . ."

"We're not oarsmen or helmsmen or smiths or cooks. Sineus and I, we're men of words."

"Words," said Red Ottar with no great liking.

"My companion can sing praise poems."

"Praising the Vikings?"

Edwin smiled. "At a price," he said reasonably. "And I . . . I make arrangements."

"Words, words, words," Red Ottar said. "They get you nowhere."

"Ah, but they do," Edwin replied courteously. "Words are bridges. With words we discuss, argue, pray, talk to ourselves, we reach understandings and make wills and write letters; with words men sell their merchandise."

"So what do you do?" Red Ottar asked him.

"Me? I'm a word trader."

"A spy? Is that what you are?"

Edwin paused. "A go-between," he said.

"What can you pay me?" Red Ottar asked.

"We can offer you contacts in Kiev—contacts you'll be glad of," Edwin told him.

The skipper put his hands on his hips. "More words," he said. "I don't deal in promises."

Then he turned around and looked at his crew. And with the exception of the two fine young women and of Odindisa, who was gazing at Sineus, what he saw were scowls and suspicion.

"I'm the mouthpiece for my crew," Red Ottar told Edwin carefully, "and in plain words, I say no. It's true, good might come of bringing you aboard, but I won't risk it. A crew takes time to pull together. If you come aboard, we'll have to begin all over again."

Edwin pursed his lips and shook his head.

"In any case," Red Ottar said, "everyone here will think that one Englander is quite enough."

"Not me," said Edith very prettily.

"This won't be our last meeting," Edwin told Red Ottar. "We wish you a safe journey."

As soon as the companions had filled their stomachs and visited the latrines at the end of the quay, Mihran came aboard. Then Red Ottar instructed everyone to sit on their chests and listen while their pilot described the journey ahead.

Mihran mounted the pile of skins in the hold, and Bard and Brita sat at his feet.

"Everyones!" he called out, raising his arms. Then he smiled gaily and with his right hand twirled his mustache. "We go together into the belly of Garthar! We go where things are strange and not always what they seem. When you come back, you will be changed."

Brita gazed up at Mihran. "What do you mean?" she demanded.

"You mean we'll change shape?" asked Bard.

"Like that girl who was changed into a fish?" added Brita.

Mihran smiled and bent down and took out of Brita's grubby hand a hunk of black bread. "See this?" he said. "Good black bread." The pilot squeezed the bread, and when he opened his fist it had disappeared. Then he closed his fist again, and when he opened it for a second time, in the palm of his hand sat a black swan, made of bread.

Brita gasped. "How did you do that?"

Mihran shrugged; his eyes were twinkling like dark stars. He gave the black swan to Brita. "First we row," he told the crew. "We row this fine boat against rapids all day. Hard works. Slow works. Our slow way is guarded by the forts."

"May the gods go with us," said Red Ottar. "May they guard us—and my boat."

Slothi crossed himself.

"Mokosh! May she go with us," Mihran said.

"Who?" asked Odindisa.

"The goddess," Mihran told her. "Damp Mother Earth. We ride the water between her banks. And the Lord of the Waters, may he go with us."

"The Lord of the Waters," Odindisa repeated.

"That's what the Rus call him," Mihran explained. "Each river has its own lord."

"Well," asked Torsten, "which god are we to trust?"

"The more gods the better," Red Ottar replied. "We're going to need them all."

"Today is the first day of May," Mihran told them. "The first trading station is Duboviki and the first town is Holmgard. That's seven days from here."

"How many days to Kiev?" Solveig asked.

"Twenty-three water days and three land days and five rest days," said Mihran.

"What are land days?" asked Solveig. "Are they for trading?"

"No, you trade in the evening after you arrive. Land days are for portaging."

"What's that?" asked Solveig.

Mihran pushed the air in front of him with both hands—he pushed it so vigorously that he toppled off the pile of skins. "Pushing!" he called up, still on his knees and laughing. He rubbed his hands together and scrambled to his feet. "You see," he said cheerfully.

When Torsten untethered the boat, the port oarsmen eased her away from the quay with their blades. The whole crew cheered, and on board their barrel-shaped boat, the Bulgars waved and Solveig felt a surge of excitement.

"Look!" she said to Edith, sitting opposite her. "The banks! Bright yellow."

"Crocus," Edith told her. "Flags, maybe."

"Bright hopes," Solveig said. "But I do wish Edwin and Sineus . . ."

"Me too," said Edith.

As she pulled strongly at her oar, Solveig felt her right wrist jar against a lump in the pocket of her tunic.

My bead, she thought. I must cut a leather strip for it and wear it. Then it'll see Vigot. If he stole it, he must have stolen Bruni's scramasax as well.

Red Ottar, meanwhile, was thinking about his helmsman and blacksmith. And later in the day, he cornered the two of them. "If I'd known before we left Sigtuna what I now suppose," he said, "neither of you would ever have set foot on my boat. I can see there's something bitter between you, but your first duty is to honor your companions. If one of you creates trouble, I'll make both of you pay for it."

At the end of the first day, when the boat nosed toward the mooring at Duboviki, most of the crew were skin-sore and bone-weary.

"Ah!" cried Mihran, pointing to the people gathered on the quay. "Who do I see?"

"Well?" said Red Ottar irritably.

"Just the man to lift our spirits," Mihran replied.

"I'd as soon drown mine in a hornful of ale," Torsten said.

"Easy now!" Mihran called out. "Easy!"

And as gracefully as a swan, a black swan, the boat glided alongside the quay, and Mihran expertly noosed a bollard and jumped out.

As soon as he saw Mihran, one of the men on the quay yelped. Then he got down on his haunches and—both feet, both hands, both feet—he hopped toward the river pilot. Mihran got down on his haunches too, and then the two of them pretended to box before standing up, laughing.

"Smik!" exclaimed Mihran. "My old friend!" And he told the crew, "Smik's a laughter maker."

"A what?" asked Brita.

Smik took hold of Brita's earlobes and gently pulled at them. "Bigger ears!" he told her. "That's what you need. Like us hares."

"A laughter maker," Mihran repeated, "even though he's half Swedish."

Smik pulled a long face. "No laughing matter," he said. Then he turned to Bard. "Hello, creature!" he said.

"I'm not."

"What not?"

"A creature."

"Of course you are. A human creature. Each and every feature from your topknot to your ten toes. The whole lot. We're all creatures."

"Even dragons?" asked Bard.

"I did tell you," Mihran said. "This is Garthar. The crossing place. Where human creatures can become wild beasts . . ."

"And beastly creatures become humans," added Smik. And then he reached up, took out his right eye, and popped it into his mouth.

Bard and Brita gasped.

"Want a taste, Big Ears?" he asked.

Brita screwed up her face.

Then Smik took the eye out of his mouth and slipped it back into his eye socket, and both children laughed.

Smik looked around the crew. "Any of you got a glass eye?"

"I have," Solveig heard herself saying in a clear voice. Then she just glanced at Vigot under her eyelashes and saw how the muscles on either side of his mouth tightened and twitched.

"Have you, indeed?" said Smik.

"A third eye," said Solveig. "An eye that can see who a person really is."

"Mm!" hummed Smik. "You're a deep one."

Everyone waited, but Solveig chose to say nothing more. Not now, she thought. The time will come.

That evening, they sat around a driftwood fire with some of the people living at Duboviki, and Smik told everyone a story.

"A Viking story," he said, "to welcome this boatload of Vikings to Garthar. But remember, half the people living here come from Sweden and Norway and Denmark—or at least their grandparents did."

Smik's story was about hot-tempered Thor and how he was tricked by the giant king in a drinking contest. When Thor supposed he was drinking ale from a huge drinking horn, he was actually draining the sea, and when his companion Loki had an eating contest with a young giant, he was actually competing with Fire, and when his boy servant ran races against a young giant, he was actually racing the speed of Thought, and when Thor himself wrestled against a horrible toothless old crone, he was really grappling with Old Age.

Many of the people listening to Smik laughed and clapped each time mighty Thor or one of his companions was worsted by the giants. But Solveig thought of all the shape changers in the forests of Garthar around her, and when Thor and his companions had escaped with their lives and the story came to an end, she shook her head.

"Well?" asked Mihran.

"The right story," said Solveig.

"I was watching yous," the pilot told her.

"If Thor can't be safe, how can we?"

Mihran spread his hands and shrugged.

"It matters," said Solveig. "Choosing the right story."

"It does. In the forest around us the bogatyrs . . ."

"Who?"

". . . the giants, they were listening too."

Solveig nodded.

"So were the spirits. The fire spirits. The water spirits."

Solveig wrapped her arms around her waist.

"They were part of Smik's story," Mihran told her, "and so they were listening to be sure it was told right."

"I know a story," Solveig said, "about a young woman who told a story at the wrong time and paid a terrible price. I'll tell you some day."

"On the right day!" said Mihran with a cheerful smile.

"Yes," agreed Solveig. "'Everything has its own time.' That's what a priestess told me once."

Then the whole crew trooped back to the boat. Though the days were slowly getting warmer, the nights were chill. Solveig curled up under her reindeer skin, but it was some time before she grew drowsy.

We all laughed at Smik, she thought. Well, everyone except Vigot. Laughter's a kind of medicine. He made us all contented.

14

"You thief!" exclaimed Bergdis. "Take your hand out of my pot!"

Vigot jerked back his right hand and licked his fingers.

"Just checking!" he said.

In the narrow confines of his boat, Red Ottar seldom missed anything. "A man with light fingers . . ." he began grimly, "a man who steals something small may well steal something larger."

Vigot avoided Bergdis's eye. He started to hiss a tuneless tune and then tied one of Oleg's shining bronze hooks to his fishing line.

Before long, Red Ottar was embroiled in a heated discussion with Odindisa. Solveig could hear them as they paced up and down the quay.

"No means no!"

"You asked me!"

"Woman!" yelled Red Ottar. "I changed my mind."

"You'll regret it."

"No."

"I'll put a curse on it."

"Don't you threaten me," Red Ottar shouted.

"Red-haired," Odindisa taunted him. "Hot-tempered. You're as bad as Thor."

"I'll sew your lips together."

"And just as stupid."

Solveig listened with a mixture of fear and admiration. Odindisa and Bergdis are the same, she thought. They're as spirited and strong as he is.

She knew what the row was about, of course: the four-eyed brooch, the one Red Ottar had intended to give to Edith before he changed his mind.

"He's always changing it." Solveig could see herself lying in Odindisa's lap and listening. "Like a weather vane. To begin with he'll be angry . . ."

"You witch!" roared Red Ottar, and he turned his back on Odindisa and stamped back aboard.

Solveig couldn't help herself: she just laughed.

Gorodishche, Gorodok . . . on they went, on, stopping overnight at bleak little trading stations with names chock-full of consonants and growling gutturals.

"I can't say them properly," Solveig told Mihran. "They're as lumpy as porridge."

The crew had to row most of the time because there wasn't enough wind to fill their sail, and by the midafternoon of the fifth day after leaving Ladoga, they were so

weary from struggling upstream that Red Ottar told Torsten to usher the boat to the riverbank.

Mihran sprang from deck to bank as if he were a goat.
Then Torsten threw him a rope, and the pilot wrapped it
around the trunk of an obliging silver birch.

Half the crew spread-eagled themselves in the bows and
stern, Bergdis complained that a cook's work was never
done and men were nothing but scrots and stomachs and
bigmouths, Slothi began to play a drifting song on his flute,
and Solveig opened her sack of bones.

It's time I finished this comb, she thought. It just needs
whittling and sanding. This walrus, it's so hard.

Before long, Red Ottar came over to inspect what Solveig
was carving, but then Mihran jumped back over the gunwale and landed lightly beside them.

The river pilot held up four fingers. "Dangers," he said.

"Well?" asked Red Ottar.

"Portages . . ." said the pilot, ticking off his first finger.
"Wild beasts . . . Ruffians . . . Fourth danger!"

"What fourth danger?"

"Water."

Red Ottar frowned. "What's dangerous about water?"

"Too much," Mihran said. "Mokosh keeps us safe, but
the Lord of the Waters, he is too strong." Mihran raised
his arms level with his shoulders. "I've never seen so much
water in this first week of May."

Red Ottar frowned. "Why is that dangerous?"

Mihran put two fingers to his lips and whistled, and Torsten came over to join them.

"I try to explain to yous," Mihran said. "The current is so strong we go too slow these days. Already we are two days late."

"Too late for what?" asked Torsten.

Mihran sighed. "If we come to Kiev too late, we do not have waters to come back. Water is very high now, but quickly it sinks very low."

"So what are we meant to do?" asked Red Ottar. "Fly?"

"We must come to Kiev as soon as we can," Mihran replied. "Then you have plenty of time to buy and sell."

"In that case," said Torsten, "we mustn't stop for long at Novgorod. Not for three days, as we planned."

Mihran nodded. "Is your decision," he told Red Ottar, his dark eyes shining. "Is your boat!" And with that, he politely backed away and gave the skipper space to talk to his crew.

"We don't know these waterways," Red Ottar said. "Mihran does. What's the point of hiring a river pilot if we ignore his advice?"

"None," said Torsten.

"What do you say, Solveig?"

"Me?" said Solveig, surprised.

"You," said Red Ottar.

"Well . . ." she began, "well, if you asked Odindisa, she'd say we must make a sacrifice. To the water spirits."

"I'm not asking Odindisa," said Red Ottar.

"Oh!" said Solveig. "I say what my father says: ask someone who knows, then follow his advice."

"Provided you trust him," the skipper said slowly. "Provided he's not giving you advice to profit himself."

"How?" asked Solveig.

"In this instance," said Red Ottar, "so he could pocket my money and be free for hire again."

"Is that what you think?"

"No," Red Ottar said, "probably not. All right, it's decided. But I can't say I welcome this turn of events. Just when everyone needs a rest, we're going to have to redouble our efforts."

Mihran showed all his white teeth. "Better prices in Kiev!" he exclaimed. "Skins yes, amber yes, brooches yes, weapons yes."

"Yes, yes," said Red Ottar, swatting him away.

"Slaves yes."

"We have no slaves," said Red Ottar. "Not for sale."

Mihran shrugged his shoulders. "Slaves no, honey yes, wax yes."

"River pilots yes," added Red Ottar. But his mouthful of sarcasm escaped Mihran.

"Unless . . ." he began, but then he paused and wound his mustache around his right forefinger.

"What?" asked Red Ottar.

"Unless," repeated Mihran, "yous like to go to Miklagard."

"Never!" retorted Red Ottar.

The pilot gave him an inviting smile. "Prices not better. In Miklagard, prices are best!"

Red Ottar snorted.

"Best best."

"Like your skins, Ottar," Torsten told him. "Everything's good but some things are better, and a few . . ."

"No," the skipper said. "I won't consider it."

"Won't," asked Torsten, "or haven't?"

"Both," Red Ottar snapped. Then he rounded on Solveig. "Did you put Mihran up to this?"

Solveig gazed at Red Ottar wide-eyed and shook her head.

"Yous come home with silk satins spices silver . . ." Mihran continued.

"Satins! They'd suit you, skipper," scoffed Vigot.

"No!" said Red Ottar very definitely. "How far is it, anyway?"

"Downstream," said Mihran. "All the way from Kiev to the Sea Black."

"Black Sea," Torsten corrected him.

"Yes, downstream . . ."

"And upstream all the way back," Red Ottar said.

Solveig made so bold as to lay her good right hand on Red Ottar's arm. "Will you . . . think about it?" she asked him hesitantly.

"Stop all this chatter," the skipper told Mihran, "and guide us to Kiev. That's what we're paying you for."

As Red Ottar had foreseen, his crew was unenthusiastic about having to hurry on. When they berthed overnight at Novgorod, except for Vigot they all felt too weary to go ashore at all.

"Yous see everything when you come back," Mihran promised them. "Now, we stay like one short breath. Next time, one hundred breaths."

Just a little south of Novgorod, the River Volkhov reached its source—the wonderful shimmering sheet of Lake Ilmen.

"Fifty-two rivers feed her," Mihran told the crew. "Only this river drains her. You'll see."

What the crew saw was that they would be able to sail across the lake. Bruni and Vigot and Slothi found new energy in their tired limbs to unroll the sail, haul it, and secure it.

For days it had been so dark, so narrow, as the boat plowed her way slowly upstream through the canyon of the dense forest, and now the world around the boat was open and breezy.

Solveig leaned over the gunwale and peered into the limpid depths. The boat skipped along, creaking and flapping and yapping, and then Brita excitedly called out to Vigot that she'd caught a huge fish. He helped her haul it in, and Solveig thought of times she had been out fishing with her father and stepbrothers in Trondheim fjord.

Blubba, she thought, you knew how I felt after my father had gone. And when you told me what your wish was, you made me weep. Well named, you are, wrapped in your own fat. I'd be glad to see you again.

Oh! Spring will be shining in the fjord now.

Spring, when we prop the door open. We lift the rushes, sweep out the cobwebs and ashes, we ransack our long room. Then we brush the dairy and the forge and clean out my father's shed on the staithe . . . I bring to the table aconites, violets . . . and I strew them on my mother's grave. Spring, and we sing, we dance . . .

Solveig's heart ached.

Edwin's right, she thought. I must ask myself questions. Questions are the best way of preparing, so that whatever happens, you're half ready.

Sailing across Lake Ilmen, the crew told each other they had never seen such light—light so bright, said Odindisa, that it would surely be too strong for night. Hope lifted their hearts, and around them Solveig counted eight little skiffs. The man fishing in the nearest one waved to her, and she smiled and waved back.

A flock of small birds kept them company. Solveig and Brita watched the way they skimmed so close to the surface of the water that their wing tips almost touched it, and they saw how they all rose and swooped as one.

"How do they do that?" asked Brita.

Solveig shook her head. "They just know," she said.

It took the whole day to cross the lake. Before the boat entered the mouth of the River Lovat, Mihran called the crew around him: "Better you know. In Garthar we say, 'Better the witches and demons you know.'"

"Better than what?" asked Brita.

"The ones you don't know," Mihran said, and he gave her a flashing smile. "Now! Lovat is twice as long as Volkhov, and each day is more difficult. River narrow and narrower." Mihran squeezed his neck and opened his mouth. "We sail for two days. Then you row and row and I guide you between rocks, past mud banks."

Odindisa looked at her husband, and he grimaced. But they weren't the only ones to wonder whether Red Ottar had been wise in deciding to travel as far as Kiev.

"And after this," Mihran went on, "we have to pull and push and roll this boat—"

"What do you mean?" demanded Bard.

"Over dry land. Wet-dry land. We come to the headwaters . . . you say headwaters?"

"Get on with it," Red Ottar told him.

Mihran nodded. "Headwaters of the Dnieper, the great river that runs you downstream." Mihran was opening his arms, and his voice was rising. "Downstream to Kiev. Downstream to the . . . the Black Sea."

"How long?" asked Red Ottar.

"Gods willing," said Mihran, "twenty-two days to Kiev."

"Twenty-two!" exclaimed Bergdis, and she gave a low whistle.

"If this river is not too much water, we reach Kiev on the last day in May. Soon we must row and pray Mokosh goes with us, but now we sail, we talk, we laugh, we eat, we drink, yes?"

"Can we fish again?" Brita asked Vigot.

"Onward!" said Red Ottar gruffly.

Once more Solveig opened her sack. After she'd felt in the bottom to check that her gold brooch was still there, she rummaged around for her violet-gray glass bead and a piece of leather. She cut off a fine strip, strung the bead, and slipped it over her head. It swung between the swell of her breasts as she worked at the half-carved pin, the one she had been trying to pierce when she had jabbed her awl into the heel of her left hand, and before long the shining bead caught Vigot's eye. He didn't want to look at it, and he couldn't take his eyes off it.

"What are you looking at?" Solveig asked him.

"Nothing."

"Liar!"

"A sweet country," said Vigot.

Solveig immediately blushed and crossed her hands over her growing breasts.

Vigot gave her a lingering smile.

"Seen this bead before?"

"No."

"You have," said Solveig, her voice rising. "In Oleg's workshop."

"Let's have a look at it."

"Keep your hands off me!"

"Keep your temper!" retorted Vigot, grinning.

"And on the quay?" persisted Solveig. "When the dogs attacked me."

By now, Solveig was speaking so loudly that most of the crew was listening.

"I told you," Vigot replied, "I've never seen it before."

"You're lying," cried Solveig. "You know you are! This is my third eye, and your eyes, they're thief eyes."

Vigot sucked in his cheeks and spit onto the deck.

"Swear you didn't pick it up. Swear you didn't sell it."

"There's nothing to swear."

Bergdis stood up. Like a large, tubby cat she reached out her claws toward Vigot. "Ahhh!" she growled very slowly and deliberately. "But there is, Vigot. There is."

Vigot stared at Bergdis with stony eyes.

"I know something you do not," she gloated.

Then Bergdis rolled down into the hold, and Red Ottar ordered Vigot and Solveig to follow her. The crew surrounded them—all except Torsten, who stayed at the helm.

"Right!" said Red Ottar. "Solveig, you've accused Vigot of stealing and selling your glass bead. And yet you're wearing it . . ."

"If he stole the bead," Bruni said thoughtfully, "he could have stolen something larger."

"And you, Bergdis," Red Ottar went on, "you know something."

Bergdis bared her teeth and slowly sucked air between them as if she were sharpening them. Then she leveled her gaze at Vigot.

"Scum!" she hissed.

"All right," Red Ottar told Solveig. "You first. You can't make accusations without good reason. Not on my boat."

Solveig took a deep breath and looked up at Edith. Edith pushed out her lower lip, then she slowly nodded.

"When I went to Oleg's workshop," Solveig began, "he gave me a glass bead. He said it would be my third eye. It was in my right hand when the dogs attacked me. In the morning, that's when I missed it . . ."

"She did," said Odindisa. "Solveig asked me whether she'd been holding anything when Bruni carried her back, but she didn't say what."

"And then?" asked Red Ottar.

"I searched on the quay," Solveig told him, "but it wasn't there. When I went to the market with Edith and Bergdis, we met Oleg again. He told me he'd seen my bead on a market stall."

Bergdis's eyes were glittering like fish scales.

"Did you hear Oleg say that?" Red Ottar asked her.

Bergdis shook her head. "No, no. I'd gone off to buy . . . things. I had work to do."

"What else did Oleg say?" Red Ottar asked Solveig.

"He said the stallholder told him a tall young man had sold her the bead. 'A tall young man. Very watchful. Like the blade of a knife.'"

"And Oleg bought the bead and he gave it back to Solveig," added Edith.

"And today," Solveig said, "I decided to wear it around my neck so it would see the thief and the thief would see it."

Vigot didn't move. He looked quite expressionless.

Red Ottar took a deep breath. "Well, Vigot—" he began, but Edith interrupted him.

"That's not all Oleg said. He told us the young man had sold the stallholder several things."

There was a silence aboard the boat. Each of the crew heard their own heart beating, the prow slicing through the water, around them wild birds shrieking.

Bergdis rubbed her hands together. "I stopped at that stall too," she said slowly. "And what did I find?"

"What?" asked Red Ottar.

"A scramasax," hissed Bergdis.

Bruni Blacktooth braced his huge forearms and levered himself to his feet. He roared.

"Yes," said Bergdis. "With your maker's mark on it."

Bruni looked as if he were about to hurl himself down onto Vigot.

The skipper raised his right hand. "So, Blacktooth," he said levelly, "it wasn't Torsten after all."

The blacksmith growled.

"And it wasn't the Bulgars."

Everyone stared at white-faced Vigot, and he began to clench and unclench his right fist.

"Clench it while you still can," Red Ottar told him in a bitter voice. "What have you to say?"

"What difference will it make?" Vigot replied. "You've ganged up against me since we left Sigtuna. All of you." Vigot sounded desperate. "All of you!" he yelled.

"Nonsense, Vigot," Red Ottar said. "What else did you sell?"

"I didn't sell anything."

"What was it Mihran said?" mused Red Ottar. "The real danger is inside, not outside . . . The one who's afraid. The one who falls ill . . . The one who's a thief."

"You thief!" Bruni shouted. "Look me in the eye!"

But Vigot didn't respond.

"It took me a month to make that scramasax," muttered Bruni between clenched teeth. "A whole month."

"For a start," Red Ottar told Vigot, "you will pay Blacktooth whatever the stallholder gave you. And pay Solveig for the glass bead. Where are the coins? In your chest?"

Still Vigot didn't respond.

"You've shamed yourself and dishonored us all."

"You scum!" growled Bruni. "Hel's spawn!"

"We have days and days of rowing and portaging ahead of us," Red Ottar told Vigot in a grim voice. "The truth is we cannot do without you any more than we can do with you. We'll have to keep you in one piece until we reach Kiev."

"If he stays aboard," screeched Bergdis, "he'll knife us all in the night."

"Thank you, Bergdis," Red Ottar said. "When I need your advice, I'll ask for it." Then he turned to Vigot again. "And when we get to Kiev," he said, "by law you will lose your right hand."

Vigot blinked. "It wasn't me," he said. "Anyhow, Bruni can have all the coins for his scramasax, and Solveig's got her glass bead already, and she can have the coin for that as well. So where's the justice?" he asked, his voice rising. "Where's the justice in your taking my hand?"

Red Ottar grimaced. "And from now on you'll sleep in chains," he told Vigot, "so you cannot escape or wound any of us."

15

Lightning sizzled across the darkening southern sky. And then far thunder bumped and blundered around the horizon.

The old waterman looked up at Torsten. "Go on, then!"

So Torsten, standing at the prow, threw the rope, and the waterman caught it and expertly began to haul the boat in.

Torsten jumped down onto the staithe. "Strong as a tree stump, that's what you are," he said approvingly.

"An old one," grunted the waterman.

"A lesser one would have been dragged in."

The waterman nodded. "You have to stand right," he said. "Come on the right day, you have."

"How's that?"

"The gods are drawing close. Thor and Perun—we've called on them both."

"Thor and who?"

"Perun!" exclaimed the old waterman. "The god of thunder and lightning."

"Ah!" said the helmsman. "One god with two names, then."

"The same but not the same," the waterman told him.

"Where is everyone?" asked Torsten. "This place looks like a ghost village."

The old waterman pointed upstream, and Torsten saw a pointed tent pitched on the green fringe between the river and the forest. Several people were walking along the riverbank toward it. "The shaman's here," he said. "She's eaten the mushrooms and gone into her tent."

As Solveig approached the peaked woolen tent with Odindisa and her children, she could hear the double thump of a big drum: as regular as a heartbeat. She had to duck her head to get inside, and at once she saw that just about everyone living at the little trading post was already crammed into the tent. In the center, a woman wearing a headdress of eagle feathers was chanting and slowly turning around and around. Sometimes she reached out, reached up, up, sometimes she sidled and almost slithered, sometimes she moaned and sometimes screamed.

At length the shaman sank to her knees. She put her head between her hands. She balled herself into a nut and fell silent.

No one spoke or whispered. No one took their eyes off her.

Then the woman began to rise to her feet. She rose like a column of smoke.

"Strangers!" she called out, neither speaking nor singing but something between the two. Not quite a human voice, but not the voice of a bird or an animal either. "Strangers! Who are the strangers?"

Everyone turned around to look at Solveig and Odindisa and her children.

"For you," the shaman warbled, "for you and your companions I see one new life. I see one dying alive. I see what I see: one new death."

The drumbeats began again. Double thump. Double thump. They quickened, they began to throb, and Solveig was dry-mouthed.

For a second time there was silence, and outside, the thunder gods took over. The shaman subsided; she drew into herself again.

She's a woman, thought Solveig, but she's a sea eagle too, with thrashing pinions and hooked talons. She keeps changing shape.

Brita stood close to Solveig and took her hand.

"One new life." Edith's baby? Solveig turned to Odindisa, but she had her arms around Bard and her eyes were closed and her mouth was open—as if she too were in a trance or riding on the back of a dream.

One new life, thought Solveig. She must mean the baby. "One dying alive . . . I see what I see: one new death." In the stifling tent, Solveig shivered. That can only mean what it means. One of us is fated. One of us is soon to die . . .

Solveig sighed and closed her eyes, and out of the dark she saw a shining woman advancing toward her, step by step, brandishing a huge pair of shears.

"No!" she cried, and then she clamped her left hand over her mouth.

Once again the shaman flowed upward, then reached high above her headdress.

"I see what I see," she moaned. "I see one who says she's strong as the sun."

Me, thought Solveig. Does she mean me?

"Strong as the sun," repeated the shaman, her voice rising. Then she cupped her hands over her mouth: "But is she strong enough? Is she as strong as she'll need to be?"

Solveig listened. She listened as if her life depended on it.

"The golden girl!" the shaman moaned. And with that she sank to the ground and into a sleep so deep that no one could have woken her.

Days passed. Around Red Ottar's boat, summer quickened. The girlish pale green leaves of birch and lime and hazel grew up. The climbing sun beat the bounds and drove the darkness back into its forest kingdom.

One dawn, Slothi imitated the cooing song of a forest bird with his flute, and one early morning, the river unexpectedly grew as bulbous as an onion, so that Torsten was able to hoist the sail; one midday, Vigot grew angry, murderously angry—he howled like a wolf—so Bruni and Torsten tied him to the mast for fear he might harm someone or throw himself off the boat, and only Brita went near him, carrying a bowl of water in case he was thirsty; one afternoon, Solveig and Edith saw a wedding party on the riverbank, the bride and groom garlanded with red and white wildflowers, and they begged Red Ottar to stop, just for a breath, but he wouldn't; and one blue hour, Solveig and some of the crew went into the forest mushrooming, and they came back with at least a dozen kinds, some they'd never seen before, but they didn't eat any of those for fear they might send them into a trance and down on a journey into the always-darkness; one evening, Edith saw the wraith of a mermaid rising from the water, and Mihran told her it was a girl who had drowned herself for love, and she'd been seen before at that place; and one night, Solveig and Edith sat and listened while Mihran told them about the woman made of gold with another woman made of gold inside her who had another gold woman inside her who had . . .

"A girl!" exclaimed Edith, almost laughing. "A golden girl inside her!" She patted her stomach.

"Oh, Edie!" cried Solveig. "Golden and growing!"

When Solveig talked to Odindisa about the shaman and what she'd said, Odindisa told her: "I could have stayed there forever. Everything was alive. The air, the trampled grass, the woolly skin of the tent, they were all alive and somehow connected. I can't explain it."

"You are explaining it," said Solveig.

"I mean," said Odindisa excitedly, "they're all part of something bigger than they are, like a thumb and four fingers are part of a hand."

That made Solveig think of Vigot, though, and she winced.

"It was the same the next morning," Odindisa went on. "That mist floating above the river—it's born to change shape, and it's alive! Then I saw the sun herself caught in a trembling drop of dew, a drop of dew on the grass."

Solveig smiled and sighed. "You say things," she told Odindisa, "like I feel them."

"Sometimes it's best to say without too much thinking," her companion replied. "Thoughts can get in the way of words."

"What did the shaman's words mean?" Solveig asked her. *"One new life. One dying alive. One new death."*

Odindisa slowly shook her head. "Three prophecies," she said. "But each could have more than one meaning. And Solveig, the golden girl—didn't she mean you?"

"I don't know," said Solveig.

"I do," said Odindisa.

"She asked if I was strong enough, strong as I'll need to be. But I feel stronger than I have all my life."

"Your journey is making you stronger," Odindisa reassured her.

"Maybe our journey will tell us what her prophecies mean," Solveig said. "The drop of dew trembling, and the grunt of the elk, and the satin river. Everything."

Odindisa smiled. "New life and dying alive and new death," she said, "they're all connected."

"Tomorrow," said Mihran, "we portage." He smiled so widely that he bared all his white teeth.

Solveig clicked her tongue. "I keep hearing portage, portage," she said, "but I still don't really know exactly what it means."

"For all your long journey," the river pilot said, "this boat has carried yous. Now yous carry this boat."

"Nonsense!" said Solveig briskly. "You can carry a skiff or a small coble, but you can't carry this boat. We're not giants or bogatyrs or something."

For miles and days the river had meandered until she was no more than twenty paces across, but then, rowing around a bend still quite early in the morning, everyone saw a kind of landing stage, a broad wooden ramp.

Almost at once they heard a horn winding, then bellowing, and at least a dozen men and women quickly assembled on the bank.

"Portagers," Mihran told Solveig. "Old friends."

Two men came slithering down the slimy ramp, carrying between them a pine roller—it looked like a giant's rolling pin. They walked straight into the water up to their hips and stood facing each other across the boat's prow while two more pairs of men stood ready on the ramp with their rollers.

Torsten told the crew to straighten the boat so that it was facing the ramp.

"Bend your backs!" he shouted. "Forward!"

The first pair of men knelt in the water so it came up to their necks, and Red Ottar's boat glided over their roller onto the second and third ones.

At once the portagers started to tie ropes to the prow and along the gunwales (one of them noosed his line right around the carved stem post), and while the boat was still half in the water, one man heaved himself up over the stern. Mihran was there to give him a hand.

"Foreman," the pilot told Red Ottar. "Truvor."

"Truvor?" repeated Red Ottar.

"His name," Mihran explained.

Solveig stared at him, astonished. The foreman was stripped to the waist, and the upper part of his body and his arms were covered with tattoos. On his upper left arm there was a dragon, and on his left shoulder a large star, on his ribs . . .

Solveig looked a bit more closely, and Truvor laughed. Then he turned to Mihran and said something.

"You want?" Mihran asked Solveig. "He says you want?"

"Want what?"

"Him!"

"Him?"

"No, no!" Mihran waved his hands. "Same with him." Mihran motioned to Truvor to turn around, and Solveig saw his back was tattooed with an open-armed tree.

"Each tattoo is to mend him," Mihran said. "Broken arm, broken shoulder, broken rib . . . Truvor has seventeen tattoos, he says."

The foreman looked quite proud as Mihran enumerated all his wounds, and then he laughed and thumped his chest.

"The only part not broken is his heart," Mihran told Solveig with a flashing smile. "Truvor says his wife, she has the hammer and pins."

"Ah, yes," said Red Ottar. "Generations ago, people in Sweden used to be tattooed for all their aches and pains."

"What does he mean?" asked Solveig. "Hammer and pins."

"That's how you're tattooed," Red Ottar said. "Ask Odindisa. She'll know."

Solveig flinched. "But—"

"Enough!" said Red Ottar. "We're not here to discuss tattooing. Truvor, I suppose, wants to talk about payment."

Red Ottar supposed right. And although he waved Solveig away, she could still hear him arguing and eventually saying, "Well, you've got me over your rollers, you have. No choice, have I?"

As soon as Red Ottar and Truvor had agreed on terms, Torsten untied Vigot, altogether calmer now, and the crew disembarked. They jumped down one by one from the prow onto the ramp and helped the portagers push and pull the boat until the hull emerged from the muddy water, dripping and covered with globs and strings of green weed, here and there decorated with barnacle shells.

She looks so strange, Solveig thought to herself. Almost naked.

"Here," announced Red Ottar, "we wait. My poor boat has to drain and dry out. She'll be much too heavy otherwise."

"Even then," said Torsten, "we may need to unpack our merchandise and carry it."

The skipper rounded on Vigot. "As for you . . ." he began. "Bruni! Tie him to that tree and make sure he can't work the binding loose. I'm taking no risks."

That night, Red Ottar asked Bergdis to give the crew double rations to fortify them for the backbreaking work ahead. They all slept on deck except for Vigot—he slept standing up, and Bruni untied him again soon after dawn.

"Give him bread and water," Red Ottar told him. "And keep a watch on him, you and Slothi."

Twelve portagers worked alongside the crew as they started to pull and push the boat up the muddy track and away from the water. As soon as the boat had run clear of a roller, a pair of men picked it up and carried it ahead of the prow again.

While they worked, the portagers joined in a kind of song, repeating it over and over again, until they stopped after noon at the top of the long slope.

There Truvor and his team ate the rations they had brought with them while Red Ottar and his crew devoured the ribs of elk left over from the previous evening, washed down with cloudy ale.

Mihran wiped his mouth and carefully wound the ends of his drooping mustache around his right forefinger. "Behind us," he told everyone, "all the rivers flow north. Garthar is north! But here . . ." Mihran opened his arms most expansively and smiled. "This is the watershed. You say watershed?

"After here, Garthar is south. River Dnieper flows south. Trees change, flowers change, fruit change. Yous see."

After eating and drinking, most of the crew went off into the woods to do their business, and then it was back to work again. Half a dozen portagers went around to the stern of the boat and tied restraining ropes there while the other six continued to carry rollers from the stern and place them under the slowly advancing, creaking prow. Each of the crew, meanwhile, stood alongside their own oar holes and put their shoulders to the hull to steady her on her journey downhill.

To begin with, Bard and Brita hopped around and joined in the chanting, but then Red Ottar told them they were quite old enough to lend a hand. Several times they helped carry a heavy pine roller from stern to prow, staggering under the weight of it.

"Watch your step!" Odindisa called out to Brita. "You'll drop it on your toes."

"I'm getting used to it," Brita called back.

"You too, Bard!" warned Slothi. "It's muddy here."

But just a moment later, as Brita tried to position their roller beneath the hull, her right foot slipped forward. Then her left foot slipped backward, and she fell right in front of the advancing keel.

Brita screamed.

The ground was so mushy, she couldn't even lever herself onto her knees.

She screamed again, and standing at the oar hole nearest to the prow, Vigot immediately saw what had happened. While the portagers pulled on their ropes, he leaped forward, yelling, and threw himself on top of Brita. He drove her face and little body down into the marshy mud, and his body protected hers as the boat rolled right over them.

Odindisa howled, and Truvor yelled a string of orders to his portagers. First they stayed the boat, then those who had been pulling began to push, and those who'd been pushing began to pull, and slowly, very slowly, they rolled the boat back . . .

Vigot lay motionless, his shoulders bloody, his white ribs exposed.

Truvor and Solveig carefully lifted him, and Solveig's eyes were blurred with hot tears.

Then Slothi and Odindisa fell to their knees and lifted their daughter from the mud. They raised her, black-faced and choking, and Odindisa sobbed and embraced her.

"She's all right?" Red Ottar asked.

Slothi nodded. "I think so."

"Come and help Vigot," Red Ottar instructed Odindisa. "Put a dressing on his bones."

Then Solveig and Truvor gently laid Vigot down, and Truvor grimaced.

"If he lives," Bruni growled in a dark voice, "he'll be a half man."

"A better man than I thought," Red Ottar replied.

"The gods punished him before you could," Bruni observed.

"They've punished us all," the skipper replied. "We were nine—and now we're eight."

16

Mihran was right. As soon as the crew set off down the Dnieper, they felt as if they were going downhill. The water was willing them on.

But before this, they had been obliged to wait for another whole day while the boat rode at anchor and her timbers drank and swelled again.

"Taking up," Torsten told Solveig. "So she won't leak."

"We do the same with my father's boat," Solveig replied.

All day, Vigot lay in the hold facedown, arms outstretched. To begin with, Odindisa smeared the same ointment into his ghastly wounds that she had applied to Solveig's bites, but then she changed her mind, and when they next disembarked she started to jab and stab with her spatula at the soft riverbank. Before long, she dug out a pair of worms, knotted together, then another pair, and triumphantly waved them in the air.

Solveig followed her back up the gangplank and watched her lay the worms on a thin iron tray and hold them over

Bergdis's fire. Before long, the worms stopped wiggling. They became crispy. Then they fell apart and turned to ash.

"Poor Vigot," said Solveig.

"This will help him," Odindisa said.

"Yes, Asta does the same."

"Who?"

"My stepmother."

"The worms have to be knotted," Odindisa told her, "otherwise the medicine won't work. The sinews won't knit together."

"I know," Solveig replied. "But Vigot's ribs cracked as well. I heard them. And he's all crushed."

Odindisa gave a deep sigh.

"Will he ever mend, do you think? Ohh!"

"He saved Brita," said Odindisa, "so I'll do all I can to save him. This worm powder, and I'll sing the healing runes and . . ."

"So brave!" whispered Solveig, and she stroked Vigot's right hand. "If only I hadn't accused you."

Odindisa took the tray away from the heat and tipped the worm ash into the palm of her right hand. Then she rubbed it into Vigot's gouged back and began to sing over him.

Vigot didn't stir. He didn't make a sound. Now and then he jerked his hands and arms, but he didn't move his legs at all.

"Will you teach me?" Solveig asked Odindisa. "I know the runes but not how to heal people with them."

"Runes for an adder's bite or a filthy stomach or for swollen knees, runes for nosebleed and blotches and boils: there are healing runes for each malady."

"I want to learn them," said Solveig.

"You want to do this and want to do that. You're so restless. Bergdis says you're like a horsefly, buzzing around and feeding off the blood of one beast after another."

"That's not true," said Solveig indignantly, and roses flared in her cheeks. "Is it?"

"You know Bergdis," Odindisa replied. "Yes . . . I'll teach you healing runes if you'll teach me how to cut them. How's that?"

Solveig smiled, but she felt upset. Bergdis is always making trouble, she thought. She's the one with the sting. But I won't let her see she's gotten under my skin.

First the boat swallowed the fresh spring water of the Dnieper, then she swallowed its miles. Mihran required only one pair to sit at their oars—Bruni and Slothi, to begin with—while the remainder of the crew attended to small duties.

Torsten filed the oarlocks that had become splintered, and then he worked on two of the knees that had come loose from their thwarts. Mihran said he thought the boat might be off balance, and so Red Ottar got Bard and Brita to crawl behind all the packages in the hold to check that the stone ballast had not shifted. Odindisa hovered around Vigot. As usual, Bergdis busied herself with preparing the next meal, and Edith helped her until Red Ottar summoned her.

And Solveig, she carved. She scratched and scraped and gouged and whittled and shaped and fashioned and sanded as if her life depended on it. Pins and combs, dice, bone beads. Now I'll really show Red Ottar what I can do, she thought.

Once Solveig glanced toward the bows, and there she saw Edith and Red Ottar. He was holding her face between his hands and kissing her on the mouth until Edith broke away from him, gasping and laughing.

Then Red Ottar attached something to the top of Edith's woolen tunic . . .

"Your brooch!" exclaimed Solveig as soon as she and Edith were alone together.

"He gave it to me," Edith told her wonderingly, as if she could scarcely believe it.

"It looks like two hammers laid end to end," Solveig told her. "And here, these studs at each end, they're like pairs of eyes."

"He won't tell me where he bought it," Edith said.

"Maybe he didn't," Solveig replied.

"What do you mean? He did, and he says charms have been sung over it. To protect us." Edith quietly joined her hands together over her stomach.

"You must show Odindisa," Solveig told her, and then she smiled a little smile, surprised at herself for being so sly.

Later that day, Solveig got to work on a pair of elk shin bones. I'll make them into skates, she thought. I can do that quite quickly and Red Ottar will be really pleased.

As she began to work, Solveig daydreamed. She was a thousand miles away, skating with her father and Blubba across the fjord where it narrowed and froze each winter. The light was so dazzling that Solveig had to keep her eyes screwed up, and they kept watering. Then her father unwrapped his auger and pointed it at the ice . . .

A shadow passed between Solveig and the sun, and she looked up. It was Mihran.

"Skates," she told him. "A pair of skates."

"Ahhh!" exclaimed the pilot, and he lifted his right foot and showed it to Solveig as if he were a horse waiting to be shod.

"That girl who told the story at the wrong time," Solveig said. "Do you remember?"

Mihran nodded.

"It was about Skadi, the goddess who always wears skates or skis. This girl lived on our fjord, and she told a story about how the winter was so bitter that even the gods were famished and Skadi herself had to go ice fishing and hunting. But she told it on the eve of the spring solstice. Her words stopped the sun from warming the earth!"

"Was she punished?"

"My father said all the farmers called her a witch and stoned her."

"There's a right time for a story," observed Mihran, "and a right place for skates."

"What do you mean?"

The river pilot gestured to the pair of shin bones. "Skates are for north," he said, "not much for south."

Solveig stared at the bones.

"Not good price in Kiev," Mihran told her.

Solveig picked them up and banged them against each other, feeling cross with herself.

Mihran gave her a sympathetic smile. "Making," he said. "Never easy."

"Kiev's south," said Solveig. "And the Black Sea and Miklagard are south from Kiev. But if you sail south from south, what then?"

"What then!" Mihran echoed her. He gave Solveig a flashing smile and sat down on the deck beside her. "Then, Solveig, the land of the Saracens."

Solveig looked at him, wide-eyed.

"Some Saracens have eighty wives."

"Eighty!"

"And they sleep with each of them each night! Their magicians can turn themselves into angels. And that's where Jesus was born."

"In the land of the Saracens?"

"Yes, and his mother Mary, she was afraid her baby wasn't the son of God at all but the son of a magician."

"And south from that?" asked Solveig, agog.

"Amazonia!" exclaimed the pilot. "The Land of Women. No man can stay there for more than seven days and seven nights." Mihran gave Solveig a knowing smile. "Boy babies are sent away to their fathers in other countries. And the girls . . ." The pilot opened his eyes very wide.

"What?"

"When they're full-grown, one of their breasts is burned off."

"Burned off!" cried Solveig.

"With a red-hot iron."

"Why?"

"So they can fight and hunt. Women who carry shields—no left breast! Women with bows and arrows—no right breast!"

Solveig stared at Mihran, uncertain whether to believe him.

"Miklagard is the end of your journey," Mihran told her. "But that's where south of south begins."

"I wish we were all going," Solveig said. "Can't you change Red Ottar's mind?"

"I try again," Mihran promised her.

Solveig was spellbound by Mihran's stories, and each day he told her more. As the sun rose in the June sky, Solveig carved and heard about the country of Libya, where people's shadows fall on the wrong side and there are no fish because the sea is so hot that it boils, and the country of Ethiopia, where the children are yellow but adults are black, and many of them have only one foot.

"That's like unipeds!" exclaimed Solveig.

Mihran frowned.

Solveig told him how Vikings sailed west from icy Greenland until they came to a country where one-legged people hopped along the rocky strand and yelled and shot arrows at them.

Mihran grimaced. "Unipeds," he said darkly. "Ruffians, Pechenegs, wherever we are now, we must keep watch."

For her part, Odindisa kept watch over Vigot, each day rubbing new powders into his wounds. And while Solveig and Brita redressed them with linen strips soaked in fish oil, Odindisa sang quietly over him.

Lying on his side now, Vigot opened his eyes from time to time, but he didn't seem to recognize anyone or anything, and he didn't move his legs or his feet.

"If he doesn't eat soon . . ." Odindisa told Bergdis.

"There's no fat on him," Bergdis replied. "That roller saved him. Otherwise the keel would have cut him in half."

Odindisa screwed up her eyes. "His spine is injured."

"With his mouth open," said Bergdis unfeelingly, "and his eyes glazed, he looks like the trout he's so fond of catching."

One evening, while everyone was sitting around a fire on the riverbank, Solveig asked Bruni whether he knew about the unipeds.

"Not really," said Bruni. "One of them shot an arrow right into Thorvald's groin."

"Ooh!"

"Erik the Red's son. He died of the wound. I know about the Skrælings, though."

Maybe Torsten thought Bruni was being too boastful or disliked the attention Solveig was giving him, or maybe he had drunk too much. In any case, the helmsman cleared the grog from his throat and spit into the fire.

"What's wrong with you, Torsten?" Bruni asked.

"You!" Torsten retorted. "You're what's wrong with me."

"Oh?" said Bruni loudly.

"A Skræling! That's exactly what you are. Small and evil-looking. Coarse hair."

"Torsten!" Red Ottar warned him.

But the helmsman got to his feet and walked around the fire, and Solveig looked up at him, wide-eyed. "You know what a Skræling is, Solveig?" he asked. "Brave men have sailed east to Miklagard," he told her. "Your father, he's one of them. Brave men have sailed west to Vinland. But one Norwegian, one miserable coward—"

Red Ottar leaped to his feet. "Torsten!" he shouted.

Everyone held their breath. But nothing happened. The fire crackled and spit. The helmsman slouched back to his place. Bruni Blacktooth turned to smile at Solveig, but Solveig was gazing into the hot-eyed fire.

It's getting worse, she thought. Their feud's festering. How long will it be before they fight? Not before Kiev. Please not before then.

As Solveig trudged back across the gangplank, she kept thinking of another of her father's sayings: *"The truth will out. Truth's a clear bubble that always rises to the surface."*

Then Solveig lay down between Bergdis and Odindisa. As soon as she closed her eyes, she began to drift. She sighed and drowned in sleep.

Perhaps because the crew's duties were nothing like as demanding as before the portage, almost everyone was becoming more fractious.

We've all been cooped up on this boat for too long, thought Solveig. That's what it is. That, and Vigot, and Torsten and Bruni.

Brita sensed the crew's discontent. She kept picking arguments with her brother, and then she refused to help her mother change Vigot's dressing.

"There's no point," she said. "He's not getting better."

"You ungrateful whelp!" exclaimed Odindisa. "Vigot saved your life, and you refuse to change his dressing."

And with that she slapped her daughter so hard that both of Brita's ears burned for the remainder of the day.

Bard, meanwhile, became more and more excitable. He gabbled, he got in everyone's way, he laughed too long and too loud. He insulted his father.

"Go away!" said Slothi wearily. "Just go away!"

So Bard did go away. He walked into the forest while everyone was eating around the fire, and although Slothi and Odindisa kept calling for him, he didn't come back.

"He will," said Red Ottar grimly. "And he'll go to bed hungry."

That was exactly what happened. And as soon as Bard woke with a hole in his stomach, a devil crept into his head. While everyone else was still asleep and a raft of mist hung over the river, he began to scale the mast. To begin with, it was quite easy because there were wooden pegs, and then Bard found a footing on some lashing, and above that on a paddle-shaped piece of wood secured to the mast to reinforce it. But higher up it was more difficult. Bard had to use all his strength to pull himself up on the lanyard, because his legs kept slipping when he wrapped them around the mast. Up near the top, though, there were several eyeholes, and Bard used them as finger holds. With a yell, he grabbed the very top of the mast and snapped off the wind pennant.

"Cock-a-doodle-doo!" he crowed as loudly as he could.

Red Ottar screwed up his eyes and got to his feet.

"Cock-a-doodle-doo!"

"Come down!" shouted the skipper. "At once!"

"Cock-a-doodle-doo!"

But after the cock had crowed for the third time, Bard's courage began to ooze out of him. His stomach lurched and loosened. The wet brown glue slipped down the mast.

When Bard did at last come sliding down, his tunic and hands and legs were fouled. Red Ottar made him bend over, bare-buttocked, and he whipped him. Then he picked Bard up, light as thistledown. "Wash yourself!" he barked, and he dropped the boy overboard.

"You can be sure," Red Ottar told Odindisa and Slothi, "this is the last time any child sails on this boat." The skipper glared up at the mast. "As for that . . ." he said.

"Rain later," Mihran reassured him. "Rain will wash it."

"No," said Red Ottar. "The pennant."

"I'll make do," Torsten told him. "I'll lash a strip of cloth to the prow until we reach Kiev."

From day to day, the river broadened. It grew so wide—fifty paces maybe—that not even Bruni or Torsten could throw a stone across it. Then it grew again, so that the crew could no longer exchange greetings with people fishing on the riverbanks.

As the gloomy pines and firs drew back, they swept past pretty green willows lining the banks, solitary farmhouses, huddles of huts, and here and there meadows of scarlet poppies and golden mustard flowers.

And when they dropped anchor early each evening to eat and rest, the light was still bright, the air mild and quite sweet.

"Chestnut," Mihran told Bergdis. "Flowers of chestnut. You know?"

Bergdis shook her head.

"The nuts are good to eat. In Kiev you see."

"Kiev," said Bergdis tartly, "it's made of your promises." Then she held up her hands and clapped them and pretended to blow the whole city away.

Mihran turned to Red Ottar. "I will arrange you to meet Yaroslav, king of the Rus," he said thoughtfully. "I try." He rubbed his right thumb and forefinger together. "Merchants favored by the king make much money."

Bruni hiccupped. "Is he the king who chose to be Christian, so we can all drink good ale and not milk or moldy water?"

"No, no," said the river pilot. "That was his father, King Vladimir."

Bruni hiccupped again and raised his drinking cup to good kings.

"Half alive, half dead," Odindisa told Red Ottar.

The skipper gritted his teeth. "The worst of both worlds," he said. "What am I to do?"

For a while the two of them looked down at Vigot.

"I doubt he'll stand again," Odindisa said. "Not without sticks. He can't move his legs." Then she took Red Ottar's arm. "Sometimes," she said warmly, "not deciding is best. Sometimes we know tomorrow what we don't know today."

Red Ottar sniffed.

"Pray to the gods."

"I will not strike his hand off," the skipper told her. "It's the law, I know, but it would be dishonorable." He sucked in his cheeks. "So what's my choice? To leave Vigot in Kiev . . . or carry him home."

"Wherever that is," said Odindisa.

"Either way," observed Red Ottar, "we'll have to find a man to take his place."

As the River Dnieper swept down to Kiev, Red Ottar and his companions could see mile after mile of earthen banks lining the eastern shore.

"Snake Ramparts," Mihran told them. "King Vladimir built them to slow down the raiding Pechenegs and their ponies."

After this, the river stretched wider and wider.

"Floodplains," Mihran explained. "Water meadows. Now this river is five miles across. In winter, just one half mile."

Since the portage, Solveig had seen no more than a few little fishing boats each day, but now she saw more and more skiffs and coracles bobbing along the skirts of the river, with one or two men fishing from each of them.

And then . . . then they were there!

A whaleback of a hill rose behind the west bank of the river, and at its foot were crowded quays with single-masted and two-masted and three-masted ships tied up alongside them.

Quickly Bruni and Slothi pulled down the sail; then they sat to their oars, with Red Ottar and Bergdis in front of them. Solveig watched eagerly as Mihran and Torsten allowed the boat to slip just a little past a landing stage before swinging her around and having the oarsmen paddle back upstream.

Around them, the water spit and sparkled and spun in whorls off the ends of oars.

Father, thought Solveig, did you see all this? All the people? All the boats? What did you think? What did you say? Did you know what this journey would be like before you began it?

Solveig was aware that Edith was standing on one side of her, Brita on the other. She saw all the people milling on the quay, some shouting, some waving, and she choked with excitement and felt almost tearful.

Then Mihran threw a line to one of the harbormasters, and Edith fiercely clutched Solveig's arm.

"What?" asked Solveig.

"Look!"

Solveig looked where Edith was pointing, and at once she saw.

"Edwin!" she cried. "Sineus!"

Red Ottar shipped his oar and stood up.

"In the name of the gods," he roared, "how did they get here before us?"

17

Red Ottar was standing with one foot on the gangway, talking to Edwin, when Mihran came hurrying—skipping, almost—along the quay.

"Yaroslav, king of the Rus, will see you," he announced. "He will receive you at noon."

"Today?" asked Red Ottar.

"Today," said Mihran. "Noon or never. This afternoon he will be fitted."

"Fitted?"

"His new armor. And early this evening he shares his table."

"Ah, yes," said Edwin. "With me."

"With you?" exclaimed Red Ottar.

"Me," said Edwin with a bucktoothed smile, "or another man with the same name."

"What are you up to?" asked Red Ottar.

"Many a loaf," Edwin replied, "has been spoiled for being lifted from the oven too early."

"You schemer!" said Red Ottar, not wholly without respect.

"And tomorrow," Mihran continued, "the king sails north."

Then Solveig and Bergdis and Slothi all came trooping off the boat with wares for their stall, and the skipper made way for them.

"King Yaroslav will see me," he told them. "At noon."

Bergdis dropped the furs she was carrying and threw her arms around Red Ottar. "Praise the gods!" she screeched.

"I will," said Red Ottar drily. "But first, I'll praise Mihran."

"Will the king buy from us himself?" Bergdis asked. "And his queen?"

"Time will tell," Red Ottar replied.

Then Mihran held up his right hand. "King Yaroslav also require you," he told Red Ottar, "to bring with you Solveig, Halfdan's daughter."

"Solveig!" exclaimed Bergdis angrily. "Why her?"

Solveig could scarcely take her eyes off King Yaroslav. He wasn't particularly tall or short, fat or skinny, hairy or bald, but he had the brightest blue eyes she had ever seen, brighter even than Torsten's.

A large circular earring hung from his left ear, and it was inlaid with a stone that matched his eyes.

The king was sitting on a very high golden bench, and beside him perched his twelve-year-old daughter, Ellisif. She was wearing gold necklaces and gold armbands, and her fair hair was swept back and braided so that it looked like a whole cluster of swirling snakes. She couldn't quite touch the floor with her pointed shoes.

Red Ottar and Solveig, accompanied by Mihran, knelt in front of the king, and all around them in the great hall of the palace stood groups of counselors, retainers, and servants.

"Stand!" King Yaroslav told them. "Welcome!"

How deep his voice is, thought Solveig. Like an ox. Mihran says he has been king since before I was born.

To begin with, the king almost ignored Red Ottar. He gazed at Solveig with his deep-set eyes, and then he beckoned her. Scarcely daring to breathe, Solveig stepped up to him, and he nodded and rubbed his trimmed beard.

"Mmm!" he rumbled. "Light-footed, not limping. Whippety. Quick-fingered, not clumsy . . ."

Solveig began to shiver.

"But," said the king, inspecting Solveig further, "the way you tilt your head a little to the left. The way you watch."

Now Solveig was trembling.

King Yaroslav smiled. "Like father, like daughter," he growled. "If you'd come into this hall with one hundred other girls, I'd still recognize you. Halfdan's daughter!"

"Oh!" gasped Solveig, and her legs almost gave way beneath her.

The king patted the bench beside him, and Solveig sat down on the padded purple velvet.

She swallowed loudly. "You met him," she whispered.

"Any friend of Harald Sigurdsson is a friend of mine," the king replied. "But your father—he was much more than that. At Stiklestad, he saved Harald's life. Isn't that so?"

Solveig nodded and swallowed again. She felt quite sick.

"Look at me, girl," said the king.

Solveig raised her eyes.

"Yes," said the king, with a wry smile. "'A bit of change-ling. Eager as a colt. Her voice clear and bright as a ray of sunlight.'"

Once more, Solveig was trembling. She couldn't help it.

"Your father is well," King Yaroslav told her. "He came here at the end of autumn on his way to Miklagard. He was in the company of Earl Rognvald—"

"I met him," said Solveig. "For one night I did. But I was only nine then."

"Earl Rognvald and twenty Norwegians," continued the king. "They'd planned to meet in Sweden—"

"Over the mountains!" exclaimed Solveig, but then she put her hand over her mouth. "I shouldn't interrupt you."

"Some thoughts matter so much," said the king, pursing his lips, "there's no stopping them. As things turned out, they all made their own way to Ladoga. Yes, Solveig, your father was eager to see Harald again. Harald Sigurdsson, leader of the Varangian guard!"

Solveig gasped and clapped her hand over her mouth again.

"Yes," said the king. "That man! So, Solveig, I praised your father's resolve, his loyalty, his honor . . ." He paused and turned to Red Ottar. "This girl," he said, "is the daugh-ter of a determined, loyal, honorable man, and she is no less so herself. A young woman, traveling from Trondheim to Miklagard—I've never known the like of it."

Red Ottar inclined his head and slowly nodded.

"I rewarded her father," the king told him. "I gave him a saber."

Red Ottar frowned and pushed his head forward.

"A curved blade," said Mihran under his breath.

"Made by one of my own smiths," the king went on. Then he turned back to Solveig and considered her carefully. "I asked your father," he said, "whether he had any regrets.

"'One,' your father told me. 'Only one.'"

Solveig gazed at the king, unblinking.

"He said he had left a fine woman behind."

Solveig blinked.

"A fine woman," the king repeated slowly.

Then Solveig lowered her eyes. Asta, she thought. Asta. My father spoke of her.

"A young woman with one gray eye," the king went on, "one violet. Wide apart."

"Oh!" gasped Solveig, and she shuddered. "Ohh!"

"Ahh!" sighed the king. "He said he left without telling her. Without explaining. He said he would regret it for as long as he lived."

Solveig kept gulping, and for some time King Yaroslav sat quietly beside her. Then he turned to Ellisif. "You see how it is?" he asked in his deep voice. "Fathers and daughters."

Without bothering to look over his shoulder, the king raised his right hand and beckoned. Two servants hurried forward, one carrying a tray with a pitcher and three little gilt cups on it, the other a silver platter decorated around the rim with wildflowers and laden with little cakes and roasted nuts.

The king waved again, and the servants brought stools for Red Ottar and Mihran.

As one servant poured liquid from the pitcher, Solveig saw that it was pale red and transparent.

"You know this?" the king asked her.

"Lingonberry?" said Solveig.

"Try it."

So Solveig took a sip and immediately screwed up her face. "Sour!" she exclaimed.

"Cranberry," the king said. "Good for thirst. Good for safe childbirth."

"I'm not pregnant!" Solveig protested.

"I'm glad to hear it," the king replied, and with that he turned his attention to the two men.

"Well, Ottar," he said. "Red Ottar. Why Red?"

Red Ottar ran a hand through his red-gold hair.

"And a hot temper?"

"I know how to keep it, King. And I know when to lose it."

"And blood on your hands?"

"No," said Red Ottar. "Not spilled unjustly. Not the blood that stains."

The king nodded. "A good reply," he observed. "So, now! Miklagard!"

Red Ottar gave Mihran a sideways glance. "No," he replied in a guarded voice.

"No?" exclaimed the king, and he was either surprised or very good at pretending to be so; Solveig wasn't quite sure. "Why no?"

"It was never my plan," Red Ottar said.

"If Solveig can go," the king said, "you can go." He planted a firm hand on Solveig's shoulder. "You can watch over her . . . like a daughter."

"My crew will say we have come far enough already."

"Only weak men," said the king, "blame their followers. Strong men have supple minds. I would have expected better of you, Ottar."

Solveig listened, astonished. For the first time, she saw Red Ottar having no choice but to be submissive and heard him being put in his place.

"As it happens," King Yaroslav said, "you've arrived here at a crucial time. A time that can be very profitable for you. Once more, the Pechenegs are gathering, thousands of them, and before long they'll attack. I've sat on this throne for eighteen years, and this will be the greatest battle of all." King Yaroslav made the sign of the cross on his chest. "May God guard me," he said, "so that it's not also my last."

"Where are they now?" Red Ottar asked.

"North from here," said the king. "North of the Snake Ramparts. Massing already on the banks of the Dnieper. You? You can scarcely go back. Upstream, rowing all the way. The Pechenegs will pick you all off. You can wait here, or you can go on." The king paused. "Ottar," he said, "Red Ottar, I need your help. I'm asking you to carry my messenger to Miklagard as quickly as you can. For me—my family, my followers, my kingdom—I believe it's life or death."

Red Ottar inclined his head, in submission or in thought. "Your messenger," he said.

"I will send him to your boat."

"King," said Red Ottar, "you must allow me to talk to my crew. To do so is not a weakness but a sign of strength."

"You can be quite sure I will reward you all handsomely," King Yaroslav told him. "Not only that, the prices your furs and wax and honey will command in Miklagard . . ." The king shook his head as if there were no words to describe them. "Whatever cargo you've brought, buy even more. You will not be disappointed."

"I'll come back in the morning," Red Ottar promised him.

"Come this evening," King Yaroslav said sharply. "Send one of your crew to speak to me. I'll have my men watch out for him."

"As you wish," Red Ottar said.

"And then you can leave in the morning."

"King," protested Red Ottar, "we've only just arrived. We've come all the way from Ladoga, and my crew is worn out. One of my men is badly injured. We'll have to find someone to replace him."

"Ah!" interrupted Mihran.

King Yaroslav nodded. "I wouldn't ask so much of you if things were not desperate. But once you've passed the cataracts—"

"Cataracts!" exclaimed Red Ottar, looking wildly around him as if he expected them to hurl themselves right through the palace hall.

"Then," the king told them, "you can all rest. Mihran, you will guide them?"

"I will," said Mihran with a small bow, and Solveig wondered just how much of the king's intentions the river pilot already knew.

"In this way," the king told Red Ottar, "you will assist me and all the Rus—all the Vikings—here in Garthar. You will make yourself rich, and not only rich but honorable. You'll always be welcome at my court, just like Halfdan and his saber!"

There was so much Solveig wanted to ask. About her father. About Harald and his two years serving King Yaroslav in Kiev. About the Vikings who guarded the emperor in Miklagard by day and by night.

But King Yaroslav stood up. All his counselors, retainers and servants bowed low. Then the king gently put his hand on the small of Solveig's back and ushered her back to her companions.

Red Ottar and Solveig and Mihran all bowed to the king. Then they shuffled backward out of the great hall.

The dusty track from the palace to the quay was so steep that Solveig whooped and skeltered down it.

Red Ottar and Mihran followed at a more sedate pace.

"You have a daughter?" asked Mihran.

Red Ottar shook his head. "No," he said, as much to himself as to the river pilot. "No son. No daughter. We've made sacrifices, we've offered the gods gifts . . . I don't know."

"But your baby is coming now," Mihran said warmly. "Coming quickly."

When they had set off for the palace before noon, the quay had been seething with merchants and customers, children, cattle and asses, cats, dogs.

Solveig had looked longingly at the wares on the stalls, so many more than at Ladoga—colored glass cups and plates, bronze bottles as tall as she was and material so filmy that it seemed to float, little pyramids of colored powders . . . Red Ottar wouldn't stop, though, and kept hurrying her up.

Edie and I, later on we'll look at every stall, Solveig resolved. We will.

But now! Solveig could scarcely believe her eyes. The same quay was deserted. A few mangy dogs were ranging around, sniffing and barking, one boy was trying to fly a kite, and a dozen or two people were drifting from stall to stall. As she looked more carefully, Solveig saw that most of the merchants and their wives were lolling beside their stalls in the shadow of their awnings. Some of them were dozing, some snoring, though Solveig supposed they'd wake at once if anyone came close to their wares.

"Here," said Mihran, stretching out his arms, "everybody rests in the afternoon. They eat and drink and then . . ." The river pilot couldn't help yawning, and that made Solveig yawn too. "The heat of the day," Mihran told her. "That's what we call it."

"Today is the first day of June," Solveig said.

The river pilot nodded. "And now each day will be hot and more hot. You see."

Solveig closed her eyes, and what she saw was a little boat crossing molten gold water. There was a man in the bows and another smaller figure amidships, both of them looking forward. Solveig's heart was bubbling with everything the king had told her . . . She opened her eyes again.

Mihran smiled. "You go on a journey?" he asked her.

"Sometimes I scarcely know where I am," Solveig replied. "I'm here in Kiev, but at the same time I'm at home on the fjord and I'm in Miklagard."

Red Ottar's crew was resting too. Torsten had hauled the sail a little way up the mast, and most of his companions were dozing in its shadow.

Before long, though, Red Ottar clapped his hands several times and summoned everyone. He said the king had welcomed him, and Solveig too, because he had already received and honored her father.

"The king gave him a curved sword," Mihran told them.

"And that's why King Yaroslav wanted Solveig to accompany me," Red Ottar told Bergdis.

Bergdis simply thrust out her chin and lower lip.

Then Red Ottar told his crew about how the Pechenegs were massing upstream, and how the king had asked them to assist him and promised to reward them all, and about the rich pickings to be had in Miklagard. And he said that he wanted any decision to be as much theirs as his own.

"This is my boat," he told them, "and I have the last word, so you can't do without me, but I can't do without you. In the end, we have to agree."

Slothi and Bruni were of one mind. They said at once that they favored continuing their journey to Miklagard if the boat was fit to make the journey.

"Fit, yes," the river pilot said, looking at Torsten. "But she is large."

"Large?"

"For cataracts."

"What's cataracts?" asked Bard.

"Rapids," Slothi told him. "Rushing water."

"Seven," said Mihran thoughtfully. "Many Vikings leave their large boats here and buy smaller boats. Barges."

"No," said Red Ottar. "I'm not doing that." He looked up and down the length of the deck. "She's . . . she's my sea wife."

"I think," said Mihran, "she is large but not too large. We portage the fourth cataract. All boats must do that."

Memory of the last portage was sufficiently recent and painful for some of the crew to begin to have their doubts, but then Red Ottar and Mihran said that the Pechenegs were an even greater hazard than the cataracts.

"Our choice," the skipper told them, "is to wait here or to continue our journey."

Odindisa pointed to the inert figure lying in the hold. "What about Vigot?" she asked.

"If we go on," Red Ottar said, "we'll have to leave him here."

"Infirmary," said Mihran promptly. "Monks."

"At least the Christians are good for something," Red Ottar observed. "And when we get back, we'll decide whether or not to take him with us." He gave Odindisa a nod. "You're right. Not deciding is sometimes best."

"Do you want to know what I think?" Bergdis demanded.

"Of course," said Red Ottar.

"You do surprise me."

Red Ottar snorted.

"We should make live sacrifices and look at the omens," Bergdis declared.

"There's no time for that."

"No time for the gods?"

"Later," the skipper replied. "If we're going, we must leave as soon as we can. And if we're fated, we're fated."

At once Solveig remembered the shaman and her third prophecy: *I see what I see: one new death.*

The thick, sweaty smell in the shaman's tent filled her nostrils.

"Fated, are we?" said Bergdis. "Is this the same man who has always called on the gods for their help?"

Red Ottar growled.

"Jesus helps us to help ourselves," observed Slothi.

"We're not talking about Jesus," Bergdis retorted.

"It's not only the rich rewards," Slothi went on. "I want to see Miklagard with my own eyes. It's the greatest city except for Jerusalem in this whole middle-earth—for Christians it is."

"Why?" Solveig asked.

"Don't start him," Red Ottar cautioned her.

"I want what's most safe for my children," Odindisa said. "The same as any mother."

Red Ottar glanced at Solveig. "No point in asking you," he said.

And Solveig gave him a smile full of such lightness and brightness that Red Ottar couldn't help laughing.

Around and around circled their talk and argument, and as the quay began to throb and hum and seethe again, Red Ottar and his crew at last agreed to continue their journey.

"In which case," said the skipper, "we must pack up our cargo."

"We've only just unpacked it," Brita protested.

"Haven't you been listening?" Red Ottar demanded. "All our merchandise will sell in Miklagard for double the price."

"And if we can pick up anything more here," added Blacktooth, "we must do so."

"You and Slothi," Red Ottar told him, "you go around the stalls as soon as the cargo's stowed."

These evenings, thought Solveig, closing her eyes, what will they be like in Miklagard? With my father.

"Solveig!" Red Ottar barked. "Did you hear what I said?"

"Oh!" exclaimed Solveig.

"This is no time to dream. I said I wanted you to help Mihran and the monks carry Vigot to the infirmary. And then we must find someone to replace him."

"Not difficult," said Mihran. "King Yaroslav will help."

"I see," Red Ottar said with a grim smile. "So you and he have already talked about it. And doubtless the king has already rewarded you for . . . your services."

"No, no," said Mihran.

"Yes, yes," Red Ottar retorted, and he turned to Bergdis. "So now! You wanted to see the palace."

"I have never seen a king," Bergdis replied.

"No," Red Ottar said. "Most unusual. Four legs."

"Is that true?" asked Bard. "Do kings have four legs?"

"What do you think, Bard?"

"Smik had four when he wanted to."

Red Ottar slapped his thighs. "Very good!" he exclaimed. "Kings have as many legs as they say they have." Red Ottar turned back to Bergdis. "You wanted to see the king," he said, "and so you shall. Better than that! You are to speak to him."

Solveig had never seen Bergdis so taken aback, let alone so nervous.

"He's a man," Red Ottar told her. "You know how to talk to men. Say Red Ottar greets King Yaroslav. Say I've spoken to my crew and we're of like mind . . ."

"Like mind," repeated Bergdis.

"Say we'll sail to Miklagard and carry the king's messenger."

"Please," said Mihran, "I will go to the palace with Bergdis."

"No," said the skipper. "You're taking Vigot to the infirmary."

Mihran fingered his mustache. "Infirmary is in the palace," he replied.

"Is that so!" barked Red Ottar. "Is there anything left for me to arrange? This message must be extremely important."

The river pilot shrugged.

"Or is no other boat prepared to shoot the rapids so early in the year?" Red Ottar demanded. "Is that the truth of it?" Then the skipper looked around his crew. "We must buy provisions," he said.

"Several seams need caulking and mossing," Torsten added, "and those knees have come loose from the thwarts again. Odindisa, will you mend those splits at the bottom of the rig?"

"What about the new vane?" asked Odindisa.

"That too," said Torsten.

"And then," said Red Ottar, glaring at Bard, "we're sending you back up the mast again. And this time we won't let you down until we reach Miklagard."

Bard looked up at Red Ottar and grinned.

"All this," said Red Ottar, "and with or without the king's help, we have to replace Vigot." He turned to Bergdis and nodded. "Tell the king I await his messenger."

Some members of the crew were glad to see the back of Vigot—Red Ottar because Vigot was such a liability, Bruni because Vigot had stolen his scramasax, and Bergdis because she despised him.

But others surprised themselves by feeling sorry for him and almost reluctant to let him go. None more so than Odindisa.

She dropped to her knees beside his litter. "You saved Brita," she told him. "You saved her life. That matters more to me than any amount of wrongdoing."

"The monks will look after you well," Slothi told him later. "And if anyone can help you mend, they will. Heaven knows, you've been punished enough."

Brita overheard her father. And on her own, unbidden, she just stole up to Vigot, knelt beside him, and planted a kiss on his brow.

Vigot opened his dark eyes.

"Daystar," he murmured.

"What?" asked Brita.

But Vigot had closed his eyes again.

With the help of two monks, Solveig and Mihran carried Vigot on his litter up the hill to the monks' infirmary, and Bergdis helped them before proceeding to the palace on her own.

The world inside the infirmary's thick walls was cool and quiet and shadowy.

It's like a world inside the world, thought Solveig.

The monks already knew all about Vigot's injury.

"I prepare the way," Mihran told her, nodding seriously.

"So I see!" said Solveig.

Solveig sat on the cool flagstones beside Vigot. "Red Ottar says he'll come and find you when he gets back," she told him quietly. "You know he won't punish you further," she said. "You know that, don't you?"

Vigot nodded.

"I think he'll try to get you back home," she said.

"You?" Vigot whispered.

"What?"

"Home?"

"Oh, I don't know. Wherever my father is."

"My lines," Vigot said. "All my hooks."

"Yes?"

"Yours," he said in a weak voice. "Yours now."

"Oh, Vigot!"

"I wish . . ."

"What?"

Vigot's dark eyes shone in the gloom. "I wish I hadn't. Your bead . . . your eye."

Then Solveig just dipped her head so that her lovely fair hair caressed Vigot's chest. She paused for a moment, and then she stood up, and, with hot tears in her eyes, she turned away.

In the almost-dark, two white faces ghosted along the quay. One stopped short of Red Ottar's boat in the shadow of an upended skiff, but the other walked right up to it. He put his right foot on the gangplank.

"Ottar!" he called out.

Red Ottar grunted. He and his crew were all sitting around the mast, some drinking ale, some dozing. Bruni and Slothi were talking about their new purchases, and Odindisa was saying that although Vigot had been no use to man or beast since his terrible injury, it was still not the same without him.

"Red Ottar!"

Red Ottar growled and got to his feet. He grasped the flaming brand and lifted it from its metal stand beside the hold. "Who's there?" he called out.

"The king's messenger," said the voice.

Red Ottar took several steps down the gangplank and waved the brand in the man's face.

It was Edwin.

18

Edwin was aboard. Sineus was aboard. And although he grumbled, Red Ottar wasn't displeased.

"When we reach Miklagard," he told Edwin, "you're the king's messenger, but on board this boat, you and Sineus are oarsmen."

"Half oarsmen," Edwin said firmly.

"Vigot rowed opposite me, and that's what you and the Slav will do. Alternate shifts."

"We'll do our best," said Edwin.

"You will," Red Ottar replied. Then he rounded on Mihran. "You knew about all this."

The river pilot held up his hands in front of him as if he were weighing and balancing them.

"You rogue!" Red Ottar said, but as much with admiration as with disapproval.

Solveig and Edith were delighted to have Edwin and Sineus for company. And so was Odindisa. More than once, Solveig saw her and Sineus exchanging lingering smiles.

"Do you remember what Edwin called us?" Solveig asked Edith.

"Fine young women!" exclaimed Edith, smiling.

"And then Red Ottar said I was a half-baked girl on a half-baked journey and you were a slave woman."

"Well, I am," Edith replied.

"The first cataract . . ." Mihran told everyone that evening, and then he took a swig of ale and began again. "The first is the Gulper. Some pilots call it 'Wake Up!'"

"On a journey like this," Red Ottar said cheerfully, "every day's a cataract! Difficulties, dangers, choices . . ."

The river pilot wagged his finger and shook his head. "Not difficult," he warned Red Ottar in a dark voice, "very difficult. Not dangerous, very dangerous. Tomorrow."

From the safety of the bank, Red Ottar and Solveig stared aghast at the cataract.

At their feet the milky water was slip-sliding fast between ugly rocks and making huge gulping noises, like a giant in a hurry to eat his breakfast. The rocks cut the river into ribbons, and beyond the rocks the water was rollicking and somehow cartwheeling back upstream.

It's making me dizzy, Solveig thought. The rapids at the head of our fjord are nothing like as fierce as this.

"Why didn't you warn us?" Red Ottar yelled.

"If I warn you," Mihran called back, "you will all be afraid."

Once the stern of the boat had been very firmly double roped to a stout oak tree, Mihran drew everyone around him and gave them instructions.

"That water," he said, pointing midstream. "Terrible! But here . . ." The pilot pointed at the water swirling and surging at their feet and nodded confidently.

Then Mihran told the men to strip down to their drawers and the women to take off their woolen tunics and wear only their long sleeveless shifts.

"You mean . . ." said Odindisa, appalled.

"No brooches," Mihran told them. "The water's a thief; it will rip them away. No belts, no one. I know one Viking strangled by his belt."

Then Mihran issued each of the crew with one of the pine poles he had brought aboard in Kiev. "We are twelve," he said. "Two of us stand by the prow, two on each side of the waist, two by the stern. Four of us tie and untie the ropes. You all understand?"

Seeing the fear in everyone's eyes, the river pilot gave them a flashing smile. "I do many times," he reassured them. "You find your way with your poles, yes? And if you trip, if you cannot hold the boat . . ." Mihran paused to make sure everyone was listening. ". . . then float," he said, bouncing his left hand up and down and away. "Float and paddle yourself to the bank. Never, never try to find your feet or hold on to a water root. The water will flatten you, and you cannot stand up again."

"Come on, then," said Red Ottar. "The sooner we start, the sooner it will be over. You, Torsten, you come to her bows with me."

"No," said Mihran. "Torsten on the bank. He knows ropes and knots."

"I will," said Solveig eagerly.

For a moment Red Ottar hesitated. "All right!" he said. "You, Solveig."

Early June it was, but the water was bitingly cold. It churned and frothed around Solveig's feet, and she wiggled her toes and tried to get used to it.

And then, ribbon by rock by root by rope, the companions slowly began to nudge their boat downstream. Once the boat was grazed by a rock, and once it slewed sideways, so that the bows were pointing at the bank and Bergdis and Edwin could do nothing as they were dragged behind the stern through deep water, thrashing their legs. There was no respite, and only when Red Ottar and his crew had cleared the first cataract, and the shadows were lengthening, did they realize their hands were blistered and their feet torn.

"You're trembling, Edwin," Solveig said.

"Like a newborn lamb," he replied.

"Ale!" cried Mihran. "Food! Tomorrow, first the Island, then the Clanger."

All that night, waking and sleeping, Solveig heard rushing in her ears. River voices rushing and splashing and singing and gulping.

As soon as they reached the second cataract, Solveig could see how it had gotten its name.

In the middle of the river, there was an inviting green island strewn with wildflowers, but on either side of it the water raced through dark channels.

I can't run that fast, thought Solveig. No one could. Not even Thialfi when he raced against the giant.

"Come on, girl," Red Ottar told Solveig, peeling off his clothes. "You and I, we'll take her bows again."

Solveig's heart swelled. She knew this was almost a compliment.

This cataract was less hazardous than the first, and the crew worked their way around it quite quickly, but then they came to the Clanger.

"Hear that?" Torsten asked Solveig.

"A battle sound," said Solveig, swallowing and closing her eyes. Father! Father, I wish you were with me now.

As the river water charged at one of the rocks midstream, it kept clanging—not a mellow boom but the flat of an ax ringing against a shield.

At their feet, however, the water was only yapping and stabbing, and for a third time Red Ottar and Solveig picked their way downstream, prodding with their poles, and led everyone to safety.

That evening, though, the crew was far from comfortable. Their clothes were still sopping, and the air hung so heavy that they were unable to dry them. Biting flies smelled the damp crooks of their elbows and backs of their knees and hollows of their necks and drank their blood.

"Very fair-minded, flies are," Edwin said, trying to keep up everyone's flagging spirits.

"Why's that?" asked Odindisa.

"They like men as much as women and Vikings as much as Englanders. They even like children."

"They like me most," Brita wailed.

"I don't mind enemies I can see," growled Red Ottar, "but I keep thinking we're being watched."

Everyone stiffened, and Solveig felt Brita jam herself firmly against her.

The river pilot cupped his ears and closed his eyes. "Is possible," he said at length.

"Bears?" asked Red Ottar.

Mihran shook his head.

"Pechenegs!" several voices exclaimed.

"But King Yaroslav said they're massing upstream," Red Ottar said.

"They are," Mihran replied. "But Pechenegs are everywhere." He looked around the crew. "You are safe," he said. "You are safe in the dark."

"Safe . . . in the dark," Bruni repeated slowly.

"Pechenegs are archers, and in the dark they cannot see." Then Mihran told a story.

"When Prince Svyatoslav reached these cataracts," the pilot said, "the Pechenegs were waiting. They stickled him with arrows. Like a hedgehog. All over his body. The Pechenegs cut off Prince Svyatoslav's head. With their sharp knives they shaved his beard and all his hair."

Brita wedged herself even more firmly against Solveig. She was trembling.

"And then," said Mihran, his voice lowering in disgust, "the Pechenegs, they are beasts, they make a drinking cup out of the prince's skull."

"No!" cried Brita.

"I know a story like that," said Bruni. "About the smith to the gods . . ."

"Not now, Bruni," Slothi told him.

"Tonight we are safe," Mihran told them again. "Tomorrow is tomorrow."

"Brita," said Odindisa, "Bard, both of you go down into the hold."

"We are so early," Mihran said, "maybe the first boat in this summer. I thought we reached here before the Pechenegs . . ." He sighed and shrugged, as if the archers were simply another discomfort like drenched clothes and bloodsucking flies. "Tomorrow," he said, "is the fourth cataract. The most dangerous."

"And what's this one called?" asked Bruni.

"Ah! Several names. Ever-Fierce and Ever-Raucous. Impassable."

"If it's impassable . . ." said Bruni, but Mihran cut him short.

"We portage," he said. "Same as before."

The crew was already very anxious; now they were dispirited too. Bergdis sucked a withered parsnip, and Slothi's back teeth were aching, and down in the hold Brita picked a fight with Bard and Odindisa snapped at them both.

Solveig remained steadfast, intent on reaching Mikla-gard. But all the same, she was afraid they would never come through the cataracts or survive the Pechenegs.

"Same as before," Mihran reassured everyone. "Rollers. Men to help us. Yous see."

Solveig thought the portagers at Impassable looked like woodwoses—men who had lived so long in the wild that they were more like two-legged beasts than human beings. Long hair, long beards, even long eyebrows. They wore filthy rags, some so torn that Solveig blushed and looked away.

Nonetheless, the wild men were just as obliging as Tru-vor and his gang. They told Mihran that they had seen no Pechenegs yet that year, but for all that, Solveig saw that while some of the men inspected the grazed keel and hull, others were keeping a sharp watch on the dark woods around them.

As Red Ottar's crew and the portagers edged the boat along the riverbank, Solveig looked down through the trees at the rapids, hurling and lashing.

"What's that?" she cried. "Down there."

"Where?" squealed Brita.

"Where I'm pointing. On that rock."

"Oh! That bird, you mean?"

"Brita!" screeched Odindisa. "You're portaging. Watch your footing."

Slothi looked angrily at his daughter. "Everyone makes mistakes," he scolded her. "Only fools fail to learn from them. You don't want to go under again, do you?"

Before long, though, the wild men called a halt, and everyone was able to look. Sitting on the rocks were two huge white birds with long hooked bills, and hanging from their bills they had enormous pouches.

"For all the fishes they catch," Mihran explained.

"They look," said Bard, "well, I can't explain it." Then he began to laugh.

"Like laughter makers," Mihran told him with a smile.

The river showed its teeth, grim and gray. It clashed its cymbals and thrashed and foamed beneath them, but the wild men were sure-footed and strong-shouldered.

Step by step Red Ottar and his companions rolled their boat along the portaging track, and slowly their spirits caught up with them again. Before daylight failed, they had passed Impassable.

"Impossible, Impassable, and I'm impatient!" exclaimed Red Ottar. "Let's press on at first light and have done with these cataracts."

"Cataracts and Pechenegs," said Bruni, looking all around as he had done so many times that day.

"She'll leak unless we take up," Torsten warned him.

"As much as comes in, we'll throw back out," Red Ottar replied. "We only need one pair at the oars. The rest of us can bail."

The helmsman's eyebrows beetled. "A boat is a being," he said. "She needs to slake her thirst."

"What!" said Red Ottar. "While we sit on our hands and get picked off?"

To begin with, the boat fairly bounced downstream. Slothi and Sineus sang a praise song together, the water streamed and chortled under the keel, and Red Ottar and his crew skipped their way around the next rapids.

"A pair," Mihran had told them. "Together they are White Wave. Then there's a water bubble . . ."

"What's that?" asked Solveig.

"A lake," said the river pilot. "And then is another pair. The Seether . . . some travelers say the Boiler or the Laugher."

By the time the boat had been tied up, she was heavy with water, as Torsten had predicted. So while Bard and Brita ranged around, gathering pads of dry leaves and firewood, and Bergdis and Edith lit a fire on the riverbank, all the others had to bail, and down in the hold, the water came up to their hips.

"I know," Red Ottar told his exhausted companions. "Tonight I'm thankless. But tomorrow night you'll thank me. Tomorrow night we'll be cleared of these hellish cataracts . . . and the stalkers. The stalkers we can't even see."

"And then Sineus will sing you a praise poem," Edwin told him.

Red Ottar gave the Englishman a knowing look. "As a gift, I hope," he said.

"The last cataract is Strok," Mihran told them.

He picked up a stick and scraped several lines on the ground as if he were keeping a tally.

"It looks like combed hair," said Brita. "After it's untangled."

"And before it's braided," added Odindisa.

"That's what Strok's like," Mihran said. "Each of the streams is very thin, very deep, very fast."

The pilot looked around at everyone as if he were telling them the most terrible story. To begin with, Solveig couldn't take her eyes off him, but then she pretended that she too had a mustache. She pulled at both ends, then she began to curl it. "Yous see!" she announced, mimicking Mihran's voice, and several of the crew guffawed.

The rocky banks on either side of the river rose into sheer walls and then into high granite cliffs. The river narrowed and darkened and raced as if its very life depended on it.

Ripping, thought Solveig. Tearing. Sluicing. I can sometimes feel my blood sluicing around my own body.

Higher soared the cliffs, and when she stared up at the strip of sky, Solveig saw how bright and white it was. As if all the color has been squeezed out of it, she thought. The cliffs are getting higher and higher, and over there they're even hanging over themselves. Down here, it's like a gloomy, echoing passage.

Then Torsten swung the boat around upstream. Mihran jumped onto a rocky ledge, and Sineus followed him. Quickly they roped the boat to a granite stack, and the pilot told the crew to be very careful as they lowered themselves into the water.

"Just enough water," he said. "Shallows between bank and deep stream."

"One more time!" Odindisa cried. "Seven's the most powerful number. Seven and nine."

Red Ottar stripped and stood in the bows brandishing his pole as if for battle.

"Come on, Solveig!" he bawled. "River maiden!"

Solveig gave him a slow smile, cautious and then trusting.

"Golden girl!" Red Ottar pronounced.

Solveig looked at him, quite astonished.

Then Red Ottar swung himself over the bows and lowered himself into the clutching water.

"Hurry up!" he told Solveig. "We started this together, and now we'll finish it."

Solveig pulled her grubby woolen tunic over her head and then, throwing modesty aside, untied her sleeveless shift, rolled it up, and pulled that off as well. She followed Red Ottar into the water and took her place on the opposite side of the bows from him, nearer to the rocky ledge and the cliff.

Solveig stared out across the racing deep streams. She stared at the gloomy cliffs. Then she threw back her head. She squinted.

And up on the high, bright skyline, she saw what she saw: men and horses.

"Look!" she gasped, jabbing her pole upward.

At once a whistling arrow spit into the water just in front of the bows. Then another stabbed into the mast and stuck there, quivering.

Sineus yelped. A third arrow had passed through his left foot and pinioned it to a crevice on the rock ledge. The Slav just gaped at it, wild-eyed.

Torsten yelled and kept yelling, frantically waving to everyone to take cover.

Red Ottar raised his eyes and he roared. He roared at the Pechenegs. Then he called on Thor to save him and his companions.

The arrow went straight in through his open mouth. It pierced his windpipe, and Solveig could see the point sticking out at the top of his spine.

Red Ottar's grip on the bows loosened. He turned toward Solveig and tried to say something, but all he could do was to blow a bubble of poppy-bright blood. Choking, he slipped into the water, and the quick, cold current shipped him downstream.

19

Mihran took over.

He hoisted himself on his forearms, swung both legs over the gunwale, stood up on the deck, and commanded everyone to get back into the boat; he ordered Bruni and Slothi to sit to their oars. He helped Edwin drag Sineus back from the rock ledge, screaming with pain, and he instructed Torsten to steady the boat until everyone was aboard, then to push off and grab the steering paddle as soon as he had tumbled in over the stern.

At once the nearest of the swift, dark streams clutched the boat. The silken water sucked at her, straightened her up, and Solveig saw the boat quickening, quickening until she was racing between rocks and boulders. For a moment, it seemed as if she were no longer floating but flying, rapid and silent, like some great seabird, just above the surface of the water.

But then the boat slewed sideways, and Torsten dug his paddle into the stream and tried to swing her around again.

He wasn't to know a submerged rock was lying in wait. The paddle crunched and smashed, Torsten was pitched onto his face, and the boat swung right around and was carried downstream stern first.

Then Solveig saw the river was widening. The soaring cliffs stepped back, and the water slackened. It snuffled and chuckled around them, and Solveig grasped the gunwale, light-headed.

She felt an arm being planted firmly around her shoulders. It was Edwin, and for a while the two of them stood side by side and gazed at the almost dawdling water.

"As if it had never been," Edwin said slowly.

But they both knew it had, all of it, the arrow through Red Ottar's windpipe, Sineus's wound, the seventh terrifying cataract, and they knew nothing could be the same again.

Solveig turned to Edwin. "Sineus?" she asked.

"I snapped the shaft and pushed the arrow right through," he said, gravely crossing himself. "Thy will be done."

Ashen-faced and without further bidding from Mihran, the crew went quietly to their stations. Bruni and Slothi repositioned their chests and manned their heavy oars, Torsten lowered himself into the hold to search for his spare steering paddle, Odindisa knelt at the side of another stricken young man, Bergdis unhooked her swinging cooking pot and stared grimly into it . . .

"You were in the bows," Edwin said to Solveig. "What happened?"

But Solveig had only just begun to tell him when they saw a body, spread-eagled, lying in the arms of an oak tree that had fallen into the river. It was Red Ottar. The Pecheneg arrow was still sticking out of his mouth.

Edwin and Solveig called out, they pointed, and it was as if they'd woken their companions from a sliding dream. Bruni and Slothi back-paddled fiercely, and Odindisa and Solveig sat to the second pair of oars. The four of them swung the boat right around again, Brita and Bard ran to the bows, and Bergdis reached out her arms and held them there as if she were a goddess welcoming Red Ottar to Asgard.

The oarsmen rammed the boat right into the heart of the tree, and the thicket of branches stayed her just as they had cradled and stayed Red Ottar's body. Torsten and Mihran both went over the side, and, keeping their balance on the slimy trunk, they edged toward Red Ottar and grabbed him under each shoulder.

Many hands reached down, many pulled him up.

What now? thought Solveig. What next? What are we going to do?

For a while the companions stood shoulder to shoulder around their leader's corpse. Everyone was silent. Everyone felt unguarded and uncertain. They felt naked and afraid.

"Row," Mihran told them, "row and keep rowing. Now water is calm, but Pechenegs still . . ." Quickly he checked each bank, and so did all the crew. "We row until dark, then we'll be safe, we can tie up."

"We must build his pyre," Bergdis told them that evening in a husky voice. "We must set Red Ottar free." Then she landed a heavy, scaly hand on Edith's left shoulder. "Poor girl!" she said.

Edith gave a start; then she gulped.

"Saint Gregorios," announced Mihran.

"What?" asked Bergdis.

"The most holy island."

"A Christian island?"

Mihran shook his head. "The emperor of Miklagard calls it that. It is most holy because all the Rus and the Vikings make sacrifices there."

"Where is it?" asked Bergdis.

"Two days from here."

Bergdis looked around at the circle of her companions.

"There's a great oak tree," Mihran told them. "As old as this world, almost. All travelers make sacrifices there."

"A sacrifice of our own leader," muttered Bruni.

And for once Torsten agreed with him. "Yes, that's a sacrifice too many."

"We're like-minded, then," said Bergdis. "We must wrap him in skins and lay him in the hold."

"Away from the flies," Odindisa said.

"Is it safe on the island?" Brita asked.

"No more Pechenegs," Mihran told her. "They are behind us. All the Pechenegs are behind us."

"But what's ahead of us?" asked Edith, shaking her head.

Bergdis stared at her. "Our fates," she replied.

"At such times," said Torsten, "it's unwise to scan the horizon. We'd do better to be sure of the next stretch."

"From Saint Gregorios," Mihran told them, "is only four days to reach the Black Sea, and from there . . ."

Bergdis swiped his words away. "Who says we're going on?" she demanded. "Many of us believed it was a mistake to sail south from Kiev." Once again, she closed her hand over Edith's shoulder. "Torsten's right. First things first."

Several of the crew averted their gaze and stared at their own feet, as if they knew what she was about to say.

"I will not ask who wishes to die with Red Ottar," announced Bergdis in a stony voice. "I will not ask . . ."

Torsten gave a heavy sigh and shifted his weight from one foot to the other.

". . . because there is no choice."

"What do you mean?" asked Solveig.

"I mean," said Bergdis in an expressionless voice, "that Red Ottar had only one slave."

Solveig turned to Edith. She stepped right over Red Ottar's body.

"Your shadow!" cried Odindisa. "Keep away from him!"

Solveig gazed lovingly at Edith: her cheeks rosy as apples, her dark eyes rounded, glistening like blackberries. She thought of the baby kicking inside her.

Solveig grasped Bergdis's right hand and removed it from Edith's shoulder.

No one said anything. Not one word.

Solveig rounded on her companions. "Torsten! You, Bruni! Slothi!"

"Quiet, girl!" said Bergdis in a cold, rasping voice.

"Aren't you going to stop her?" Solveig demanded. "Aren't you going to say anything?"

"This is how it is," Bergdis said. "This is how it has always been."

"Who says so?" Solveig challenged her.

Then Brita bravely crept up to Solveig and clutched her right hand.

"Who?" wailed Solveig.

Bergdis gave Brita a freezing look. "From now on," she told her, "you must wash Edith's feet. You, Odindisa, you must ready her clothes for the pyre. You, men. You know how it is. Each of you must say to this . . . slave woman: 'Tell your master this is because of my love for him.'"

Solveig listened, horrified.

"Slothi!" she screeched. "You're a Christian. You can't just stand by."

"Solveig," hissed Bergdis.

Solveig took no notice. "Edwin!" she wailed.

Edwin at once raised both hands. "You are Norsemen," he said. "I am not." Then he fixed Solveig with a long, calm, meaningful stare.

"Edith's English," said Solveig rather more calmly. "You're English. She's Christian and you're Christian."

Now Edwin gave Solveig a warning look.

"Gag her!" rasped Bergdis. "How dare you speak against me and against the gods?"

But just as no one had spoken up for Edith, no one moved against Solveig.

"Men!" said Bergdis contemptuously. "You're not men. You're half men."

Still no one moved.

"Unless," said Bergdis slowly, "Solveig wishes to take Edith's place."

In the branches of the fallen oak, little birds twittered.

"Or to die with her."

"No," said Torsten. "That's not right. Solveig's the daughter of a freeman; she's not a slave."

Bergdis thrust up her chin and turned her grisly attention back to Edith.

"Men," she said, "you Torsten and Bruni, Slothi, Mihran . . ."

"Not me," said Mihran.

"Edwin."

The Englishman shook his head. "Not I," he said.

Bergdis snorted. "Sineus! He's groaning down in the hold. You then, Bard. Be a man! All of you, grip each other's hands so the slave woman can stand on them. I'll give her the words to say."

The three men and Bard did as Bergdis ordered them, and so did Edith.

She's like a sleepwalker, thought Solveig. Like her own ghost already.

When Edith repeated the words that Bergdis gave to her, she sounded as if her voice came from the Otherworld.

"Look!" she intoned. "I see my mother and father."

And then: "Look! I see my master sitting in Asgard. How green it is, how beautiful. Men and young boys are sitting there with him. Red Ottar has summoned me, so let me go and serve him."

"Put her down!" Bergdis ordered, and Bard at once scuttled back to his mother's side.

"What was that?" asked Solveig in a woeful voice.

"What do you think?" Bergdis retorted.

Solveig just trembled.

"She was looking from this world into the next," Bergdis told her.

That was when Solveig saw that Bergdis was wearing the same bracelet—the one made of the bones of little fingers—that she had worn when she sacrificed the chicken after they'd escaped from the ghost ship and the night storm.

Solveig gulped and sobbed. She turned away, but Edwin caught her by the elbow.

"Comfort Edith," he said in a low voice. "Yes, comfort her. But don't challenge Bergdis. She's very dangerous."

Then the Englishman guided Solveig back to the circle standing around Red Ottar.

"Raise your eyes!" commanded Bergdis in a harsh voice. So Solveig lifted her heavy lids, but Bergdis was speaking to Edith. "Raise your eyes to Asgard, where your master awaits you."

Edith obediently raised her eyes.

Why, thought Solveig, her heart banging in her chest, it's not now, is it?

But then she remembered they were going to build a pyre . . . She remembered the most holy island . . . two days downstream.

Around Solveig, her companions were already beginning to go about their business. Torsten went over the side and unlashed the remains of the smashed steering paddle and fixed a new one in its place. Brita and Bard halfheartedly bailed out the hold. Edwin and Odindisa were kneeling on either side of Sineus. And before long, Bruni and Slothi pushed out the boat from its green cradle and then sat to their oars.

This life, thought Solveig. So sweet. So fearsome. So painful. What was it Edith said about expecting the worst and grasping whatever joys there are?

She stared at the dizzy little whirlpools made by the end of Slothi's oar each time he pulled it through the water, and then she looked up at the lamb cloud almost immediately above her head. She breathed in the fragrant scent of the linden blossom, and tears streamed down her cheeks.

When Solveig went to sit in the bows, Edith was as cheerful as she was subdued.

I couldn't be brave like that, thought Solveig. Not if I was going to die. How can she be? She can't escape. Not in this wilderness. Where could she go? Or does she suppose we'll be able to save her? Why did the men say nothing? Slothi's a coward—he doesn't believe Edith should be burned, even if the others do. But they don't, anyhow. I think they're afraid of Bergdis.

A cataract of thoughts tumbled and raged through Solveig's head while Edith sat beside her and told her how she wouldn't have to cook another meal in her life; and how she believed she would see her own husband and not

Red Ottar in the afterworld; and how she was going to ask Edwin, if ever he went back to England, to find Wulf and Emma and tell them everything that had happened; and how she knew a woman who could actually have conversations with birds. And Edith pointed out all the bride-white blossoms and blood-red berries and death-dark yew trees they passed on their way downstream.

During that day and the next, more reasonable now but no less troubled, Solveig sometimes talked quietly to her companions.

She asked Bruni, then Odindisa, and then Torsten how it could be right to sacrifice Edith. She told them she understood men died in battle for their beliefs or to follow their leader, as so many had done at Stiklestad. She said she knew women and children often got caught up in a fight between men, as Edith herself had been when Swedes raided a Danish village in England.

She said that if a man had been killed for no good reason, it was right for his family to avenge his death. But why, asked Solveig, why is it right, how can it be right to put someone to death who has done no wrong?

"How will Edith's death help Red Ottar? He was so pleased . . . Wouldn't he have wanted Edith to mother his child? Edith's innocent. How can it be right?"

Again and again Solveig asked her companions, but answers came there none.

"It's the good and bad Red Ottar did in his life that matters to the gods," Solveig declared. "Isn't it? How can Edith's death help him? How can it?"

Slothi agreed with Solveig. "It's wrong," he said. "It's against God's law. The Bible tells us 'an eye for an eye and a tooth for a tooth,' but Edith's blameless."

"You said nothing," Solveig accused him. "Not one word."

Slothi nodded. "You were brave," he said. "Maybe braver than you realize."

"I said what I felt," Solveig replied.

"Exactly," said Slothi. "But Solveig, you must learn what you can do. And can't do."

Solveig didn't reply.

"You can do nothing for Edith," Slothi told her. "Accept. You have to accept. That doesn't mean you think it's right."

Solveig shook her head furiously.

Then she talked to Edwin.

"I've seen this before," he told her. "You haven't."

"What happens?" asked Solveig in a small voice.

Edwin shook his head. "There's no need for you to know," he said calmly. "It is foul."

Solveig started to tremble.

"To take away a life—that's sometimes necessary. In England as in Norway, there are laws, and to commit the worst crimes means you must die. But no, not like this. Never like this."

"Tell me," said Solveig, shuddering.

Edwin put his hands on both her shoulders. "Torsten and Bruni . . . the men may have heard about it," he confided in her, "but I could see by their faces they've never witnessed it. Never taken part in it. If they knew what they've got to do . . ." Edwin paused. "I'll tell you again, Solveig. Beware of your own life. Beware of Bergdis."

Solveig nodded, and Edwin raised a forefinger to her left cheek and wiped away a tear.

"The Angel of Death," he said very deliberately.

Solveig gave a start.

"With her bracelet. Her filleting knife. You understand?"

Solveig nodded.

"You must leave her to me."

Bergdis was the first to disembark at the island of Saint Gregorios. She marched everyone to the massive old oak tree, and there, with Edith standing next to her, she told them, "The oak tree rises, the oak tree falls. Here and now, it's our duty to build the pyre at once, to make our sacrifice and set Red Ottar free."

Edith gave Solveig a fond look. A lingering look.

She's giving me her strength, thought Solveig. It should be the other way around. She swallowed loudly. My name is Sun-Strong, but I'm not.

But then Solveig saw Edith give her fellow countryman a wild look, a flicker of sheer terror, as if she could see her death and the manner of it. Edith put her hands to her throat, then slid them to her ribs.

Edwin drew in his breath. He lurched forward. He pushed his bulky body between Edith and Bergdis.

Bergdis's eyes glittered.

"No!" said Edwin very clearly, very loudly. "Red Ottar can make his own peace with the gods."

Bergdis hissed.

"He needs no help from this woman. This blameless woman. This loyal woman, with Red Ottar's own baby leaping in her womb."

Bergdis stared wildly around her. "Men!" she barked, beckoning them with both hands. "Silence him! This stranger. In the name of Red Ottar! In the name of the gods!"

"This blameless woman," repeated Edwin, his voice rising. "Your companion. Your friend."

Bergdis reached for her belt. She grasped her knife, but Edwin at once gripped and stayed her hand.

Then the Angel of Death screamed. She kicked Edwin's shins; she banged her head and left fist against his broad chest.

But Edwin refused to let her go. He gritted his teeth. He tightened his grip, and she was helpless.

20

Solveig closed her eyes.

She could see herself standing hand in hand with her father, staring into the heart of the hilltop fire. Asta and Kalf and Blubba were there, and so were a dozen fjord farmers and their families.

The fire was so fierce that Solveig felt her cheeks, her whole face, burning. The cool night air sizzled with sparkling fireflies, and the deep orange ball of the sun sat on the horizon.

Midsummer, she thought. There's no dark. There's all the time in the world.

Solstice. The day I love best in the place I love most—my hand wrapped inside my father's . . .

Solveig wrinkled her nostrils at the acrid smoke.

Then the singing began. But it wasn't the raucous chorus of fjord farmers and not their cheers and hullaballooing as the huge ball of the sun slowly bounced up from the horizon. It was chanting, the same words over and over again,

"He rises to you, he rises, we must remember him. He rises to you, he rises, we must remember him."

Solveig squeezed her father's hand; she dug her nails into his palm.

"Ow!" said a voice.

Then Solveig opened her eyes and at once recalled where she was and who was singing. Edwin frowned at her and wrung his right hand.

The dark wood smoke rose in a steady column from the pyre, and Red Ottar's companions stood in a circle around his burning body. Solveig stood to Edwin's right, Edith to his left; Bergdis was kneeling on the other side of the pyre.

"Red Ottar!" exclaimed Torsten. "I'd gladly have sailed with you on many journeys. My first journey with you was my last."

Many of the companions joined hands. They stepped around the funeral pyre, chanting again, "He rises to you, he rises, we must remember him."

"Red Ottar told me the truth," Bruni declared, "and that's true friendship. Nothing's worse than a liar, and no true friend tells you only what you want to hear."

Once again all the companions except for Bergdis side-stepped and shuffled. "He rises to you, he rises, we must remember him."

"Red Ottar!" Odindisa called out. "Quick to anger. Quick to forgive. You were always forthright, fair in your blood, fair in your bones."

"He rises to you, he rises, we must remember him."

When it was her turn, Edith said simply, "Red Ottar! I didn't care to die with you, but I came to care for you." Then she placed her hands over her womb. "Red Ottar," she sobbed, "now and in days to come, you're with me, quick and dead."

Around and around. "He rises to you, he rises, we must remember him."

"Red Ottar!" said Solveig. "I've cut these words for you." She tossed into the flames a wafer of ash wood incised with runes. "Red Ottar!" she repeated, and now she was singing. "Clear-minded. Fair-minded. You honored your word. You barked at me and made me strong. My foul-weather friend."

"He rises to you, he rises, we must remember him."

Bergdis was so wild with fury, so racked with pain, she was unable to praise Red Ottar. All she wanted to do was to pour venom and gall on the heads of her companions, but what she actually did was glare and grind her teeth and say nothing. Not one word.

The thick gray plume of smoke rising from the pyre began to waver and wobble.

Once more the companions rubbed their smarting eyes and joined hands. "He rises to you, he rises, we must remember him."

Bergdis tore at her own face. She gouged it. She screamed, and her scream cut Solveig to the heart.

One by one, Red Ottar's companions sat down on the grass around the pyre.

They had unlocked their thoughts; they had poured out the feeling in their hearts. But now, as the day's light faded, there was silence. Silence and, hidden in the ancient oak tree, one crow cawing.

For a long time, the companions sat staring into the pyre.

The acrid smoke dwindled. At last it thinned to no more than a silver stream.

Heaven swallowed it. The air began to clear.

When Solveig and her companions slowly straggled back to their boat, they saw little orange-green balls bobbing all over the horseshoe harbor.

How strange, thought Solveig. First I saw the heavy orange solstice sun, and now I can see hundreds of little suns in the water.

"Oranges," Mihran told Solveig.

"Are they markers for nets?"

The river pilot shook his head and spoke with his hands.

"You can eat them?" exclaimed Solveig.

"Very tasty," Mihran told her. "Sweet, bittersweet."

Solveig pursed her lips and sniffed at her grubby tunic and bare arms. "Like that smoke," she said. "Oranges . . . why are they in the water, then?"

"Rotten," replied Mihran. "One goes green and soft, then many more go green."

"It's the same with apples," Solveig told him. "In Norway we say a person's a rotten apple."

"Better get rid," the pilot said. "These oranges were going from Miklagard to Kiev, Novgorod, maybe. They were thrown overboard."

"And we're going to Miklagard," Solveig said, "but not Red Ottar. Not Vigot."

"Who will come?" asked Mihran. "Who not?"

"What do you mean?" asked Solveig, startled.

It wasn't long before the arguing began.

"How long do we have to hole up here?" Bruni demanded. "Let's get the wind in our sail."

"That's what I think," Edwin agreed.

"Onward!" exclaimed Bruni. Then he turned to Mihran. "How far is it, did you say?"

"Three four days to the Black Sea," Mihran replied. "After that, seven days most to Miklagard."

Solveig bit on her lower lip. Eleven days, she thought.

Torsten searched the faces of his companions one by one and then cleared his throat. "No!" he said in a loud voice.

Everyone looked at him.

"I'm not going on."

"Why not?" asked Bruni.

"And neither is this boat."

"Who are you to say?"

Torsten drew himself up. "I'm the helmsman," he replied.

"That's just what you are," Bruni retorted. "The helmsman, not the skipper."

"We're in great difficulty," declared Torsten. "Red Ottar. Sineus. We're two men short."

"It's downhill from here," asserted Bruni. "Mihran says so."

"He said it was downhill when we reached the Dnieper," Torsten replied. "We've already overstepped the mark. Only a fool oversteps it even further." The helmsman turned to Slothi. "Well?"

Slothi tugged nervously at his wispy mustache. "We can't go on unless we all agree," he said, "but we can't go back unless we all agree."

"In which case," the helmsman said, "we'll be tied up here forever. Bergdis?"

"Back," snapped Bergdis without raising her eyes.

"We've come this far for one reason," mumbled Slothi. "We've come to trade. That's why we've come. But . . ."

Odindisa waved his words overboard. "Torsten's right. We're in danger. As it is, we may never get home."

"I want to go with Solveig," piped Brita.

"Think again," Bruni urged them. "We're Vikings, on the doorstep of Miklagard. The best market on middle-earth. Isn't that true, Mihran?"

"True," said the river pilot.

"Life's for living!" declared Bruni. But then he looked at Bergdis and the rest of the crew and wished he hadn't said that. "To go forward may be dangerous," he added, "but it's dangerous to go back. The cataracts. The Pechenegs."

"It's dangerous to keep company with you," Torsten said in an even voice. "That much I know."

Bruni snorted.

"No!" declared Torsten for a second time. And then, in his ringing voice, "I'm not going on."

"Well, now," said Edwin with a thoughtful smile, as if he were playing a game of chess and trying to work out a tricky move. "I have to go on myself. I've no choice. I'm carrying a message for King Yaroslav."

"Someone can carry it for you," said Torsten.

Edwin shook his head. "I fear not," he said ruefully. "I am the messenger and I'm the message."

"All your fine words," the helmsman told him. "One day you'll tie yourself in knots."

"But Sineus," said Edwin, "I think he'll do best to stay here. When I get back, I'll help him . . . hobble back to Kiev."

"Well, now, Solveig?" asked Torsten.

Solveig returned his gaze. "I'd like us all to be able to agree," she replied. "I do wish we could. You know, all of you, why I've come. Do you think I can turn back now?"

"So that's three of us," said Edwin.

"Three?"

"Where I go, Edith goes," the Englishman declared in his reasonable, good-humored way.

Solveig's heart lifted. "Praise Freyja!" she exclaimed.

Edith gave Solveig a look of relief, exhaustion, sisterliness.

"Four," announced Mihran. "Four of us. I will help you, Solveig. That's what I promised you in Ladoga."

"You did," said Solveig.

"You're not telling me you're going to Miklagard just because of Solveig," Odindisa accused Mihran. "You're Edwin's guide. The king has already paid you."

Mihran chose to ignore Odindisa. Instead, he informed everyone that he knew the harbor men on the island and could recruit a river pilot and volunteers to help Torsten get the boat back to Kiev.

"I can't go on without this boat and without our merchandise," said Bruni angrily, "but I don't want to go back. Back through the cataracts! Back through the arrow storm!"

Odindisa held up her fists. "Will you two men hold fast to your promises to Red Ottar? Can you not keep the peace? 'We must remember him'—that's what you chanted. 'We must remember him.' If you want to honor Red Ottar, do as he asked of you and make peace. At least until we all get home."

Torsten gave Bruni a level look and rubbed his chin.

"The feud's yours, not mine," Bruni muttered.

Quite late that evening, Mihran walked right around Saint Gregorios with Solveig, Edith, and Edwin, and Brita came too. "I've hired a small boat for us," he told them.

"Already!" exclaimed Solveig.

The river pilot snapped his fingers. "Very small. Just a tree trunk, hollowed out. A little sail."

"It's all we need," said Edwin.

"You, Edwin, you help me paddle and sail her."

Edwin put his hands together in prayer.

"Joke!" said Mihran. "You, Solveig."

"Yes," Solveig said eagerly. "Yes, I will. Can we see her?"

"Too dark," said Mihran, waving his arms. "It's that one over there. Tucked in at the end, next to the bigger one. Yous see in the morning."

"When can we leave?" Edith asked him.

"Dawn," said Mihran.

"Tomorrow!" exclaimed Solveig. "But I wanted to carve a rune stone to Red Ottar."

"The sooner the better." Mihran narrowed his eyes. "Bergdis!" he muttered.

"Where?" asked Edith, alarmed.

"Here," replied Mihran, "she is everywhere."

"I'm watching her," said Edwin.

"You sleep on shore," Mihran told him and Edith. "Somewhere safe. But now, go aboard. Make your farewells."

Aboard again, Solveig pulled out her bag of bones from her chest and just squeezed the bottom of it to check that her gold brooch was there. She wrapped up her bits and pieces of grubby clothing inside her reindeer skin and put her hand to her throat and fingered the glass bead Oleg had given her. Then she looked lovingly around her.

This boat, she thought. I know every inch of her, and how she moves, and the sounds she makes. What will happen to her without Red Ottar? Who will love her as he did?

I think he cared more for this boat than for any of us. How proud he was when he showed me around and slapped and stroked her. Once, I saw him standing alone in the bows, talking to her.

Edith told me that Red Ottar had no children, and that's why he was so glad about their baby. So who will own the boat now? Slothi and Bruni? Not if Torsten has any say in it.

While Solveig was standing and thinking in the half dark, Torsten approached her. She knew it was he by the way he walked. Even when the boat was tied up, he rolled along as if he expected the deck to lurch and shudder at any moment.

"Torsten!" she said, and she put a hand on his left arm.

Torsten waited. Around them, the warm night air breathed lightly.

"I'll come back to Sigtuna."

"With us?" exclaimed Torsten.

"No, no! I mean . . . after."

Torsten grunted.

"When you told me you'd sailed east with my father, I knew it was an omen. Like a red sky at night. That's when I believed the fates were on my side."

"The fates blew us together," the helmsman observed, "and now they blow us apart."

"Tomorrow, at dawn," Solveig said.

"So soon?" said Torsten. "Well, it's better that way. This is a sorrowful place. None of us has any reason to stay."

Then he wrapped Solveig in a bear hug, and when she stepped back from it, she told him, "You've been . . . well, my guardian. Almost my boat father. I hope that you and my blood father will meet again one day."

Then Mihran joined them, and Solveig listened while he told Torsten about finding four men willing to join the crew.

"And a river pilot," Mihran told him. "They'll come to see you early in the morning. Now I tell you what you pay them."

"Ah!" said Torsten. "Slothi can count better than I can. Slothi!" he called out. "Come over here."

Solveig slipped away into the darkness. She heard murmuring and then made out Edwin and Edith kneeling beside Sineus, tending to his foot wound.

"It's still so black and swollen," Sineus said. "Like a bloated bladder, all the way up to the knee."

Edwin reassured Sineus that he would return to Saint Gregorios within the month and help him back to Kiev before the leaves turned.

Seeing Solveig, Edith stood up and linked arms with her, "I don't want to but I must," she said, and she firmly led Solveig and Edwin toward the stern. Bergdis was sitting there on her own.

In the dark or almost dark, the two women stared at each other.

Solveig could hear Edith's breath quickening. She could feel the tightness of her forearm and elbow, locked now with hers.

"Unless I say this," Solveig heard Edith say, "I'll regret it until the day I die."

Solveig looked down at Bergdis. Her eyes were darker than the dark, yet they were glittering.

"I know what you were going to do," Edith said in a low voice. "Edwin told me. The men . . . the strangling . . ." Despite all her efforts to stay calm, Edith's voice was rising.

Solveig gripped her arm to give her strength.

"The men . . . the strangling . . . the knife . . . your knife . . ." Edith swallowed and broke off.

Bergdis didn't move. She just looked up at Edith with her burning, freezing eyes.

"Your gods . . ." Edith went on. "I don't know how to say it . . . Your gods, they're nothing to me. Less than nothing. Your beliefs, they're violent and cruel." Edith paused. "And yet . . . the way you believe, Bergdis! The way you believe.

Not like a lily liver but with all your head and heart. With such a passion!"

Edith paused, and Solveig could hear how she was speaking more with awe than revulsion.

"What binds us," said Edith, more calmly now, "is our care. Your care and my care for Red Ottar."

Red Ottar, thought Solveig. His Angel of Death. And her victim.

"That will never change or die," Edith said.

Edith's a healer, Solveig thought. Bergdis and I pray to the same gods, but I can't believe in such a sacrifice. It's so violent. So unjust.

Edith wants to make her peace with Bergdis, and I admire that. Women must be healers.

Again the women gazed at each other. Again the night breathed, almost easy.

"Go!" said Bergdis in a biting, cold voice.

Then Edith and Solveig wheeled away with Edwin right behind them, still watching his back. They padded along the deck, glad it was over, glad of each other's company.

It was Edith who broke the silence. "Bard will be up and about at dawn," she said. "He's always first."

Solveig gave a prodigious yawn.

"I won't wake him now," said Edith.

"Or Brita," agreed Solveig. And she yawned again.

But at that moment, Odindisa loomed up in front of them, holding a horn lantern, looking haggard. "Have you seen her?" she cried.

"Yes," said Edwin. "Yes, Edith's just been talking to her."

"Where?"

Edwin looked over his shoulder. "There! Slumped in the stern."

"No!" cried Odindisa. "Brita! I went to check her, but she's not there. Her fleece is." Odindisa sounded quite bewildered.

"We'll find her," Edwin assured her.

"She's not on this boat. I've searched everywhere, and Slothi has crawled to both ends of the hold."

"We'll find her," Solveig repeated.

"She knows she's not allowed ashore," wailed Odindisa. "Not after dark. What if . . . ?"

What if she's gone overboard? thought Solveig. She can't swim. We would have heard her. What if she's gone back to the pyre? What if those men loitering down the far end of the harbor . . . ?

"Please," begged Odindisa, and like white moths her eyelids fluttered.

"Ask Mihran," Edith said.

"I've asked him already."

"Tonight," said Edwin patiently, "we'll use our voices. At first light, we'll use our eyes."

"We'll leave the gangplank down," Solveig added.

"I'll kill her," Odindisa said fiercely. And then she begged: "Please . . . Not Brita."

21

Solveig lay very still. She took slow, deep breaths and tried to drift herself to sleep. But she was too aware of her companions, some sniffing, some snorting, some tossing and turning after the troubled day that had begun with the lighting of the pyre and ended with the search for Brita in the darkness.

Despite walking right around the little island and going back to the pyre where the embers were still glowing, Odindisa and Slothi couldn't find their daughter. Torsten and Bruni and Edwin all called for her, but their voices fell into night's dark pit.

I know sky's made of air, thought Solveig, but sometimes when it breathes it's so thick and heavy and smooth. It's like that roll of material I saw in the market in Kiev. Velvet!

Skin can be like velvet, too. Brita's cheeks, they are.

Where is she?

Flying late, a curlew cried out its loneliness and longing. Then a warm night wind got up and the giant fig tree growing beside their mooring flapped its leathery hands.

Then Solveig heard Brita's voice, mellow as the low notes of Slothi's pipes, saying: "I want to go with Solveig."

Solveig sat up in the dark.

"I want to go with Solveig."

She knew then where Brita was. Where she must be hiding and waiting.

Why didn't I think of it before? she asked herself. And why didn't I just stop thinking and let my heart tell me?

In the moonlight, Solveig stood up. She slipped on her shoes, padded down the gangplank, and picked her way to the huddle of little boats at the far end of the quay.

"Tucked in . . . next to the bigger one at the end." Isn't that what Mihran said?

The little boat was covered with some kind of skin—sealskin, maybe—glistening silvery in the moonlight.

Solveig listened. Nothing. Nothing but the sips and kisses of the great river against the sides of the boats lying side by side in the darkness.

"Brita!" said Solveig, under her breath almost.

Nothing.

A little more loudly: "Brita!"

Nothing.

Then Solveig got on her knees and reached down and grasped the skin. She lifted it and peeled it away from the stern.

And there, with Solveig peering down at her, the moon gazing down at her, lay little Brita—eyes shining, white-faced, and shivering.

Solveig reached down to her, and Brita reached up to Solveig.

Then, with her strong arms, Solveig lifted Brita into the air, up and out onto the quay. Without a word, the two of them embraced: Brita with her arms around Solveig's waist, Solveig with her arms around Brita's neck.

"I want . . ." whispered Brita, and she swallowed loudly.

"I know," Solveig replied. "I do know."

For a while, Solveig went on holding Brita, and Brita went on shivering.

What were you going to do? wondered Solveig. Cram yourself into the bows? You didn't really think . . .

"Can I?" whispered Brita.

"Sometimes," said Solveig in a low voice, "we have to do things we wish we didn't have to." She paused, trying to find the right words. "I mean, I wish I didn't have to take you back. Brita, I wish you didn't have to accept this. I wish I didn't have to go to Miklagard without you."

Brita buried her face in Solveig's arm.

"Come on, now."

"Third wishes," sobbed Brita, "come true sometimes."

Back aboard, Solveig let Brita find her own way back to her mother, and as she listened to their murmuring and sniffing and cooing, she felt so lonely. She thought of her mother's grave by the stony, yapping shore. She thought of Edith's children in far England. She thought of all the children on this middle-earth divided from their mothers by distance or death.

I know how much I want to see my father, she thought. He's been father and mother to me. I'm traveling halfway across the world to be at his side, and there's not been one day when I haven't thought about him. With love, and with such longing, with everything I want to tell and ask him.

But then Solveig began to wonder what Halfdan would think when he saw her.

That dream I had when I saw my grandmother, and she was warning my father: "*You should have left her out on the ice . . . You mark my words, the day will come when Solveig's weakness will harm others—maybe her own father.*"

He will be glad to see me, won't he? What will he say? What if he's living with Harald Sigurdsson and all the other men . . . or with another woman? With her own children, like Kalf and Blubba? What if . . . ?

As Solveig left the sad island of Saint Gregorios, she almost took wing. Sitting alongside Edith and across the boat from Edwin and Mihran, she waved. She waved and waved until all she could see of her companions were pink hands, waving.

"Poor Brita!" she said. "I wish I'd given her a bone pin or something. I hope she'll get back to Kiev safely."

"So do I," said Edith anxiously.

Solveig turned to Mihran. "But now!" she said, her voice lifting. "Now! Three days?"

"Three four," said Mihran.

"Is the water black?" Solveig asked him. "In the Black Sea."

"Darker than the Baltic," Mihran told her. "Darker than Marmara and the Great Sea."

"Why?"

"Because it's so deep. So deep there are mountains under the sea."

"How do you know?"

Mihran shrugged. "Everyone knows."

"Have you heard of the White Sea?" Solveig asked him.

"I have," said Edwin. "It's north of Norway, north of north. A traveler came to the court of King Alfred and told him about it."

"Sometimes it's covered in ice and snow," Solveig explained. "That's why it's white."

"And the Red Sea," Mihran told them, "is next to Egypt. The shores are red, and the people there have red skins."

"Is there a Yellow Sea?" asked Solveig.

Mihran screwed up his face. "I hope not," he said. "A whole sea of scummy piss!"

The boat was much as the river pilot had told them: just the hollowed-out trunk of an oak tree, shaped to have a shallow keel, fitted with a small mast, a single sail, and oarlocks and oars and a steering paddle in the stern. And if he and Solveig and Edwin and Edith had lain head to toe, head to toe, they would have been longer than their boat.

"Long and narrow," said Mihran, "Easy to capsize. Bend your knees when you're moving around, keep as low as you can."

"And turn your backs," said Edwin, "when one of us has got to turn the Black Sea yellow."

When he smiles like that, thought Solveig, his buckteeth stick right out. He looks as much like a rabbit as a human being.

"I've never seen a boat like this before," she said. "It's not a smack and not a skiff, not a scull and not a shell and not a canoe, not a coble and not a coracle."

"You could call it a dugout," Edwin suggested.

Mihran nodded. "That's what it is."

The farther the little boat skipped and slid, skated almost, the wider the Dnieper became.

Solveig could see people on the banks, but she couldn't really see what they were doing. And the light was so bright that for much of the time she had to screw up her eyes.

"Hot and damp," said Edith, pink-faced and squirming. "It makes me sweat."

"All the same," said Edwin, "better than a black wind. Better than a skriver or scouring of hail."

"Today's like a sponge," Mihran said.

"What's a sponge?" asked Solveig.

Mihran smiled. "Sponge!" He opened his hands, slowly squeezed his fists, opened them again. "Grows in water."

Solveig shook her head.

"We use for cleaning us. Washing us. Blue sponge."

So the hours passed, not so much with thinking about everyone they'd left behind and everything that had happened as with responding to the smells and sights and sounds around them. And when Solveig trailed her fingers in the water, her whole body felt how quickly the boat was skimming downstream.

In the evening, Mihran and Solveig rowed the dugout to one bank or the other and bought food from the villagers. They scooped out a fire pit and grilled river fish on it. They ate grainy bread and summer fruit—plums and cherries. They drank ale. They slept unafraid.

"I told yous," Mihran said. "Downhill. Tomorrow, the Black Sea. And the last danger."

"What danger?" asked Solveig.

But Mihran didn't reply.

So the river opened her arms to the sea. Beneath the boat the water began gently to rock, and Solveig could feel it was at one moment holding them back, the next drawing them forward.

Some days pass so slowly, thought Solveig, some so fast. It's only four days since we left Saint Gregorios, but I've seen so much that it seems a long time since I found Brita nestling here.

"Black Sea," announced Mihran very proudly, almost as if he owned it. "No more reeds rushes."

Edith gently shook her head. "No more water lilies," she said, remembering something.

"But fields," said Edwin. "Crops. What's that over there?"

"Flax," said Mihran. "Blue purple flowers. And there— how do you say?—tea."

Solveig frowned. She'd never heard of it.

"Drink," Mihran told her. "Hot. Very good."

Solveig smiled. "I want to try it," she said eagerly.

"Now," Mihran told them, "we sail west. We stay close to shore. All the way to the river."

"Another river?" complained Edwin.

"Danube," said Mihran. "Long as Dnieper." He pulled a long face.

"No!" said Edwin, looking concerned.

Mihran grinned. "We go past her," he told them.

It's true, thought Solveig. The Black Sea is much darker than any water I've seen before—the mountain streams dashing and clattering down to the fjord, and the many-fingered fjord itself, and the Baltic Sea between Sigtuna and Ladoga, and the rivers of Garthar, and Lake Ilmen.

"Many moods," Mihran told her. "Sudden wind. Sudden rain."

"Squalls," said Solveig.

"But now . . ." the river pilot went on with the most expansive gesture.

"Sunlight," said Solveig. "Calm seas."

"Jason sailed from here," Mihran said.

"Who?"

"Jason!" repeated Mihran, as if everyone in the world had heard of him. "He could only win his kingdom if he found the Golden Fleece."

"Fleece?"

"Golden," said Mihran.

"It sounds like sheep grazing up in Asgard," Solveig said. "The realm of the gods. Did he find it, then?"

"He did," said Mihran, "and he sowed the dragon's teeth, and he came into his kingdom."

Will I? wondered Solveig. Will I come into my kingdom?

To starboard lay fields and more fields, fields of flax and maize, apple orchards, pear orchards and, on the slopes above them, woods of beech and alder. To port lay the subtle black and silver sea. Above and around stretched the crown and girdle of the sky, crisscrossed by black cormorants and red-breasted geese.

"I saw a wonder!" announced Edwin. "That's how one English poem begins. Here, there are wonders everywhere! Red-breasted geese, water mint, bald ibis, tamarisks."

"It's how you see," Edith said. "If you're sharp-eyed, anything and everything becomes a wonder."

Before long, Solveig rummaged in her bag, pulled out a little slat of bone, and began to carve. And as she did so, she talked to Edith.

"Do you keep thinking about Red Ottar?" she asked her.

Edith's brow tightened, and she sighed. "Yes . . . well, no. More about his baby."

"Oh, Edie! If it's a girl, will you keep it?"

Edith gave Solveig a startled look. "Of course! Of course I will. I'm not a Viking."

"Where will you go?"

"When?"

"After Miklagard?"

At once Edwin replied, "Back to Kiev."

"Kiev!" exclaimed Solveig.

"Until I can ship you back to York," Edwin told Edith. "Back home, back to your children."

"Emma and Wulf," said Solveig. "I remember."

Then Solveig told Edith she kept thinking about her father, wondering what he'd say when he saw her and whether he'd be glad. "And then I start to worry," she said. "I mean, what if he's not there? Harald Sigurdsson's followers are fighting men. They may have gone away. To fight."

Edith placed a warm hand over Solveig's carving hand and her metal pin.

"Or to die," said Solveig in a dark voice.

"What did you suppose before you left home?" Edith asked her.

"Not those things. I was so miserable and so lonely. That's why I decided to come. But I was still afraid. Afraid and yet hopeful."

"That's how you have to be now."

"I know, but what if he wishes I hadn't come? What if . . . ?" Solveig's bright blue eyes were full of doubt. "I keep telling myself I'll be all right, and I've come here on my own from Trondheim, so I must be strong enough to look after myself. I keep saying I can ask Edwin and Edith to help me." Solveig could hear her voice rising. "But you're going back to Kiev."

"What about Mihran?" asked Edith.

"He'll go away too. He's a river pilot."

"If you were back at home now," Edith asked, "would you still choose to make this journey?"

"Oh, yes!" cried Solveig.

"Everyone would say you're brave," Edwin chipped in, "but some would say you're foolhardy."

"What's that?" asked Solveig.

"Almost unwise. I don't think that, though. You knew this journey would be long and difficult."

"And dangerous," said Edith.

"But unless we take risks . . ." said Edwin. "I mean, you can sit at home by the fire and stir the stew pot and nothing much will change, or you can say your prayers and step out and face what's unknown."

The nearer they came to their journey's end, the more precious to Solveig her companions became. You're my life-blood, she thought. I can't wait to reach Miklagard, but I can't bear to think of being without you.

How strange I am, all made up of opposites: brave and afraid, and laughing and crying, and friendly and lonesome, turn by turn, or even at the same time.

Solveig went on shaping the bone slat, and as she did so she gave a secret smile. Yes, she thought. That's what I'll carve. I won't tell Edith, though.

But she did ask Edith two questions. The first was: "What was your mother's name?"

"The same as mine," said Edith. "Why?"

"So if your baby's a girl, will you call her Edith too?"

"How should I know?" said Edith. "I won't decide until I've seen it."

On the fourth evening after they had reached the Black Sea, Solveig was fishing with some of the hooks Vigot had given to her when she noticed that although the east wind was still shouldering them toward the shore, the water beneath the boat was pushing them away from it.

"Danube," said the river pilot, waving at the shore. "Huge river. The river water pushes us."

"I can feel it," said Solveig.

"Now last danger," Mihran said. "We must cross open sea."

"Not in this . . . tree trunk!" exclaimed Solveig.

"We sail overnight," Mihran told them. "We sail across open sea, very far from land."

"Do we have to?" Edith asked, alarmed.

"No choice," said Mihran, shrugging his shoulders. "The Danube is our strong mistress." He reached forward and patted her lap. "We do it."

"We can!" insisted Solveig. "We've come through the cataracts." But then she wished she hadn't said that and avoided Edith's eye.

"The danger," said Mihran, "is black wind, sudden storm. The danger is . . . we roll over. If the wind gets up and snatches us, I take our sail down."

"What if we do?" asked Edwin.

"Do?"

"Roll over."

The river pilot pursed his lips. "Very far from land," he said in a flat voice. "No other boats . . ." Mihran didn't complete the sentence.

"Couldn't we right her?" asked Solveig. "I think we could."

"Next morning," said Mihran. "Maybe. Sleep now. Try to sleep. I am your guide."

But Solveig couldn't sleep. She stared into the dark until her eyes ached. She sniffed the thick scents of a summer night in the south. She listened to the whirr and slap of the water passing under the boat, and the boat itself groaning, the mast cracking, the sail straining and easing . . .

In the middle of the night, Solveig and her companions were sprinkled by a shower; the raindrops were warm.

Then Solveig remembered Asta telling her that each day, childbearing women must drink a little of the dew that falls from Yggdrasill, the ash tree with arms spread out over the whole world.

I think Edith should drink some of this sweet rain, she thought. It will keep her baby safe.

Before long, there was a second shower, sharper than the first, and as it died away Solveig could see lightning on the eastern horizon. Not forked sticks or sharp spears but whole sheets, momentarily lighting up the whole sky, the sea, their little boat.

Mihran cleared his throat. "You, Solveig," he said quietly. "You boat woman. What you think?"

"You're asking me?" Solveig replied, not taking her eyes off the eastern horizon, not for one moment. "The lightning and thunder aren't going away, but they're not coming closer. Don't take down the sail yet. Otherwise we won't be making any headway."

"Boat woman," Mihran said again, and Solveig could hear the approval in his voice.

"I'll keep watch with you," said Solveig. "One is one. Two is better."

In the darkness, Mihran smiled. "Two is better," he repeated. "For them, too, I think. Edith and Edwin."

"You mean . . ."

"Yous see," said Mihran.

When the danger came, it wasn't in the shape that Solveig or Mihran had imagined. It wasn't a lightning strike, it wasn't a sudden squall or a half-submerged tree trunk, it wasn't a leak or a ravening sea monster or the rocky shore of a floating island.

As day began to dawn in the murky eastern sky, while Edith and her baby and Edwin still slept the sleep of the English, Solveig spotted a boat coming up astern.

Mihran gazed at it intently.

"Who?" asked Solveig. "Who are they?"

The river pilot shrugged.

The boat was a good deal larger than their dugout, in fact not much smaller than Red Ottar's boat. It had two sails as grubby as the dawning day, and after a while Solveig and Mihran were able to count at least thirteen people.

"There may be more," said Solveig. "In the hold. Why do I feel afraid?"

"Wake Edith and Edwin," Mihran told her. "Tell them I change course."

Without letting go of the sail, Mihran grabbed hold of the steering paddle. He dragged it to one side so that the dugout lurched and swung right around from the south to the west.

At once the boat behind them changed course too and quickly closed in.

The men aboard the boat began to yell, and as soon as she'd woken Edith and Edwin, Solveig scrambled down to the stern.

"No weapons," she told Mihran. "Not as far as I can see."

Then Solveig and Mihran heard wailing.

"Women!" exclaimed Solveig. "Women as well!"

Solveig saw two of the men were holding long grappling hooks. They waved them at the wicked sky, they reached toward the dugout . . . And only then did Solveig see the rotting faces and club hands of the passengers.

"Lepers!" growled Mihran, and he covered his eyes in terror.

The witch fingers of the two hooks grabbed the inside of the dugout and hoicked it sideways. Still rubbing the sleep out of their eyes, Edith and Edwin were thrown back into the bottom of the boat.

"Away!" cried Mihran. "Away!" And he warned his companions. "Don't touch their hooks! Don't look at them! Don't breathe the air they breathe!"

The passengers moaned. Some of them grunted.

Solveig did look up at them. One man was reaching down toward her, and Solveig could see he had only two fingers on one hand, three on the other, and they were more green than white. She looked up and saw one woman with bluish-red nodules all over her face, each as big as her own glass bead, and another whose face was twitching on one side but stiff as ice on the other, and a man without a nose and no eye in the left socket.

"Don't look at them!" Mihran begged her. "You become one of them."

"No," said Solveig. "That can't be true."

One of the lepers called out in Solveig's language. "In the name of the gods," he bawled, "in the name of whichever god you believe in, Mokosh or Odin, Christ, Allah . . ."

Around him, all the passengers cried and wailed and tore at their own bodies.

"In the name of all the gods," begged the man, "give us alms. Give whatever you can."

Edwin stood up and pulled off his little wooden cross inlaid with silver from around his neck. Then he murmured something to Edith and tore a narrow strip from the bottom of her tattered shift. Edwin wrapped the cross in the material and threw it up to the leper boat.

Seeing this, Mihran dug into a pocket and pulled out a bronze coin and tossed that up too without looking exactly where he was throwing it.

"You," he told Solveig.

"What?"

"You throw."

"What?"

Edwin reached up toward them. "May Christ sail with you in your terrible plight," he called out. "May Christ save your souls."

"Food?" asked Solveig nervously. "Our wheaten loaf?"

"No!" snapped Mihran.

"What about the sprats?"

"No!"

While Solveig was still hesitating, the two lepers loosened their hold on the dugout with an experience born of practice. They set the dugout adrift, and it bobbed on the water like a cork.

Then the leper boat swung away from them.

"It's looking east," said Edwin with a deep sigh. "As we Christians must."

"And Muslims," said Mihran.

"Where are they going?" asked Solveig.

Mihran shrugged. "Around and around. They only come to land to buy food."

For a while the four companions sat silent, still troubled, still sorrowful.

Edith gave Solveig an anxious look. "I wish you'd given them something," she said.

Blood rushed to Solveig's cheeks. "I wanted to. I did! I even thought I'd give them my glass bead, but that would have betrayed Oleg." Solveig shook her head fiercely. "But I'd rather be dead than alive like that."

"Lepers aren't animals," Edith protested. "They're human beings. Humans in need."

"You Vikings!" said Edwin scornfully. "God will call each of us when He chooses."

My father, thought Solveig. What would he have done? Did he see those lepers? Did he look into their faces?

What if I get there and no one has seen him? Would Harald Sigurdsson help me? It's true, I've got the gold brooch. My father told me it's worth more than our farm and all our animals. If he's not there and Harald's not there . . . My father's gift, that could save me.

"I remember," said Edith in a dreamy voice, as if she were thinking of something that had happened in a far-off land long ago. "Red Ottar told me that one of the Åland Islands—where we sailed to, me and Solveig, after we left Sweden—yes, one of the Åland Islands was a leper island."

"In that case," ventured Solveig, "maybe that ship sweeping past us in the middle of the night . . ."

"You're right," agreed Edith. "When Torsten saved us. Maybe the crew weren't ghosts but lepers."

The bleary-eyed sun rose in the east.

Mihran puffed out his cheeks and dragged his fingers through his oily dark hair. "Today," he informed them, "and one more night."

"At sea?" exclaimed Solveig.

Mihran thrust up his chin and raised his eyes.

"You didn't tell us," said Edwin, frowning.

"Say one day at a time," Mihran replied.

That night, the sea breeze was light and the sea swell gentle, and the four companions gossiped and ate and drank and dozed, but then Solveig had a terrible dream. The leper boat had grappled their dugout for a second time, and because Solveig hadn't given them a gift, the lepers lifted her, dangling, with their grappling hooks. They lowered her into their own boat and began to take away the parts of her body they were missing themselves. One gouged out her left eye, and one twisted off her nose, and one snapped off most of her fingers, and one tore at her growing right breast.

Solveig was too terrified to go back to sleep again, and she jammed herself against Mihran in the stern.

But day did dawn. It dawned at last, and Solveig could see land, a blue rib to the south, steep slopes to the west.

Mihran opened his arms as wide as the world. "This!" he said rather proudly. "All this. The Empire of Byzantium."

22

As they drew closer to the shore, Solveig could see dozens of little boats, some with sails as green as water mint, as blue as herons, as pink and scarlet as the wings of flamingos. Mihran steered their dugout into a wide water passage leading south, where they were surrounded by countless vessels—just as many, thought Solveig, as all the water boatmen shooting across the pond behind our farm.

Water bottles, she thought, and waterfowl and waterlogged and water spirits and goddesses like Mokosh . . . all this journey has been water—on water and in water and near water.

"Where are we?" she asked Mihran. "I keep thinking and feeling faster and faster."

Mihran smiled. "Nearly," he said. "This waterway is Bosphorus."

"What's that?"

"Greek word," he said, and then he shrugged. "Greek to me!"

"Where does it go?"

By now Edith and Edwin were listening too. "All this land," he told them, "is the Empire of Byzantium. The greatest empire on earth. It stretches far beyond the Black Sea to the east and south to Antioch and all the way west through Greece to Italy. Miklagard is the hub, the great city at the center. And here is the waterway to Miklagard."

Solveig hugged herself, excited and fearful. Then she threw herself back against her side of the dugout, almost turning it over.

"Careful!" Edwin warned her. "Many's the mission foiled at the last footstep."

"Miklagard," said Mihran, "is a great magnet."

"What's a magnet?" asked Solveig.

"You know," said Edwin. "Lodestone."

"No," said Solveig.

"Metal stone," explained Mihran. "It pulls all other metals toward it."

"It attracts them," added Edwin.

Like the maelstrom, thought Solveig. The maelstrom at the bottom of the ocean that drags down boats and the people and grinds everything into salt.

"City . . . people . . . market . . . music . . . marble . . . money . . ." The river pilot let go of the steering paddle and waved his arms and shook his head in wonder. "Church of Hagia Sophia! Divine Wisdom! Yous see."

"The largest church in the world," said Edwin. "That's what I've heard."

"But!" said Mihran. He paused and looked Solveig straight in the eye.

"What?" asked Solveig.

"Snake pit." Mihran turned his whole body into a slowly squirming, sidling snake. "Empress Zoe is a very, very dangerous woman. Man-eater! Knives. Poison." Mihran darted a look at Edith. "Strangling! She kills as she pleases, and many people, many, would be pleased to kill her."

Edwin made a sound somewhere between a hum and a growl. "Hmmm! I'll have to watch my words, then."

"Your message is for the empress?" Mihran asked him.

Edwin nodded. "And . . . the emperor," he said carefully.

Mihran snorted. "Michael. Boy-man."

Edwin raised his eyebrows.

"Empress Zoe is old woman. Fifty-four . . . fifty-five. Michael, nineteen!"

"So I've heard," said Edwin thoughtfully.

"Empress Zoe and boy-man have Viking guards," Mihran said.

"I know," replied Solveig. "The Varangian guard. My father told me."

"What's Varangian?" asked Edith.

"Viking guards who serve the emperor," Solveig said. "Harald's their leader."

"Man-man!" said Mihran. "Harald is only one year more than Michael, but he is man-man!"

"My father . . ." mused Solveig, "I think he's one of those guards."

Mihran nodded. "Where Empress Zoe is, Harald Sigurdsson is. And where Harald is, your father is. All Norwegians."

For a few minutes, Solveig sat in the hazy sunlight and watched the way in which Mihran so expertly threaded their little boat between the swarm of craft advancing toward them, sometimes only narrowly missing them, and she kept looking from shore to shore, astonished at the way both sides of the channel, sometimes no more than eight hundred paces apart, were almost completely lined with stone towers, houses, sheds, rickety piers, staithes.

"Yes," said Edwin after a while, "a snake pit. And I suspect Red Ottar's boat will be a snake pit by now." He paused and put a friendly arm around Edith. "What with Bergdis and all her venom."

He cares for her, thought Solveig, and not just because she's English. She cares for him too. He's no good at fishing or knots or rowing or anything, but all the same, he's strong and kind. So could they . . . ?

Edith smiled at Solveig as if she could read her thoughts.

"Gæþ00FE; a wyrd swa hio scel!" she said.

"Huh?"

"Oh!" Edith shrugged. "Fate goes as it must!"

"Is that what you really think?"

Edith gave Solveig a knowing look. "Well," she said with a pretty smile, "sometimes we can help it along."

"But you're Christian," said Solveig.

"Fate moves in the mind of God," explained Edwin. "Yes, as I was saying, Bergdis and her venom. But it's not just her. Torsten and Bruni, too. On their own they're each decent men."

"Torsten is," said Solveig.

"But put them together and there's trouble."

"Red Ottar told me about Bruni," said Edith.

"He did?" exclaimed Solveig.

"Yes, Bruni killed Torsten's cousin Peder and stole his wife."

"No!" exclaimed Solveig.

"Yes," said Edith. "She was called Inga. Bruni stole her and bedded her and sailed away with her from Norway to Iceland. Bruni doesn't know that Torsten and Peder were cousins. Torsten recognized him not just because of his name but by his black tooth; that's what he told Red Ottar."

"And because Bruni had lived in Norway before he went to Iceland," Edwin added.

"Red Ottar told me Torsten will avenge his cousin's death," Edith went on, "and he'll avenge Inga's disgrace."

"He must," insisted Solveig.

"But he made them both swear to keep the peace until after our journey."

"It's not our journey any longer," said Edwin. "Not now that Red Ottar's dead."

"That's one reason Bruni wanted us all to stay together," said Edith. "There's safety in numbers."

"The rat!" exclaimed Solveig vehemently. "I'm not surprised, though. Not really."

"So, Solveig," Edwin said, "is this what your gods teach you? To scheme? To kill? To blind an eye for an eye and extract a tooth for a tooth?"

"If a woman's dishonored," Solveig replied, "she must be avenged."

"With violence?" Edwin challenged her.

"And if a man's injured or killed without reason, he must be avenged. That's how it's always been."

"Until everyone is blind and toothless," said Edwin quietly.

Solveig could feel the roots of her hair tingling and an angry blush creeping down to her chest.

"You Christians!" she retorted. "You're always looking at people with lamb eyes and turning the other cheek and forgiving. At least you say you do."

"Solveig!" Edwin warned her.

"Always waffling like Slothi. Or not speaking at all."

"Don't say words you'll regret later."

"You Christians will choke on your compassion," Solveig snapped, "and murderers will roam free, free to kill again."

"Solveig, how can your feuding—violent revenge, brutal killing—ever be preferable to healing?"

"You call it feuding. We call it justice. We call it law. We call it order."

Edwin clamped his jaw and sighed. "Nothing's ever easy in the kingdom of earth," he said.

"No, it's not," cried Solveig. "And that's what Christians can't accept. People become Christian because they can't bear all the pain on middle-earth and need empty promises about high heaven. That's what I think."

"Oh, Solveig!" exclaimed Edith, so sad, so understanding. And then she clutched Solveig and tried to hug her.

"You English!" Solveig yelped. "You always think you know best."

For a while Solveig and Edwin were silent. They'd hurt each other and hurt themselves, and Edith didn't know quite how to soothe them.

But after a while Edwin began to sing and say part of a poem:

> *"Time passed. The boat was on the water,*
> *moored under the cliff . . ."*

We're not moored, thought Solveig. And there's no cliff, anyhow. Just slopes, scrubby bushes.

> *"Water streams eddied, stirred up sand.*
> *Then those brave people began their journey.*
> *Foaming at the prow and most like a seabird,*
> *The boat sped over the waves, urged on by the wind,*
> *until next day, at about the expected time,*
> *so far had the curved prow come*
> *that the travelers sighted land,*
> *shining cliffs, steep hills,*
> *broad headlands. So did they cross the sea,*
> *their journey was at its end."*

Despite herself, Solveig listened. He's Christian, she thought. And he made me angry. I think he wanted to. And yet . . .

Half listening, half thinking, Solveig began to feel almost as fond of Edwin as she had felt angry before. She smiled cautiously at Edith and shook her head.

Edwin finished his song. "Now," he said, "let's not end our long journey with an argument."

"Look!" said Mihran, pointing to starboard.

Solveig and Edwin and Edith looked. And in the hazy sunlight they saw a hill covered in buildings, most of them flat-roofed, and soaring above them a huge dome.

"What is it?" asked Edith.

At first Mihran didn't reply.

Edwin opened his arms.

"Floating," marveled Solveig. "Well, it looks as if it is."

"High on the hill," Mihran agreed.

"Above the hill," Solveig corrected him.

"Heavy stone and mortar," Mihran told them. "Hagia Sophia."

"Hagia Sophia!" Solveig and Edith and Edwin cried together. For a while the three of them gazed at it, speechless.

Mihran knew when to keep silent. He watched his companions, and the corners of his mouth twitched.

"What keeps the dome up?" exclaimed Solveig.

Mihran smiled and nodded. "Yous see," he said obligingly.

What they saw was an inlet, a wide harbor opening to starboard. It was seething with little craft, some entering, some busily crossing from side to side.

"Not just cobles and knarrs and skutes," cried Solveig. "All kinds of boats I've never even seen before. What are they, Mihran?"

"Feluccas," the pilot told her. "The little boats you can row. And dahabiahs. And dhows—they're the ones with three-pointed sails. This is the Golden Horn!"

"The Golden Horn?" exclaimed Edwin, and he all but stood up but then thought better of it and plumped himself down again. "The harbor of harbors."

Around the shoulder of land facing them beyond the entrance to the harbor, there was a massive wall, at least seven men high, stretching south from the Golden Horn along the shore of the Bosphorus as far as Solveig could see.

"This is Miklagard. It is, isn't it?" Solveig said out loud. Not really doubting it, she still needed Mihran to confirm it.

Mihran just smiled at her and rubbed his mustache between his right thumb and forefinger. Solveig filled her lungs with salty air and noisily blew it all out again. "I know," she said.

Inside the harbor, there was a hubbub: boats crisscrossing, carcasses and all kinds of muck floating in the water, people shouting, scents and stinks . . .

Solveig felt thrilled and alarmed. She was almost gagging on her own excitement.

"We each have to go our own way," Edwin told them. "I to the Empress Zoe, and Edith with me."

"Edith bazaar," Mihran suggested. "Best on middle-earth."

"Edith with me," repeated Edwin. "We to the empress, and you, Solveig, to your father."

"I will," said Solveig. She felt out of breath and dry-mouthed.

Edwin nodded. "Wherever he may be," he said. "But we must meet. We must be sure . . ."

"Yes," said Edith, taking Solveig's hands between her own.

"Oh, Edie!" whispered Solveig.

"At noon tomorrow," said Edwin. "At the landing stage where we leave this boat."

"No," said Mihran. "Too many." He thought for a moment. "There's a water pool . . ." he began.

"Water pool?" repeated Edwin.

"Underground. A sunken palace. It waters the whole city. The cistern, people call it." Mihran spread his arms. "Water! Dream!"

Water, thought Solveig. Dream. That's what my journey has been made of.

"We meet there," Mihran told them. "Noon tomorrow."

And I've become a water girl. More water than earth.

"And me," said Mihran, "I go with Solveig."

Solveig gave a start. "What did you say?"

"I go with you."

Solveig smiled with her mouth. She smiled with her eyes. Then she rubbed her face against the river pilot's right shoulder.

"I promised," said Mihran.

"You did," said Solveig. "But, Mihran . . . this journey, I began it alone, and if I can I must end it alone."

For a moment Solveig closed her eyes. She was rowing away from the farm, and it was still masked by night. Now she was under sail, running before the east wind.

"Ægir," she was praying, "don't shout at me with your rough wave tongues. Ran, don't snare me with your drowning net. Lift me and carry me to Miklagard."

23

In the milling covered market, all the merchants had their own shouts and snares.

One little dark-skinned man, like an exotic bird in his scarlet and saffron robes, was piping out "coriander cinnamon cumin" and then "ginger pepper mace" in two short bursts over and over again. One woman bowed so low to Solveig that her left fingertips almost swept the ground, and then she dabbed Solveig's cheek with perfume as delicate and yellow-green as the first day of spring. And one man actually uncurled Solveig's fingers and pressed a pearl into her palm before smiling at her with his pearly teeth and taking it away again. All around her, people were calling and shouting, jostling, sidestepping, clapping their hands and laughing, weighing, bargaining.

In the market at Ladoga, thought Solveig, I began to list everything around me. Antlers and ale cakes and apples and awls, ash wood bowls, amber, blueberries and brown cheese and bronze bottles, birch-bark carvings and bone combs, crystal beads, cockerels, crabs, crayfish. Oh! And clay cups and carrots and cornelian . . . I only got as far as C, and that's nothing compared to this market. I don't even know what half these things are. This bowl here, smoking. Thick and sweet. What is it?

"You Christian?" asked a merchant with eyebrows as coarse as the bristles of a wild boar.

"Yes," gasped Solveig. "I mean, no. I don't know."

"You Moslem," said the man encouragingly, and he beckoned her with a hooked little finger. "Come see."

Solveig walked on, feeling dazed. Unsteady on her feet after so many days at sea, she began to climb the hill toward Hagia Sophia.

The sky was curdled. The day was growing hotter. And high above Solveig the dome floated, as if it were suspended from the sky by a golden thread.

As she drew close to it and at last saw the enormous dark buttresses supporting it, she remembered what King Vladimir's envoys had said.

"We didn't know," they reported, "whether we were still on earth or had entered heaven."

Solveig took a deep breath. Then she put down her bag of clothing and bones and stretched and braced her shoulders.

At once Solveig thought of the shoulder blade. I've carried it all the way here, she thought, and I've heard the battle ghosts singing:

Cut me
Carve me

Tell me
Sing me

I vowed to carve runes for them, and I will. I will. But . . .
with my journey, with my words and tears and laughter, I
have already been singing for them. Isn't that what we must
all do?

I Sun-Strong
Sing your life songs

So you live
In my life

Your laughter
Your youth

Your quick blood
And your death

I sing your life songs
Now and forever.

Solveig sucked her cheeks and swallowed loudly.

Mihran says it's right to come here first, she thought.
Because the Empress Zoe worships here each day and her
guards escort her. He says they're all Norwegians, Norwegian to their back teeth. He knows everything, Mihran.

I feel so nervous. I haven't felt as fearful as this since I told Asta I'd gotten cramps in my stomach . . .

You told King Yaroslav about me. You said you'd regret not telling me you were leaving for as long as you lived. Surely you'll be glad, won't you?

Solveig picked up her bag. Anyhow, she thought, I don't even know where you are. You may not be here in Mikla-gard. You may be away, fighting shoulder to shoulder with Harald Sigurdsson. For all I know, you may be at the other end of the Great Sea.

Inside Hagia Sophia, it was gloomy and damp and chilly.

Solveig stopped just inside the entrance door and listened.

It's the distant ocean, she thought. Humming. Almost growling. No. It can't be that. It's every sound ever made in here, trapped and circling around and around.

Little by little Solveig grew used to the half-light. She saw that she was in a huge hall and that there was the most enor-mous dark cavern in front of her. At the far end of the hall, several men were standing at the bottom of a wide ramp lit by flickering horn lanterns.

Slowly she walked toward them, and when she drew close, Solveig could see they were fair-skinned and fair-haired. All of them! Then one of them said something, and never in her life had language sounded so sweet or so welcome.

"Look!" one man with a ruddy face called out. "Here comes an angel!"

"I could do with a real woman myself," one of his companions replied.

Their voices ricocheted down the hall.

"Look how fair and tall she is," exclaimed a third man. "A Valkyrie!"

"Almost like a Norwegian."

By now Solveig was smiling to herself, and she walked right up to the men.

"From a farm," she told them. "In Trondheimsfjord."

"What?"

"She is! She's Norwegian."

The five men stood in a ring around Solveig and marveled at her.

"I'm . . . I'm looking for Asser Assersson," Solveig said in a level voice, low as murmuring bees.

"Who?"

"Never heard of him."

"Some people call him Halfdan."

"Halfdan!"

"The old sod!"

"Some men get all the luck."

"Is he here?" asked Solveig, and her voice faltered.

The five Viking guards would happily have gone on cracking jokes and teasing Solveig, but they were interrupted by a great shout from the cavern.

"Hallelujah! Hallelujah!"

Solveig stepped backward and straight into one of the guardsmen's arms.

"Hello!" he said. "I'm Hakon!"

Solveig quickly extracted herself. "I didn't even know anyone was in there," she said, waving at the vast space under the dome.

"Hundreds of people," the ruddy-faced guard told her. "One thousand, maybe. And the empress herself."

"She's here!" exclaimed Solveig.

"Up there," he said, nodding at the ramp. "In the gallery."

"And . . ." Solveig began hesitantly.

The guards eyed each other.

"So's he," Hakon told her.

"Here?" cried Solveig, and she clamped her hand over her mouth.

"Unless he's away with the birds."

"No one's allowed up," said the ruddy-faced man. Then he gave Solveig a wink and politely stepped aside.

Solveig thanked them all and began to stride up the twisting ramp.

"So young, too," one guard called after her.

"Young enough to be his daughter."

The five men guffawed. And Solveig, steadily she rose from darkness to light.

Two guards were standing at the top of the ramp, and one immediately challenged her.

"Halt! Drop that bag!"

Solveig glanced at him. Dark-skinned. Dressed in baggy trousers. Grasping a saber.

"In the name of the empress!" the other guard countered. "She's just a girl! You see terror lurking behind every bush." Then he waved his right hand airily. "Pass!" he told Solveig.

That voice. That imperious tone.

When Solveig had stepped into the brightly lit gallery, she quickly looked back.

So very tall. A hand's height taller than a tall man. That blond beard. And one eyebrow higher than the other.

Solveig's heart lurched.

It was Harald Sigurdsson.

He didn't recognize me, she thought. Have I changed so much? She rubbed her face and ran her fingers through her tresses.

Yes. Yes, I have. I was only ten. And I've crossed half of middle-earth.

To Solveig's right as she walked along the gallery were high windows, and the walls between them were covered with thousands and thousands of little gold tiles. So was the ceiling. To her left were massive marble columns and, far below, the circular cavern and all the worshippers.

Solveig passed a crowd of people and wondered whether they were surrounding the empress herself. Empress Zoe and her lover, Michael, the boy-man. Many of the male courtiers had strange, hairless faces like plucked chickens, and Solveig couldn't tell whether they were old or young.

Solveig stared up at the soaring dome, and then she peered right over the marble balustrade into the vast body of the church. It was a dark murmuring ocean.

"Hallelujah! Hallelujah!"

The shouts echoed and answered each other. They rose and circled around and around in the dome.

Where? Where is he? Solveig's heart was battering in her chest. Next to the empress, guarding her? I can't force my way through there.

Near the end of the gallery, a face stared down at Solveig from the wall—a man's face made entirely of tiny tiles.

He looks so strong, she thought. But gentle too. So wise. So sad.

Solveig walked right up to him and examined the tiles.

Snowflake, sealskin. Cormorant. Ice-blue, flax flower, forget-me-not. Poppy and cherry and orange. Holly, water-mint green. Gold and silver . . . silver and gold . . .

Ah, thought Solveig, quite breathless now, this man, he's all the colors of my own journey.

It's so light above me, so dark below me. Like Asgard and Hel.

Then Solveig turned the corner from her gallery into a second one, leading away to the left, almost as long as the one she had just walked down.

She closed her eyes and opened her eyes.

At the far end, at least fifty paces away, a man was leaning into the balustrade. Solveig could see he was holding a knife and incising the marble.

How long did she stand there, staring at him? However many times she thought about it, she was never quite sure. For a moment. Forever. Until she was quite weightless.

So stooping. And cumbersome. I'd recognize you at any distance, anywhere.

Always I have loved you. I've never questioned that. But now I question it, and I love you all the more, strong and weak, weak but strong. Not a god. A man.

My father.

My own blood.

She couldn't wait. Not any longer. She stepped forward, she dropped her bag, and the dry bones clattered. She quickened and ran toward the man, calling, "Father! Father!"

Halfdan looked up. He looked toward her.

And without one word, father and daughter, they reached toward each other.

Solveig closed her eyes. I'm wide and deep as the ocean, she thought. Small as a hazelnut. Then she allowed Halfdan to sweep her up and lift her off her feet.

"You were carving," Solveig said at last in a husky voice.

"Look!" said her father, pointing to the balustrade and brushing a tear from his left cheek. "Solva, my Solva!"

SUN-STRONG, sang the runes. ᚴᚠᛏ ᚾᛗᛁᚻ.

Solveig's own hot tears dripped onto the marble ledge. She swept back her golden hair, and then she took the shining knife from her father's hand.

"With salt and stone," she said. "With bone and blood. I'll cut your name next to mine."

A *fair-haired young woman, tall, willowy almost, and a cumbersome man with a limp were loping down the hill from Hagia Sophia.*

She kept turning to him. Then she threw back her head and laughed, and that was the most joyous sound anyone in Miklagard heard all that day.

Waiting for them at the top of a wide flight of stone steps leading down to the ancient cistern, the water pool that supplied the whole city, were a cordial-looking man with buckteeth and such a pretty, dark-haired young woman, plainly pregnant.

The two men stared unblinking across oceans into each other's eyes. They clasped hands.

Then the two young women embraced. And without a word the fair-haired one pressed into her companion's right hand a wide, flat ring of walrus bone. A teething ring!

Again they embraced.

A swarthy little man with the most extravagant mustache came bounding up the stone steps. His eyes were liquid and black.

He pointed and led them down the steps and opened his arms as wide as this middle-earth.

In front of them stretched an immense pool of water, lit by hundreds, thousands even, of floating, flickering candles: a magical, underground night sky.

The girl with the golden hair stepped a little apart. She gazed into the water.

Water rocking and fractious and seductive and bottomless, clicking and kissing, cradling and drowning, a mirror, no, a broken mirror, a dream, this water shining, violet and gray, green as her growing.

The girl knelt and trailed her fingertips through it. The water of life.

Author's Note and Acknowledgments

I've stepped into a dozen or so buildings and ruins that have made me gasp—among them Sydney's Opera House and the Mezquita in Cordoba, the Colosseum in Rome, the sky-high Acoma Pueblo in New Mexico, and the Neolithic village of Skara Brae in Orkney. But the most stunning of all is the huge church-mosque-museum of Hagia Sophia in Istanbul. For more than one thousand years, this was the largest covered space on earth, and there on a high marble balustrade I found Viking runes reading HALFDAN (Half-Dane). They were probably carved by a mercenary in the eleventh century. That's where this book began.

A great deal has been written about the Vikings at home and in the south and west, but altogether less about their utterly remarkable colonization of Russia and their trading and military expeditions to Constantinople, where the Byzantine emperor's handpicked guard consisted entirely of Vikings. So this book has entailed plenty of research, but of course the trick for any historical novelist is to remember that he or she is a storyteller, not a historian. Anthony

Cheetham, cofounder of Quercus, suggested I should write it, and in his wake I've worked closely with my thoughtful and very supportive editor, Roisin Heycock. I also warmly thank my discerning and eagle-eyed copy editor Talya Baker, and Margaret Histed, Parul Bavishi, Emma Thawley, and Jon Riley at Quercus for all their help.

Hemesh Alles has drawn the delightful and informative map, as he did those for my Arthur trilogy and *Gatty's Tale*; once again, I'm so grateful to Richard Barber for his imaginative interest and scholarly advice, as well as for the loan of valuable books; the letter carver Gary Breeze allowed me into his dusty workshop and introduced me to Anton Englert, curator of the Viking Ship Museum in Roskilde; my longtime editor Judith Elliott has continued to care for and support my work; Geoffrey Findlay gave me a copy of Cherry Gilchrist's utterly magical *The Soul of Russia*, a book that has been at my elbow for the last eighteen months; my wife Linda's Norwegian relatives, Harald Hansen, Randi Hansen, and their families, warmly welcomed me to Trondheimfjord; and Jim Ring has generously given me advice about ships, sailing terms, and a skipper's feeling for his boat.

I'm dedicating this book to Twiggy Bigwood, who has not only expertly threaded her way through my manuscript and typed it over and over again but also researched many aspects of Viking life and lore. She, my wife, Linda, and I have very often engaged in friendly and fascinating argument about issues and characterization, while Linda could well have been an outstanding editor in another incarnation and tactfully suggested literally thousands of small textual changes. Mainly cuts! Viking women were on the whole freethinking and strong-willed, witty, capable, and loyal (I'll set aside some of their less desirable qualities). So are the two women flanking me, and this book would certainly be the worse without them.

I've found it thrilling to reengage with the Viking world for the first time since writing *The Penguin Book of Norse Myths*, and this first encounter with Solveig and her father and Harald Sigurdsson (Hardrada) will not be the last. I'm now at work on its successor, *Scramasax*.

Chalk Hill, Burnham Market
September 2010

Word List

clinker-built a method of boat building in which each plank overlaps the upper edge of the one below it

coble a rowing boat or sea-fishing boat with a flat bottom and square stern

dahabiah a large river-sailing vessel

elf-fire a flamelike phosphorescence that drifts or flits over marshy ground. Also known as *will-o'-the-wisp* and *will-o'-the-wyke*

felucca a small Mediterranean rowing or sailing boat

fjord a long, narrow sleeve of the sea reaching inland, often between banks or cliffs

frazil ice needle-shaped ice crystals—the first stage in the formation of sea ice

hack-silver small bits and pieces of silver (often cut-up jewelry), used by traders and weighing the same as Arabic or European coins

knarr	a merchant ship about fifty feet (sixteen meters) long
Lodestar	also known as the Pole Star or North Star; once thought to be magnetic and used by mariners to take their bearings
Morning Star	the planet Venus, which can be seen just west of the sun before sunrise. In the northern world, it was also known as Aurvandil
rime	hoarfrost
Skrælings	the name (probably meaning "wretches") given by the Vikings to the native inhabitants of Greenland and the eastern shores of North America
scramasax	a dagger or knife-shaped sword (about twenty inches long) used for hunting and fighting
skute	a small, light merchant ship
skuther	driving wind (more than a gentle *gurl* or a *gushle*, less than a fierce *cat-risper*)
strike-a-light	pieces of flint and steel used to strike sparks
tamarisk	an evergreen shrub with slender feathery branches and scaly leaves